ALL THE PLACES I'VE EVER LIVED

DAVID GAFFNEY

URBANE
Publications

urbanepublications.com

First published in Great Britain in 2017 by Urbane Publications Ltd
Suite 3, Brown Europe House, 33/34 Gleaming Wood Drive, Chatham,
Kent ME5 8RZ
Copyright © David Gaffney, 2017

A CIP catalogue record for this book is available from the British Library.

ISBN 978-1-911331-06-3
MOBI 978-1-911331-08-7
EPUB 978-1-911331-07-0

Design and Typeset by The Invisible Man
Cover by OR8 Design

Printed and bound by CPI Group (UK) Ltd, Croydon, CR0 4YY

urbanepublications.com

For Clare

David Gaffney

PRAISE FOR DAVID GAFFNEY'S WRITING

"Loaded with potent charges, insidious and cumulative in their effects, the stories are sometimes haunting, sometimes comic."
The Times Literary Supplement

"Sad, funny fables recalling evanescent moments of connection and happiness. One hundred and fifty words by Gaffney are more worthwhile than novels by a good many others." *The Guardian*

"A ruthless eye and pitch-black humour." *The Observer*

"It would be hard to imagine a book that scored a more penetrating bull's-eye on the target of the moment." *The Independent*

"Witty, clever and poignant, Gaffney's micro fictions work as funny routines, moving insights and illuminating character sketches, often all at the same time." *Time Out*

"Gaffney's arresting series of short stories *Sawn-off Tales* seems to operate much as Surrealist paintings do: able to strike with depth through peculiar arrangements of thoughts and ideas. Madly imaginative." *The Skinny*

"Utterly brilliant. Hilariously demented and wonderfully succinct. David Gaffney's *Sawn-Off Tales* are little McNuggets of pure gold. This is writing at its best." *Graham Rawle*

"David Gaffney is, I think, one of very few contemporary British writers who have mastered the very short form." *Nicholas Royle*

"Great read, these twisted wee tales." *Johnny Vegas*

"Elliptical, sharp, witty and dazzling, written with a poet's eye for detail and a novelist's appreciation of human faults and foibles." *Jenn Ashworth*

"Gaffney's latest is a masterful taster menu, every mouthful wickedly inventive and deliciously absurd. Brilliant." *Adam Marek*

"Sharp, poignant, surreal, lyrical and very, very funny, the collection reveals intense knowledge and control of the form, along with a desire to push the boundaries in every direction." *Emma Jane Unsworth*

'The dead don't die – they look on and help'

D.H. Lawrence

David Gaffney

ACKNOWLEDGEMENTS

Thanks to the following people whose support in writing this novel has been invaluable:

Sarah-Clare Conlon, Sarah Butler, Adrian Slatcher, Elizabeth Baines, Benjamin Judge, Christopher Burns, Phillip Coleman, Alan Cleaver, and to Nathan Lee, at whose cottage in Wales many sections of the book were written.

David Gaffney

The lesions erupted suddenly, without warning, and I sat up in bed and tugged my pyjama top over my head to have a proper look.

They were distributed evenly, covering my torso, legs and arms, and it didn't hurt when I pulled at one, but it couldn't be moved. Oddly, it felt as though it were part of my body. And it was metallic. All of them were.

I climbed out of bed, put on my dressing gown and went downstairs to the bathroom. I took off the gown, stepped out of my pyjama bottoms and stood naked in front of the mirror. I stared at myself for a long time. The lesions looked like the hard backs of curled insects, like ticks, ticks which had buried their sharp little jaws into me and locked themselves on. But ticks made of metal and engorged with – engorged? Why was I thinking they were engorged? They were round, shiny, clean metallic buttons the diameter of a half-pence piece, and they curved up out of my flesh as if they had always been there, like some sort of piercing. Someone had pushed seeds into my skin while I slept and had been waiting for the pods to burst and these metallic studs to heave up out of me.

I moved closer to the mirror. The marks were all over but there weren't many on my face, my forehead being the worst, followed by the backs of my ears. I moved my fringe so that it obscured the bad parts; if I could hide the marks, at least others would not be traumatised, because for some reason I felt that other people being able to see them was more distressing than my own awareness that they were there.

I took a long deep breath and tried to work out how I felt. Anxious. Anxious, but not ill. I was OK. I wasn't dying. At least, not right away. But I was hot and my heart was beating hard. And now I felt a little sick, yes, I felt a little nauseous. It was like an assault, like I'd been attacked. The idea of it, the idea of being covered in metal lumps.

My mother was the head-teacher at the local Catholic primary school, St Patrick's, and she came home every lunchtime, and that day, the day of the metal lumps, I was supposed to be studying in my room, having lied to her that I had coursework to complete. In fact, I had planned to spend the day finishing off the new songs for my upcoming performance at Troubadours. I was hoping that Samantha Fry, a girl from the year below who I'd been obsessed with for nearly two years, would play her bass guitar with me, but so far I hadn't been able to persuade her that folk music was cool. Samantha Fry had been drawn into the world of punk and had cut off her hair with a bread-knife died it bright green, and started wearing a camouflage vest, fluffy black jumper, tartan tights and long leather boots.

I got dressed in black school trousers and a white school shirt, black socks, no shoes, then sat on the grey vinyl armchair and turned on the television. I watched a school programme; a drama about a gypsy boy who sells a fox to a child. The fox escapes and returns to the gypsies, who immediately leave town and sell the fox again somewhere else. This pattern went on and I wondered what the story meant. It must have meant something or it wouldn't be part of the schools' programmes.

I watched *Rainbow*, with Rod, Jane and Freddy singing songs about vegetables.

I'm a potato, just a potato
I'm always covered head to foot in mud
I had become afraid to move and sat as still as if I were dead.
But if I'm washed with water

I look just like I oughta
And they will say, oh, what a lovely spud!

My mother came in while I was looking at *Pebble Mill at One*, Showaddywaddy interviewed by Jan Leeming, and I stood up and lifted my untucked shirt.

'Look.'

My mother's hand flew to her mouth. 'Oh,' she said. 'What on Earth? What is that?'

She came up close to me and poked at one of the steely blisters, moving it gently with her hand.

'What have you been doing?' she said.

'What's happening to me?' I said, in a pathetic high imploring voice that I hated the sound of.

'I'm not sure,' she said.

We were both quiet for a time, me holding up my shirt and exposing my stomach, my mother squinting at the strange eruptions. I was trying not to become distressed, but could feel water in my eyes and my throat tightening.

'Did you...?'

'Me?' I covered myself up again. 'I found them all over me when I woke up.'

My mother looked as though she was about to faint, and she sat down and squeezed her forehead with her fingers as if she were forcing out unwanted thoughts.

Seeing the effect on her was more traumatic for me at that point than the effect the condition had on myself.

Showaddywaddy pranced in their pastel drape coats and brothel creepers.

Undurr the moon of love

'Where were you last night?' my mother said.

'What do you mean?'

'Have you heard about that poor girl?'

'No.'

Undurr the moon of love

'She was… attacked.'

I had no idea what my mother was talking about, but immediately thought of Samantha Fry, who had been at the fair, as I had. She hadn't spoken to me, just stood near us, at the Octopus, and smiled across.

'Who? Was it Samantha Fry?'

'No,' my mother said softly. 'No.'

The mooon orf lurrrve

My mother went over to the television and silenced it. She lifted my shirt and peered at the strange lesions. She touched one, then absently pressed and tugged at it as she spoke.

'That poor girl, that poor girl.'

'I went to the fair,' I said. 'Me and a few others.'

My mother looked up at me and let go of my shirt, allowing it to fall down.

'She, the girl, she was supposed to be at the fair. That poor girl.' She turned away from me and went to the window where she put her hands on the ledge and looked out. Our house was on an exposed corner and rain and wind were whipping around it noisily; you couldn't see much in the grey murk, but my mother stared into it.

'What happened to this girl?'

My mother didn't say anything. She kept her back to me. She was wearing a blue dress printed with yellow flowers, and sandals. I didn't like to see her bare feet poking out.

'She was supposed to be at the fair, too,' my mother said to the window pane. 'But she wasn't. She went to a pub. The Derby Arms. They serve under age. Known for it.'

I flinched at the mention of The Derby. It was where I'd been going with Finny and, more recently, Samantha Fry and her mates, to play pool and illicitly drink pints of Hartleys.

'They found her this morning, down near the Grey Stuff in a–' My mother cried out and put her hand to her mouth again. 'In a ditch, Barry, a ditch.'

I watched the tendons in her wrists tighten as she gripped the window-ledge harder.

'Naked. In a ditch. She was 16. Everyone knew her, she was in Jenny's year, the year above you.'

'But not her class?'

'No. Her year.'

Somehow it seemed better that she wasn't in my sister's class, somehow it made it further away, like it had happened in another country.

'What was she called?'

'Philomena May. The Bowthorn Mays. I knew her, I know them all. I taught her. She was a bit, you know, wild, definitely wild. But not bad. The poor, poor girl. Her mother, her father, her brothers, her sisters. They're from Bowthorn, a family from Bowthorn.'

She turned from the window to look at me. 'The police are talking to everyone,' she said. 'They might talk to you. Where were you?'

'I didn't do anything,' I said.

My mother was silent for a time. Then she sighed, long and slow. 'This rain. I don't know if I can stand any more of it.' She looked at me intently. 'Lift up your shirt again.'

I did as she asked and she stared.

'Why am I covered in metal lumps?'

'What metal lumps?' she said. 'I don't understand, Barry.'

'These,' I said, nodding towards my chest.

'There are no metal lumps, darling. It's some skin condition. What have you been doing? What have you been doing to get like this? Could it be something to do with this girl? With poor Philomena?'

'How could it be to do with this girl?'

'I know,' she said. 'The poor girl. The police are talking to everyone. Show me again. I have to go back to school. Show me again.'

I showed her again, and again she stared.

'Can't you see the lumps?' I was raising my voice now. 'The metal lumps? They're all over me.'

'I'll get an appointment with Dr Ferguson. She's the young one, you know. Scottish. She's lovely. The whole town is traumatised. Are you saying you stuck metal things in yourself and this is what it caused? You're not one of these punks, are you?'

'No.'

'Is this anything to do with Samantha Fry?'

'No, Mum. It's not a punk thing.'

'Tell me the truth, Barry. I won't be angry. We won't be angry.'

'There is no truth,' I said.

My mother glanced over at the mantelpiece, at the plastic Our Lady full of holy water from Lourdes.

'Have you been to confession lately?'

'What do you mean?'

She stared at me for a long time. 'I don't know,' she said, and tapped me on the cheek with her palm, nodding her head firmly. 'Have a bath. Have a bath and we'll see what it looks like when I come home. Don't tell your dad yet. He seems to have other things on his mind at the moment.'

My mother went out into the roaring rain and got into her Austin Allegro. I watched her through the window. She sat in the driving seat for a few minutes, doing nothing. She yanked down the vanity mirror and brushed powder onto her face. She adjusted her hair. Then she took something from her purse and looked at it closely, turning it this way and that, as if it held some important secret that she couldn't work out. She replaced whatever it was – a small piece of card or paper, possibly – started the engine and drove away.

I went into the front room, picked up the portable record player, and took it into the kitchen. This was as near to the bathroom as I could get it. I stacked three LPs on to it, one on top of the other: *The Freewheelin'* by Bob Dylan, *The Anthology of American Folk Music*, and *Harvest* by Neil Young. These were artists that I, Barry Dyer, could be like, if I tried hard enough. They had acoustic guitars and wrote, sang and played their own songs about their own lives, just like me. And this was music that I could perform and record completely on my own if I needed to; there was no need for other band members and all the difficult negotiations that would entail – agreeing what to play, and how to play it, agreeing on a name, a type of sound, an image, meeting up all the time and rehearsing, hanging out together, all the things I couldn't be bothered with.

I dropped the stylus and Dylan's scratchy strumming and nasal vocal began.

Corrina, Corrina

Gal, where you been so long?

I went into the bathroom and turned on the taps. While I watched the bath fill, I ran my hand up and down my front, feeling the beads of metal. I thought they might vibrate, but they didn't. I imagined they might become hot or electrified, but they didn't do that either.

I been worr'in' about you, baby

Baby, please come home

I twirled the lid off my sister Jenny's bubble bath and poured a big slug into the water, paddling it about with my hands. It was red. This red froth would mean I wouldn't have to look at the weird skin condition. In the bath, I lay as still as I could. Snakes of steam rose up around me and I began to experience all kinds of uncanny thoughts. Had I taken on special powers? Had I been chosen for something? While I was terrified of being seriously ill, it felt as though I was somehow suddenly important. Would I be on the news? Would it spread to others? Was I the first?

The dead girl, Philomena May. I could picture her face. I remembered her. I had seen her at school and thought she was sexy. She had very, very dark black hair and a face shaped like a heart with jutting-up cheekbones. She was small, like a little pixie, but a pixie with a plump round bottom.

I wondered whether I could have done it. I could have killed Philomena May. I could have experienced a mental blackout. I wondered whether the girl's death and the metal lesions were related, or if it was an odd coincidence. I wondered if any of my school friends had anything to do with it. My best friend, Finny? No. Finny was as woefully introverted as a chess champion with spots and had the social skills of an oyster. Yet Finny had a deep and seemingly mature interest in sex and spent a lot of his spare time in the library looking into different sexual practices, and down the refuse tip peering at glossy pornography. But Finny? Finny? Finny would never do anything like this.

I closed my eyes. *The Anthology of American Folk Music* clonked down onto the player: *Henry Lee* by Dick Justice.

He laid his head on a pillow of down
Kisses she gave him three
With a penny knife that she held in her hand
She murdered mortal he

It was then that it happened. I experienced a very real sensation of someone lying on top of me. A weight, a definite weight. And I could feel flesh, naked flesh, pressing against mine. Warm skin. Then puffs of breath against my cheek, now strands of hair tumbling down onto my face, and suddenly, a pair of soft arms encircling me under the water. I didn't dare open my eyes. The weight seemed to be present for a few moments, like a strong sensation of something pushing me down, and the arms felt solid, real, as if I was being gripped about my body by slim female limbs.

I froze.

She took him by his long yellow hair
And also by his feet
She plunged him into well water, where
It runs both cold and deep

All of a sudden the sensation was gone, and when I opened my eyes I was alone.

Of course I was. Why was I such an idiot?

I shuddered and jumped out of the bath and looked down into the still-moving red frothy water. There was no trace of another person. I looked down on the lesions to see if they had changed, but they appeared the same. I rubbed my chest hard with the towel. Maybe they would come off if I was rough enough. I remembered Samantha Fry telling me about her skin tag – showing it me, in fact. Below her throat, low, almost at the top of her breast, a pink sac of flesh held on by a skinny stalk and she had ripped it off herself one night, after she'd got high from meditating. Meditating could get you as high as pot, Samantha Fry said.

I rubbed hard, so hard that the areas where the metal beads were embedded began to sting as if I had been flicked hard all over with rubber bands.

'Lie there, lie there, love Henry,' she cried
'Till the flesh rots off your bones
Some pretty little girl in Cornersville
Will mourn for your return'

I looked again in the mirror. The studs gleamed in the harsh bathroom light like precious stones. I thought about the nuclear plant, Sellafield, nine miles away on the coast, and the radiation everyone said was in the air, and about Brannan's thermometer factory at the top of the road. Could this infestation have been caused by them? If so, why just me? Or was it just me?

The record stopped, *Henry Lee* stopped, and I went upstairs and got dressed. The house was three storeys high and from my bedroom I could see over the ramshackle allotments to where the fairground stood, looking dull and shabby in the murky curtains of rain. Further on past the fairground was the Grey Stuff, where my mother said they'd found the girl. The girl. Philomena May. I wondered what had happened to her, but without asking anyone, I knew. Whenever people spoke like that, of a girl found dead, it was always the same thing. She must have been murdered. But before the murder, there was always something sexual. I didn't really know why the two were associated.

I chose some heavy jeans which I pulled on, noticing the way the denim slid over the shiny studs smoothly without catching, and then a thick lumberjack shirt because a thinner one might reveal the bumps through the fabric. My cowboy boots next, the ones I'd got from a secondhand shop, and then I topped it all off with my fur-lined denim coat from JanWear. Once dressed, I looked in the mirror, this time at my face, the only exposed part of my skin. The metallic lesions glinted on my forehead so I rearranged my fringe to make sure these patches stayed hidden.

Still in my coat, I sat on the floor, picked up my guitar, and played the opening chords to my latest composition. I went through the first verse, singing the words off a sheet of paper on the floor and making amendments with a Biro as I did.

I crooned the chorus softly, under my breath.

Ain't no marigold pushing its way through the tarmac

Ain't no marigold pushing its way through the tar

Over and over, gawping at myself in the mirror as I did so, making sure not to smile.

I looked serious, dangerous, despairing, bohemian. My job was to spill out my soul on the stage, and I believed that I looked the part. Maybe this metalling of my skin would be good for my image. After all, it didn't seem to be harming me, I felt fine. I decided to stop thinking about the metal blisters. I had an idea that the blisters had a collective mind, a consciousness, a will; that they were somehow plotting against me. So if I ignored them, if I showed no fear, they would subside, melt away into the air in the same secret way they had appeared.

I tossed my guitar onto the bed, took my wallet from my coat pocket and looked inside it. No money. I needed four pounds and seventy-five pence. I had worked it out exactly. That included the bus fare. Call it five pounds then. Five pounds would do.

I left the house and set off down the road towards Moor Row. The rain had stopped, but the air still felt cold and wet.

When I reached Number One Hollow, I stopped. Number One Hollow was a disused pit shaft filled with green, still water. Children had drowned in it: the Coan boys, playing on a homemade raft; a young girl called Madeline Grahame who slipped through its icy crust one winter. I stared at the solid-looking green surface, the bulrushes around the edges with their fat brown ends. A fly-tipped sofa was nearby, purple, with yellow foam splurging out of it, now coated in a film of silver from the rain. Me and Finny liked to sit on this when it was dry enough, and discuss the world and death and music and sex and drugs and politics while we smoked the grass Finny's brother brought back from Newcastle where he was a student. If everything wasn't so wet, I would have sat on the sofa and thought about things for a time. I would have thought about my songs for Troubadours, and about my next meet-up with Samantha Fry, and what I would say to persuade her to join my folk music project. I set off again, picking my way around puddles of rainwater, all red-coloured because of the iron ore which was in the soil everywhere.

Iron ore?

No. How could that be?

I stopped at a raggedy group of brown and white chickens, clucking and pecking in the dirt. A purplish-black cockerel with a crimson comb on his head stared at me, aggressively, sarcastically, almost. It seemed to know. Know about me. Barry Dyer. About the situation I was hiding under my clothes. What would an animal do if it woke up and found itself covered in metal blisters? I knew what it would do. Ignore it and get on with its life. Human beings are animals too, I thought. So if that's what a cockerel would do, that's what I should do.

I carried on past deep hedges of trees and bushes and brambles to the brown culverted stream everyone called the Water Boxes, which lay at the bottom of the track. The Water Boxes was a run of dirty water divided into two down the middle by a low concrete wall, and no one knew what the structure was for. I guessed it was in two sections because it was used to move different materials in and out of the iron ore mine. Birds hopped about on the concrete partition. Nearby, a fat sewer pipe on long metal stalks ran above the Water Boxes towards the treatment plant at Egremont. Me and Finny would sometimes climb up on to it and see how far we could walk without falling off.

I carried on past fields of trampled dirt, where nothing jutted out but the odd crisp packet or sun-bleached plastic toy, to where the path became muddier, and round the corner to where everything had overgrown so much you had to push your way through coils of thorns to get to the entrance of the tunnel through the hill.

The tunnel through the hill had been built for the small trains that used to move the iron ore about. It was long and dark, and so narrow you could touch both sides with your hands at all times. I felt a twinge of apprehension as I was about to enter. Although most of the way you could see light from somewhere, there were two curved sections in the middle at opposite angles to each other which meant that between these twists there was a small space where it was always pitch black. This was the point where whoever you were with made you stop, and said, 'Listen? Hear that humming sound? That's the ghost of Jimmy Connolly', then went on to tell you about the unfortunate fourteen-year-old miner who was trapped underground for seventeen days before he died. Everyone said they could hear him from above the collapsed mine, humming to keep himself calm, old Irish tunes his father used to play on a fiddle, and long after he had died down there – alone, of hunger, of dehydration – the humming continued, and still does to this day.

I stopped and listened.

The tunnel did indeed emit a hum; an eerie two-note drone caused, I knew now, by the wind in the ventilation shafts. It was a strange harmony that I recognised as a sixth, and the name of the chord convinced me there was nothing occult about it. A real ghost would hum a flattened fifth, the Devil's harmony – so evil-sounding, it was once banned from church organs. It would never hum a pathetic sixth, a muzak interval, which sounded nothing less than smug.

I listened harder. Between the waves of hum, I heard the dripping of moisture from the moss above my head, the scrabbling of something, maybe a bird, the tick-ticking of drying grass, the creaking of the mound of earth above as it shifted under the weight of the rain. Then, something else. A soft fluttering sound at first, then it became breathy, and then, then, it was like a whisper, like a thin, high human voice. I even imagined the words it seemed to be forming. They seemed to materialise in my mind like a photograph in a tray of chemicals.

He will ask them the time, it seemed to be saying. *He will ask them the time.*

I shuddered. An insane idea passed through my mind that the metallic lumps were speaking to me, and as I processed this thought I felt suddenly stupid, small, juvenile, vulnerable. These pathetic shiny pimples were affecting my brain. I coughed loudly to assert my presence, then moved out of the claustrophobic elbow of a space and into the final section of the tunnel, walking quickly over the gritty floor towards the faint circle of light at the end.

Outside, a gravelly path led from the tunnel's exit into the cluster of poky grey and cream terraced houses that formed Moor Row, and over the road I could see my father in the Co-op, standing at the bacon slicer.

I crossed the road and went inside the store. The main room was wide with floor-to-ceiling shelving along the back wall, a long wooden counter in front of it, and lots of loose goods dotted about in sacks and jars and barrels that my dad and shop assistant Marion Crow would weigh before putting into bags they made out of flat sheets of paper.

'Hey,' Dad said when he saw me. 'What you doing here, lad?'

'I've been doing coursework at home.'

'We were talking about the girl. The girl they found on Cleator Moor, on the Grey Stuff.'

I wondered who he meant by 'we' as I couldn't see anyone else there.

'Me and Marion,' he nodded towards the floor. 'She's cleaning out the traps under the counter.'

'Oh,' I said.

My dad looked down. 'It's our Barry, Marion,' and he smiled towards the floorboards then looked back at me.

'She says hello.'

'Hello Marion,' I called into the air. 'What do you do with the dead mice out of the traps?'

'We give them to her uncle Leo' my dad said. 'He has snakes. He has to jiggle them about though, because snakes need live food, really. He's always had reptiles, her uncle Leo. He's a biker.'

The top of Marion Crow's head appeared, then her face, then her body, and she smiled at me and brushed dust off her chest, her fingers flicking the tips of her breasts under the thin Co-op overall my father made her wear. Marion Crow was in her twenties and had a lot of jobs in the town. I had seen her working in the school canteen, at the doctors, at the funeral parlour, in the betting shop, and in The Derby Arms too. I was always astonished at how strong she was – carrying a sack of potatoes on her back like it was nothing, or once, dancing about with half a pig under her arm, singing *Chirpy Chirpy Cheep Cheep*.

'Not at school, Baz?'

I disliked being called Baz, but tolerated it from Marion because she was pretty.

'Coursework at home,' I said.

'You want to help out here?' my dad said.

'No. I need to borrow some money.'

'Oh, aye. What for, lad?'

'Records.'

'He's got loads of records,' my dad said to Marion.

'Well,' said Marion, moving away from the counter and finding some stepladders. 'It's his ambition, isn't it? Him and his guitar. You have to learn somehow. How else is he going to escape from this town?'

Marion leaned the stepladders against the tall shelves of groceries behind the counter and climbed slowly up them. My dad didn't look round, but I watched closely as she went up, up and up, higher and higher, and higher, staring at her legs, her thighs. When she was at the top, she called down.

'Bill, did you say aromatic?'

'Yes, aromatic, please.'

'How many?'

'Two pouches. For Ronnie Pep.'

She leaned across for the tobacco pouches, allowing me to get a long look at her thighs.

'Baaaaz?' she called as she descended, dragging out my name in a reproachful way. 'Baaaz? I hope you don't have any bad habits yet?'

'He's not going to smoke, are you son? We have a deal. Brand-new Washburn acoustic if he gets to eighteen never having had a drag.'

My dad banged a button on the till, the drawer flew open, and he handed me a five-pound note.

'You going to Whitehaven?'

'Yes,' I said.

'Don't let any teachers see you. It's O level year, isn't it?'

'That's next year,' I said. 'I'll be fine. What were you saying about the girl? Philomena May. Have they found someone yet?'

Marion replaced the stepladders and came back to the counter.

'She was discovered in a terrible state. I couldn't sleep last night, thinking about it. I got so hot, feverish. Dominic said I was rolling over and over. I had to take everything off, everything. The disgusting things people are saying that he did to her. Have the police spoken to you, Barry?'

'No.'

'They think maybe someone from the fair. These fair people, you know, these travellers, they are not kind of, they are not kind of rooted anywhere. It's like a different law.'

'Were you at the fair, lad?' my dad said.

'Yes,' I said.

'Did you see anything?'

'I didn't see Philomena May. Mam said that she was supposed to be at the fair, but she went to The Derby Arms instead.'

'Some are saying,' Marion continued, climbing up on to a high stool and crossing her long black nylon-clad legs, 'and I don't agree with this, but some are saying she was a bad lot, and one even said, and this was a church woman – the little skinny one who does the flowers at St Mary's, a Catholic – this Catholic woman said, people are saying, they are saying, she deserved it. That she went with this feller she shouldn't have been with and she went willingly and it all got out of hand. Who can blame a man when a young girl is offering herself on a plate and you don't know how old she is? Who can tell nowadays? With Sunsilk and nail varnish and pierced ears and everything. They are saying that's what happened and then he panicked.'

'So they know who he is?' I said.

'No. No idea yet.'

The shop bell donged and Ronnie Pep, a small round man with sticky-out yellow hair, came in for his aromatic and, as Marion wittered on to him about the murder, I saw my chance to escape.

'Dad, I'm off to town. I'll see you later.'

'Wait,' my dad said, 'come here,' and he took me into a corner. 'Your mother's been on. She's upset. Wouldn't say what it was at first. At first she said she'd found something, something upsetting. Then she said it was you. This skin thing. What have you been doing?'

'Nothing.'

'Something about your skin. She said you have to meet her at Dr Ferguson's at five. She's the nice young one. Scottish.'

'But I'm going to buy records. You gave me the money.'

'If your mother says you need to go to the doctors, then you need to do what she says.'

'I don't need to go, I'm fine.'

'She says it's your skin. What's up with your skin?'

'It's nothing.'

Dad shooed me into the stock-room where it smelt of cereal and sawdust and raw meat.

'Look,' I said, and was about to raise my shirt when Dad stopped me.

'I don't need to see it. Just tell me.'

'It's like metal things on my skin.'

'Metal things?'

'Yes.'

'And you didn't put them there?'

'No.'

'Have you been taking drugs?'

'No.'

'So,' he said, 'you feel OK?'

'Yes.'

'So it's just metal things. Are they rusty? 'Cos you'd need a tetanus injection if—'

'They're not rusty. They're clean and shiny.'

Dad went quiet and looked down at his brown overall, then at his feet on the floor.

'With this girl last night as well, it's all a bit…'

'How, Dad? How could the two things be related?'

My dad looked at the window then over at the sharp tools he used for cutting up meat.

'You're right,' he said. 'But if the police come and ask you questions, I wouldn't mention the skin thing. It just, it would just single you out.'

Marion began speaking as soon as we emerged from the stock-room.

'You know, Bill, how I was telling you about the oven? About the fact that we can't have a drop-down door because the kitchen's not big enough? Well, Dominic has solved this by taking out all the cupboards and putting up wall units without permission.'

'Oh,' my dad said.

'I think he just likes to see me bending over and looking into the cooker.'

'Can you bag up that sheep's head for Audrey Clegg?' My dad said to her.

'Oh?'

'She's gonna boil it up for the hounds. Jimmy Fleming will pick it up for her. Can you sort that out?'

Marion disappeared into the stock-room and came back with the head of a dishevelled-looking ram under her arm, its nose pressing against her breast.

'Hey,' she said, 'listen.'

She pointed the sheep's head towards us and moved its chin up and down with her fingers while she sang in a high, affected Irish accent.

Now, Patrick McGinty, an Irish man of note
Fell in for a fortune and he bought himself a goat

Dad laughed. 'Marion Crow, stop it now.'

Then Marion wiggled her hips and pretended to waltz about the room with the sheep's head, looking into its eyes seductively, while her long legs made shapes on the floor as she whirled and spun.

'Enough, enough, enough now,' said my dad. 'After you've bagged up that head, can you check on the plain flour please, and make me up a dozen two-pound bags while you're there?'

Marion stopped still. 'Right away, Captain,' she said, saluting him and bowing at the same time, before sashaying off back into the stock-room.

Outside the Co-op, I stopped and looked back. My dad was

leaning on the counter, writing in his big ledger. Marion appeared with the bags of flour, plonked them in a box, then climbed up on the counter and sat next to him, her long legs outstretched and her skirt riding high.

I thought about her thighs, and her nipples under the thin Co-op overall, and with this in mind I went back into the tunnel and walked in the damp fuggy air towards its dark centre. I thought about the five-pound note, rolled into a tube in my pocket and the thrill it would bring. Finny would be astonished when I told him I was going to go through with it.

At the dark spot in the centre of the tunnel, I had meant to pick up pace and get out of there fast, but I heard it again; the murmur, the soft fluttering syllables I thought I'd picked up before. I stopped still and focused. A white whoosh of nothing, the pulsing of my own blood.

Then the voice spoke once more, and this time it was clear.

Barry. He will ask them the time. But they should not answer

I listened hard again.

Help me

The voice was closer now, right in front of me, and I could sense a presence, sense that someone was definitely there.

Barry

It was a girl and she was in the tunnel with me, close, inches away, and now I could hear her breathing, and then – then I felt her hand on mine, and my body jerked like I'd been shot through with a thousand volts. But I didn't move, I didn't take my hand away. I tried to picture the hand, her hand. It felt small, with long fingers. She brushed my knuckles with the long fingers, then encircled my hand in hers and squeezed, and we stood still like that for a few moments.

Barry she said again, then pulled me towards her until the back of my hand touched her stomach.

It was then that I realised she was naked. I wanted to pull away, but she guided me even closer and this time I felt her breast, her naked breast against my upper arm, and I could feel her breath on my face and she spoke to me again, into my ear.

He will ask them the time, but they should not answer

Her words came slowly and deliberately as if she were speaking a foreign language she had recently learned.

My heart was pounding, my face was hot, and I wanted to run away more than anything, to be out of that space, but I felt unable to move. I pulled away a little and when I did this she let go of my hand, and, as she did so, I felt sharp little fingernails drag against me.

I need you, Barry. I need your help. We have to stop it. He will ask them the time, but they should not answer. Can you help me? Please. Barry. I need you to tether me

I tried to answer, but it was as if a lump of dry wool had filled my mouth.

'I don't know,' I said, eventually, 'I don't know who you are. I'll come back with help.'

And then I turned round and my legs seemed to work again, so I ran, ran out of the dark centre of the tunnel towards the dim disc of pale sun at the end. Outside I gulped in a massive draught of air as if I had been underwater, then staggered through the tangled vegetation to a sagging wooden fence which I leaned against, sucking in air and holding my head.

The hooter from Brannan's thermometer factory brayed, indicating the start of the three o'clock tea break.

I was going insane. I'd read about schizophrenia, a condition that made you hear voices, and I remembered Deborah Fisher from my year at school, who had ended up having medical treatment for mental ill health, at first on A Ward in West Cumberland Hospital and then, because A Ward didn't work, in Garlands, a frightening, rambling mansion just outside Carlisle.

Yet.

Her sharp little fingernails. I stared at my hand and thought I could see a faint pink line. I looked at the entrance to the tunnel. Was she completely naked? It appeared so. But she'd felt so warm. Her stomach. Her breast.

I peered into the bushes. A sodden, fading copy of the *News &* *Star* lay there.

NEW OUTFALL PIPELINE FOR WHITEHAVEN

Over three quarters of a mile long, the new pipeline has a multiple diffuser meaning higher volumes of sludge are possible with a total of 23 outlet ports.

The fur edges of my denim coat were covered in the sticky bobbles that some plants leave on you, and I brushed them off violently as I paced up the path, pausing to stare at the moody cockerel, as if it might have some sort of answer, then carrying on up to Number One Hollow where I sat on the purple sofa's soaking cushions and thought.

A cow leaned over the fence and blinked at me.

I looked at the green surface of Number One Hollow. The mist above it hung in sheets. Maybe the girl had risen up out of this murky bilge like a water nymph. Maybe – my mind raced on with thoughts fantastic, outlandish, spooky and surreal.

What did *ask them the time* mean? I thought about the girl's breasts, and then about Samantha Fry and the small pillows of fat on her chest I had eyed once when she bent down to lift her Fender Precision out of its case.

Finally, I decided that there was a normal explanation for it all. It was the metal. These metal lesions were poisoning me, like the mercury they used in Brannan's thermometer factory at the top of the road. In fact the blobs did have that strange, otherworldy consistency of molten silver.

No.

An infection, that was all it was. An attack of microbodies, an imbalance of chemicals that was affecting my brain and could be easily solved by the application of modern science.

But I didn't want to see Dr Ferguson. She might send me to hospital to have them removed. The doctors would spray me with acid to dissolve them or snick them out with razor-tipped pliers. And for some odd reason, some reason that I couldn't explain, I didn't want to have them taken from me. I pushed my hand under my shirt to see if they were still there.

Yes.

The metal studs were somehow comforting, as if they belonged to me, as if they had become a unique thing about me, the only unique thing, a thing that made me special.

3

The Grey Stuff was a slag heap of extrusions from the iron ore mines. Originally brilliant white, it had turned grey after years of exposure to Cumbrian wind and dirt, and had now been partly taken back into nature, its edges wild with long grass and small trees.

Finny was standing near the edge, rattling his fingers impatiently up and down the side of a lamppost, his long dark hair covering half his face.

Police vans were parked everywhere and a patch of land was cordoned off with blue and white tape. *The boys are back in town* could be heard coming out of the Commercial Hotel's juke-box.

'I got the money,' I said when I reached him.

'What money?' said Finny, not looking at me.

'Two pound fifty for the room and three for—'

'Oh,' said Finny.

'You got yours?' I said.

'Yeh, yeh. I've got it.'

'So we're on?'

'When were you thinking?'

'Tonight.'

'A Friday?'

'So?'

'More of a Saturday-night thing, I'd have thought.'

'Oh. Right,' I said, not disappointed that the plan could be put on ice.

'Tonight it's the school disco. Remember? Samantha Fry and Heather Fox are coming round.'

'But where's your mum?'

Finny pushed his hair out of his face. 'She's at kung fu. It's good for her nerves.'

I had always admired Finny for his individuality and his single-mindedness, and the fact that he never seemed to care what anyone thought about him and his family. He had his own way of doing things and his own way of looking at things and his own distinct taste which rarely wavered under the pressures of fashion, practicality or convenience. Ever since Finny started at the grammar three years ago, he'd been an outsider, and I suspected he liked it that way. West Cumbrians were always suspicious of anyone who had moved in from outside, and Finny's home life, with his depressed mother who was learning kung fu, had not reassured them that he would slot right in with no trouble at all. But I saw something special in Finny and began in certain ways to model myself on him. If Finny wore Pepe jeans, then I would wear Pepe jeans. If Finny said, 'That was tubular man, really tubular', I would start to say things were tubular. When Finny read *Invasion Of The Crabs, Night Of The Crabs* and *Dawn Of The Crabs* by Guy N Smith all in one sitting and said they were the best books ever, I read them and said they were the best books ever.

Finny pushed his long hair back again. 'Something to show you, by the way,' he said and looked about carefully, then, from the pocket of his tattered two-tone suede jacket that he thought made him look like Adam Faith in *Budgie,* he took out a small envelope which I recognised as one of the ones that were used to send home our end-of-term reports.

He opened it to reveal a small clump of hair with some skin attached.

The boys are back

The boys are back in town again

I felt immediately sick and turned away. 'What the hell, Finny? What the hell?'

'I found it at the old kennels over there.' He nodded behind him.

Then Finny barrelled off over the Grey Stuff, his wide denim flares flapping, and I ran after him.

We walked over to the edge of the area where the girl's body had been found. The grass and weeds looked crushed and mussed up and there were some twigs broken on the bushes. My mother had called it a ditch, but it wasn't really a ditch. Nearby lay a discarded tractor seat, the metal stem rusted, the plastic top snapped in two. There was a pile of old clothing catalogues, saturated with rain, the colours leached out. A short length of grey electrical wire coiled on a wooden bobbin. A red semi-transparent space gun that looked as though it used to have sweets in it.

I wondered if any of these items were involved.

Police were wandering about everywhere – on the Grey Stuff, in the bushes, on the pavement, in the road – stooped over, and creeping incredibly slowly as they scrutinised the ground.

I couldn't help thinking that if the murderer had been local, he would have weighed the body down and tossed it into the malodorous green broth of Number One Hollow. Or, if he had a car, driven her to nearby Wastwater, which was supposed to be 250 feet deep in parts

Finny and I stood for a while and watched the policemen searching, but nothing was found, at least not while we were there. I guessed they would be looking for cigarette stubs, or footprints, or scraps of clothing ripped off during the attack, but had no idea really, despite having watched dozens of episodes of *Columbo* and *Ironside*. The whole thing seemed hyper-unreal, happening here, in Cleator Moor, in my home town, a mile or so from my own front door.

'I saw her once coming home from dancing class. In a leotard,' Finny said.

'Me too,' I said.

We looked for a bit longer at the patch of grass, at the drooping broken stalks of plants that possibly marked the spot where Philomena May had been found, and at the wide expanse of Grey

Stuff with the policeman crawling about on it.

Then I felt a hard slap on the back of my head and turned to see Marion Crow's husband, Dominic Crow, staring at me with a big grin all over his cakehole.

'Hello poofters,' he said in a low voice. 'Wishing you'd seen her when she was naked?'

Dominic Crow was a short, wide, powerfully built man in his mid-twenties. Although he had some obscure full-time job at Sellafield, the erratic timings of the shifts meant that he was often to be seen in the daytime roaming about the town between the pubs and the betting shops, smoking non-stop and shouting loudly at people he knew in the street, or driving about in his black and gold Ford Capri with Deep Purple pounding out of his wound-down window. Today he was wearing cowboy boots, tight Brutus jeans that showed his thick muscled thighs, a T-shirt that said *War Pigs*, and a leather biker jacket with fronds that hung down from the arms.

'You sick fuckers. You know what the police are looking for in the bushes? Her nipples. Rumour is he chewed them off. The sick bastard. When they bang him behind bars, he'll have everything gnawed away. The crooks in there have no time for fellers like him. Up the arse with a sharpened toothbrush, bleed to death on your own.'

'Nice, Mr Crow,' I said. 'Thanks for that.'

'Was it you that did it, teacher's boy?'

'Uh?' I said.

Dominic Crow hawked up snot and spat a gobbet into the grass. 'You haven't got it in you.'

* * *

A pair of creepy porcelain dogs stared at each other across the fireplace as though they hadn't been moved for a hundred years. Four china plates on the wall showed seasonal images of nuns herding cows. On the dining table, which was never used for eating at as far as I could see, a glass dome covered a dead branch on which sat six stuffed birds; a carmine bee-eater, a hummingbird, a bearded parrotbill, and three described simply as 'South American'. Against the wall was a sofa with half a back, which Finny said was called a chaise longue. Every surface was tacky and furred with dust, but Finny and I liked this room because of the drinks cabinet, a bottle-shaped bureau that opened up to reveal a multi-mirrored interior, gaudy plastic cocktail paraphernalia a huge variety of differently shaped glasses, and lots of drinks for people who rarely partook – like Babycham, Advocat, Baileys and Cinzano.

Finny handed me the latest copy of *Uncanny Tales*, then busied himself in the cocktail cabinet. The cover of the comic showed hooded men doing something medical to a terrified naked woman in a glass tube. I opened its pages and was looking at a story called *Alien Brain Invasion*, in which a fleet of tiny flying saucers land inside a man's head and minuscule homunculi emerge to take him over, when Samantha Fry stomped in wearing scarlet flares, a stripy mime-artist top, heavy cork platform shoes, and a swipe of dark red on her lips.

'Heather can't come,' she said. 'She's too upset about last night.'

She stopped in the middle of the room and closed her eyes. Long seconds passed and I stared at the cartoon drawings of metallic creatures in their landscape of organs and blood.

'Philomena May,' she said finally, purring out the words like a song. 'I knew her. We used to go to the same dancing class. She was so beautiful. Gorgeous eyes. High cheekbones. Face like a rosebud.'

Water welled at the corners of Samantha Fry's eyes and I didn't know what to do. I chucked the comic onto the chaise longue and went over to her, gripping her upper arm with my hand. Her tears came soundlessly, washing down her cheeks.

'They found her without clothes,' she said, speaking breathlessly through sobs. 'How could someone do that? Think of her lying there in the cold with the rain and the wind and the insects and the quiet and the dark. The muck in her hair, the dogs sniffing around, and her lovely two eyes pointing towards the moon and stars but not seeing anything but blackness.'

Finny left his work at the cocktail cabinet and came over and gripped her other arm. Samantha let out a long low whimper and we stood in the centre of the room in silence, each boy gripping one of her arms, until she collapsed onto a chair at the dining table.

'Rosie Whelan and Karen Walsh were with her,' she said towards the ceramic dogs. 'Karen said that before they went out, they got drunk on this stuff called Bénédictine. Supposed to be gold-coloured, but this one was green and she thinks someone had replaced it with absinthe because that's illegal on account of the psycho stuff in it. Wormwood. Philomena got sick over by the Police Houses, spewed green into someone's begonias, and they had to run off. They went to the fair for a bit, but didn't go on anything 'cos that's not cool. They sneaked behind the Rib Tickler and spoke to a gypsy feller who travels with the rides. Three fingers, lost the others in the gears of the Waltzer. He gave them fags and a swig from a bottle of vodka. Rosie Whelan snogged him, Karen said, but then they all ran off laughing. They went to The Derby Arms. There were no strangers in there, Karen said, it was just all the usuals. Half ten came and they got a lock-in and they were dancing in the pool room to *Down Down*, doing the Status Quo dips with the fellers. One of the girls climbed on the pool table and danced so fast she fell off. Karen couldn't remember if it was Philomena May or Rosie Whelan. Later Philomena felt ill again and went off to the bogs to spew. They didn't see her again. They went in looking for her, knocking on all the cubicles, but she wasn't there and they assumed she'd gone home on her own.'

We sat in silence for a time, not knowing what to do or say.

'Talk to me about something else, boys,' Samantha said eventually, raising her head, and sitting upright in the chair. 'To take my mind off it. How's that song about the marigolds coming on, you miserable bastard?'

'Finished,' I said.

'I'm not forming a band with you until you write some proper tunes.'

'I'm fifteen. I'm supposed to be confused and depressed. I'll be doing it at Troubadours.'

'All the sad wee singer-songwriters whining abut their lonely, complicated lives in a world that hates them,' said Samantha.

'Exactly,' I said.

'Psycho Faction are playing Maryport Civic Hall,' she said. 'Punk is where it's at. Want to come with me?'

'If you promise to play bass with me at Troubadours.'

Samantha Fry snort-laughed. 'Maybe, Barry, maybe. But now,' she got up, flicked the giant cork structures off her feet and tossed herself full length onto the chaise longue, 'Wait on me, boys.' She took out a steel case and opened it to show a row of pink-coloured cigarettes. 'Fashionable ladies used to have these dyed the same colour as their dresses in the sixties.' She lit one and held it at a jaunty angle next to her head. 'Boys, come on, come on. I need to drink this thing out of my head.'

Finny jammed Pink Floyd's *Wish You Were Here* into the cassette player and Samantha Fry grimaced at the distinctive guitar figure.

'So this band, Dyer. When we gonna enlist the rest of them? We'll need drums. And maybe another guitar. And who's going to sing? And you're going to have to get an electric, you know that, don't you? And I'm not joining till we've agreed a name.'

The pencilled name was Cubical Domes, something I had found in a book of surrealist poetry, but Samantha Fry wanted a more visceral moniker.

'Like Twatbox. Or Mindfuck.'

'For the school Christmas party?'

I wanted to stick with my current style of music – profound, sensitive and cerebral.

I looked at Samantha Fry lying there. Could Samantha in some way have been the naked girl from the tunnel? No. The girl's voice had been higher, more wavering. It was definitely someone else. I wondered if the naked girl was in the room somewhere, invisibly watching me.

Finny handed us both a tumbler of vodka, Canada Dry and

barley wine before slurping from his own.

Then–

'What's that on your skin?' Samantha suddenly said, reaching out and brushing away my fringe. 'What the hell, Dyer? What you been doing?'

I adjusted my hair to cover it, but Finny said, 'Let's have a proper look,' and lifted up my fringe again.

'Jesus, fuck,' he said. 'It's like you've been burned then dragged along the floor behind a truck.'

I pushed Finny's hand away. 'Is that what it looks like to you?'

'Yes. Does it look different to you?'

'Yes. Listen, this is going to sound very weird, but to me it looks like I'm covered in metallic bumps.'

'Is it all over your body?'

'Yes,' I said, and lifted my shirt.

'And to you it looks like you're half metal?' said Finny. 'A metal man?'

'While everyone else sees a weird skin infection,' I said, lowering my shirt.

'Let me see,' said Samantha Fry, and she lifted the lumberjack shirt and stared, her mouth open. 'Wow,' she said, fondling the lesions, trailing her fingers over them like they were the keys of a musical instrument. She pressed one, staring me in the face while she did so, as if expecting something to jump out. 'My god, Dyer.' She smiled. 'You're a disfigured freak!' she said, and continued to finger the bumps, sighing softly as she did. Feeling suddenly fired up by the booze and my exotic patterned state, I felt so brave I put my face close to hers and unbelievably, she closed the gap, causing some dry, fumbling lip contact for a few seconds before Finny interrupted with a loud long moan.

'Oh no. We're out of barley wine,' he said. 'Barry, you'll have to take the motorbike to the offy. I can't go – they know me in there.'

The motorbike was in Finny's shed and when Finny had fought his way past broken pots, lawnmowers, garden shears and sacks of fertiliser to reveal the prize vehicle, I couldn't believe how unimpressive it was. I had been expecting something black and chrome, Harley style maybe, not this mutant. It had a big snub nosed face as if it used be the front half of a van and the body looked like a sewing machine or a Bontempi organ, all green and cream with clunky lumps and bumps.

'It's a scooter! A fucking shit scooter, Finny. Why'd your dad get that?'

'It was for Mum.'

'For her nerves?'

'Yes. It's a DKR Defiant.'

I grabbed the handlebar from Finny, wheeled it onto the grass and sat on it.

'It's a girl's machine,' Samantha Fry said, as she came outside to have a look.

'You can ride it when you're sixteen, though,' said Finny. 'It's under fifty cc so you don't need a test. Mods used to ride them.'

'Not these contraptions,' said Samantha Fry, 'Mods had Lambrettas and Vespas.'

'I don't know how to ride it,' I said.

'Have a practise in the field before you go,' said Finny.

We took it through a gap in the garden hedge and into the field at the back, which was long and wide and empty and had no animals in it because the farmer was letting it lie fallow.

'Light the touch paper like so,' said Finny turning a key, and making the machine rattle and buzz like a crushed clockwork train. I jumped on. After a stuttering start, I managed to get it to run off down the field and then, when I twisted the handgrip all the way round, suddenly I was really going some, bouncing along on the bumpy, tussocky grass like a rocket, feeling as if I was travelling exhilaratingly fast, even though the speedo said twenty-five miles an hour.

Then I felt it. Something encircling me. A grip about my waist and the weight of a body against my back. For a moment I thought it was Finny, that Finny had leapt on to the back of the scooter the way a cowboy might do onto a horse in a western. But the weight was wrong. The mass was wrong. The feeling was wrong. Too light. Too small. The arms became tighter and the weight of the body was pressing up against me hard. And I heard the voice in my ear, the same one, the one from earlier. This time, as well as hearing the voice, I felt breath on my neck and a trembling against my back as the voice spoke:

Barry. He will ask the time but they should not answer

I tried to turn, to take a look, but whoever, or whatever, it was placed a small hand firmly on the back of my head and forced me to look forwards.

Watch out, Barry

I swerved to avoid a grassy hummock, but kept control. I decided to head away from the house and, turning parallel to the hedge, sped down the slope towards the bottom of the hill, with an idea that I would stop suddenly and make the thing, the person, the whatever it was, fly off. My speed hit thirty, the handlebar shook, but the grip from my mysterious pillion passenger became firmer, more assertive, and the words kept coming.

We need to stop him, Barry. I need you to tether me. Tether me, please

It was a girl, it was *the* girl, the same girl from before in the tunnel.

In the distance I heard Finny's voice calling out – 'Barry, Barry!' – but I twisted the handgrip further and was now heading directly towards the hedge. *I'll crash,* I thought. *I'll hit the hedge, I'll do it deliberately, then everything will be fine and this creature, this tormenting voice, this hallucination in my head, will disappear in the same way it came.* I twisted the handgrip again and the scooter went faster and faster and Finny's voice retreated further into the distance and the hedge got closer and then the scooter must have hit a brick or a chunk of wood because it suddenly flew up into the air. For a few terrifying seconds I was above the hedge, suspended, and I looked down to my side and saw the road tilting up towards me, the hard tarmacked road, and when I glanced behind I saw a naked foot and a leg, a long, lovely smooth calf, and as soon as I saw this I knew I would be safe, and I was right. There was a pause, as if we had entered a pocket of sucked-out silence, then the scooter drifted down as if it was a feather, and when it hit the ground all I had to do was turn the handgrip and I was off. Whooping like a maniac, I spun the bike into Finny's drive, laughing and shaking my head in disbelief at my amazing feat of heroic daring.

'How the hell did you do that?' Finny said. 'You were fucking Evel Knievel, man.'

I switched off the engine and looked behind me. There was no sign of the girl. I pulled off my shirt to reveal the glory of my silver-studded chest and roared at the sky.

'I'm Metal Man. Half-man, half-metal!' Then I started the engine again with a delicious *vomp* and screeched off towards a country lonning that led all the way to school without crossing any main roads. Finny would have to sort out the offy on his own.

I rode fast, the cool breeze licking at my bare chest and as I rode I thought about the ghost girl. For that is what I believed her to be. She was a ghost, a phantom, a dead person walking the Earth. But who was she? Was she the spectre of the murdered Philomena May? If so, why was she haunting *me*? I hadn't done her any harm. She had made me zoom through the air like a hawk. Did this ghost girl have magic powers? I'd read that witches greased the handles of their brushes with hallucinogenic fat and rubbed their parts with them to get high; that is what was meant by flying on a broomstick. Was the naked girl a witch? Half-real, half-dead, half-fairy, half-zombie. Was the girl good? She might not be good; she might not have my welfare in mind at all. She might have some darker motive.

Maybe the metal studs were causing me to be feverish, to hallucinate, the way fermented mushrooms or rotten wheat seeds might. Or the grease on a broomstick between a witch's thighs.

Thinking this, I went blind.

I slammed on the brakes, and felt the scooter slew to the side and thump into a ditch where the machine and I collapsed together.

The girl's hands remained over my eyes and I didn't move them. I enjoyed the coolness of her skin, the strange toffee smell of her hair, the cold shush of her breath on my neck, and the stillness, the quietness, the peacefulness; a state she seemed to carry about with her like a cloud of personal weather.

Eventually she re-gifted me my sight and moved to sit nearby in the dyke, and it was then, for the first time, that I really saw her.

She was hunched up in the hedge like a brooding pixie, and it was true what Samantha Fry said; she was beautiful. Her face was heart-shaped, with cheek-bones you could slice your tongue on, her skin was as pale as uncooked pastry, and her lips were the colour of Bulls Blood wine.

This was Philomena May, this was the girl who had been – what? I didn't want to think the word. She was completely naked, yet her skin looked perfect with no sign of wounds or cuts or abrasions. Unmarked, unripped, uncut, unbruised, unmolested.

Undead.

Nothing felt real. The whole scene seemed veiled and the girl behind gauze.

Philomena May. Her name was like a five-syllable hymn.

'Do you… do you want some clothes?' I said, looking about me for a wardrobe stuffed with fashion options to choose from.

Her shapely head tilted and she appeared to address the hedge.

'Not really,' she said, 'I don't seem to need any, I don't feel the cold.' She looked at me. 'But would you be more comfortable if I wore something?'

'A bit,' I said.

'Go on then,' she said.

I stumbled drunkenly towards the edge of the path to where it blurred into a row of back gardens, and my eyes tracked along some washing lines of pegged-out items, but none looked suitable; they were mostly kids' things. Then I saw, drying on an outhouse roof, a wetsuit, a small red wetsuit, and I ran over and grabbed it.

She was examining the scooter as intently as a cave person swept forward in time, her face close to the controls, her hand twisting the accelerator. I tapped the bare skin of her back, and she turned, looked down at the garment, and gave me a big crescent smile.

'A perfect choice,' she said, snatching the sopping all-in-one and putting herself into it like a lizard slithering into a hole.

'Now, I need to do something. I need to tether you to me. Come here,' she said, and she grabbed my hands and tugged me in close to her and then kissed me hard on the lips. There was something solid and practical about the way her lips moved and the manner in which her tongue wormed about in the corners of my mouth; it was as if she were gaining a specific amount of precisely calibrated nourishment from me. Indeed, when a certain time had elapsed, she broke away and nodded her head firmly.

'That will do fine,' she said. 'For now. Now I have you.'

'Have me?'

'Yes. Now I have you and there's something we need to do. Together.'

'I'm drunk and I'm supposed to be going to a school disco.'

'I need your help.'

'Is it about the man who did it? The man who did this to you?'

She bit her lip and thought for a time.

'No,' she said. 'It doesn't seem to be that. We don't seem to seek revenge.' Every phrase seemed important, as if she was mumbling a psalm to herself. 'We prevent similar things happening in the future. Get on the,' she looked at the name on the side of the scooter, 'the Defiant. And don't be frightened.'

Her eyes were coppery with chips of green and they sent something deep inside me.

I got on and we sped away and the more I twisted the scooter's handgrip, the faster we went as if we were gliding along polished ice. On the main road, a truck swept past, dragging its giant shadow over us, but for some reason, I felt invincible with the ghost girl, and rocketed on regardless.

The ghost girl directed me by tugging on my arms and eventually we ended up tearing back up towards Crossfield Road, past the tunnel through the hill, past the fat sewer pipe on its long metal stalks, past the puddles of red water and the Water Boxes, past the chickens and the fly-tipped sofa, then down, down, down, to the edge of Number One Hollow, where she thumped me hard on the back to stop, right by the soupy green pond. The scooter's front wheel teetered over the edge, the bottom of the tyre semi-submerged in the swampy goo.

'We have to go in there,' she said. 'That's what your skin is telling me.'

'In the water?'

'Yes. Drive in, please.'

I didn't want to drive into a flooded pit shaft with the ghost of a murdered teenage girl. I would rather be drunk at the school disco with Samantha Fry. I sat on the scooter for a time, feeling the girl's warmth though the wetsuit against my bare back and found myself wondering how she worked. I could register no heart beat in her, but could feel something like breath. I hoped that if I sat there long enough, she would change her mind. But does a ghost have a mind? And can it be changed?

She leaned forward. 'Now,' she said, and slapped her hand on mine where it sat on the accelerator and banged her other hand on top of the opposite handle then her bare foot went under mine on the clutch, and she kicked my shoe away from where it was holding the brake and abruptly we flew up, up, up, up into the air, just as we had when we'd leaped over Finny's garden hedge. This time, though, we didn't fly across the pool to the other side; we landed on the surface and immediately sank.

The pool grew darker and colder as we plunged under the weight of the Defiant. I tried to let go of the machine so I could break free and swim upwards, but the ghost girl held on to me with a powerful grip. I panicked, my mind whirling from one thing to the next in a flickering showreel, jump-cutting from ghosts to skin diseases to scooters to murder scenes to pits of noxious slime.

I gave in to the terror. Closed my eyes, closed my mind. It seemed the only thing to do. Resign to the sleepy silence of the void, begin the slow, slow lapse into oblivion. But before I could help it, I had opened my mouth again and this time I sucked in a clot of dirty, weedy, stagnant water, and then more water, and I thought, no. This is what it is like to drown, this is what happens when your lungs brim with fluid and you choke to death on your own body's fumes. I tried to shout, though I knew that underwater there was no point, and even if I were able to make the tiniest of squeaks, in this dead pit of nothingness only the frogs would hear me.

Then.

It was then, while attempting to yell for help from deep at the bottom of Number One Hollow, it was then that I realised that I wasn't drowning, I wasn't suffocating, I wasn't dying.

I could breathe.

I could breathe underwater, I was alive, I was fine, and the scooter was fine too. The Defiant, the DKR Defiant, it was still working, it wasn't sinking, it was propelling us ahead through the grimy gunge, and I breathed in slowly, slowly again, deeply again, slowly again, then opened my eyes.

I couldn't see much at first. Below us, a few dark, angular shapes, which, after a longer look, turned out to be pieces of household junk – a mangled dining chair, a bulky appliance like a fridge or cooker, something sideboard-shaped. I glanced above and could make out wisps of sunlight strafing the surface. Ahead, the water appeared clearer as if we were coming out of a patch of fog, so I twisted the handgrip to speed up and the black spinach of the weed broke into clumps of greasy gunk that became further and further apart until in the end they had floated off like dark distant clouds.

Clear water. We were now in clear water, much colder water, freezing, and I looked down to see sharp black rocks a long way below and, above, a blue sky through a wind-ruffled, clean-looking, surface.

That's when I saw the man.

Roundish, heavy and not tall, he was floating in a half-foetal position with his back towards us and, as soon as he became visible, the ghost girl tapped me on the shoulder and waved her hand in front of my face to indicate that I should slow down.

We glided to a halt a few yards behind the dreamy, drifting figure and sat on the scooter, under the water, as if in a bubble.

The drifting man twisted and turned slowly, enjoying his weightlessness, delighting in mimicking a spaceman.

Was this person dead? Another ghost? I didn't think so, but I did wonder whether the man was in the process of either killing himself, or suffering from the bends, which I knew sent divers into a delirious trance before tipping them over the lip of the abyss.

The man's body turned to face us. He was wearing a scuba-diving mask and I could see his orangey face behind it, but couldn't read his expression through the breathing apparatus. The man didn't appear to notice the metallic-studded boy and the ghost girl floating on a scooter in front of him; he looked straight through us.

As he spun slowly in the water we saw that he was cradling something in his arms.

It was a garden gnome.

At the base of the gnome I could see a black plug as if the gnome held something inside it.

The diver went deeper, using his hands to follow a wire that had been attached to rocks at the bottom, where it led to a murky outcrop of sand and pebbles.

We followed him.

The silt on the lakebed swelled black from the waves we were making, but soon, through the swirling clouds of dust kicked up by the diver's flippers, you could make out a whole garden of gnomes, some semi-buried in grit and mud, many smeared with dirt and identifiable as ornamental gnomes only by the crimson tips of their pointed hats, others completely faded, and one as bright as if it had been placed on the lakebed yesterday.

The diver added his gnome to the collection, placing it on a rock at the back, and trod water for a time, staring at the miniature man sitting with his new friends.

When the clouds of silt settled enough so that the whole gnome grotto was visible, the man took out a bright yellow oblong object that I had never seen before, pointed the device at the tableau, and pressed a button. He examined a display on the device and, after consulting a dial on his watch, kicked his long orange flippers and began to ascend.

The ghost girl and I surfaced a few seconds after the man and floated on the skin of the lake, watching from a distance. The diver looked shorter and stockier when he was on land and his movements were wooden, lacking the grace he had shown when supported by the water. As he walked up the stony shore and onto the grass, he pulled off his face-mask and snorted snot out of his nose. He was heading towards a grey car parked in a lay-by. The car had the word *Taxi* on the side, and a large phone number on a yellow sticker. It was a model I had never seen before. Oddly curvaceous, strangely large, and glinting.

I looked about me at the mountains crowding in around the water, at the grey scree slopes, at the barren edges, at the sullen sheep chewing at the scrubby heather, and I knew where we were. We weren't at Number One Hollow. We were on the surface of Wastwater, the deepest lake in the Lake District, in the country even.

'I take it,' I said, turning to the girl, 'That we aren't going to the disco?'

Dr Ferguson pulled on white rubber gloves, asked me to remove my shirt, then poked at my skin for a time, frowning.

'And you describe them as metal lumps?'

'That's what they look like to him,' my mother said.

'Mam – I can speak for myself. Yes, Doctor. They even feel like metal. They seem real to me. They are real.'

'And the colour? To you?'

'Silver coloured, shiny.'

'Mm,' she said. 'Put on your shirt and sit down over there. You say you feel fine?'

'Yes.'

'And there's no pain?'

'No.'

'And have you taken anything, any mind-altering drugs?'

'He says not,' said my mother.

'So apart from it being a little unsightly, you're a fit and healthy young man. OK.' She looked at me and my mother for a short time without saying anything, then snapped off the gloves and tossed them into a metal bin that said *For incineration* on the side in wobbly red felt pen.

'Just being ultra careful,' she said, following our eyes. 'There's no need to worry.'

'But can't you do anything, Doctor?' my mother said. 'He has exams to take. He has his music. He's always been healthy. We are a good family. We eat well. We hardly drink, we don't smoke.' She looked at me for a time then back at the doctor. 'He's not always the happiest of kids, I have to say. Would you agree, Barry? You're not exactly a ray of sunshine.'

My mother was always ready to give any stranger a guided tour of all my frailties.

'Why would I want to be a ray of sunshine? There's more to life than being gormlessly happy like a village idiot.'

'No one said you were an idiot.'

'I know,' I said, 'but—'

Dr Ferguson was scouring a big book and I watched her face to see if anything registered.

'There is a condition called lupus,' she said eventually, 'which might be worth investigating.'

'Lupus?' my mother cried. 'Like wolves?'

'The word comes from lupine or wolf, you're right, Theresa. It's an auto-immune system-related condition that can cause the skin to flare up like this.'

'But what about the fact that he thinks they're made of metal?'

'That could be a kind of—' she paused and looked at the ceiling as if summoning the gods, then looked at me again and said slowly, as if speaking to an animal who would understand the tone but not the words, 'a kind of hallucination.'

'Oh,' I said. 'So I'm going mad.'

'No, Barry. I am not saying you are mad, of course I'm not. But this sort of thing is not uncommon in adolescence. Groups of teenagers have been know to faint together all at the same time, for no reason at all. Or fall into comas. No one knows why.' She began to flick through the book again, hurriedly. 'The other issue I am thinking about, though,' she said, 'is that it might be notifiable.'

'Notifiable? Notifiable?' my mother said.

'Yes. A public health risk.'

'I do worry about these factories round here,' Mam continued. 'It's not just Sellafield. There's the thermometer factory at the top of our road, Brannan's, and there's Marchon probably polluting the sea with chemicals, and Barry goes in the sea; you've been in the sea, haven't you, Barry?'

'Just paddling about, mostly.'

'He's been in the sea. And you know what they said, the people at Sellafield? *Avoid unnecessary use of the sea.* Which basically means avoid the sea. And they found cadmium, whatever that is, in a vacuum cleaner dust bag in Seascale.'

The doctor slammed the book shut and replaced it on the shelf. 'I don't think that it's a symptom of any kind of poisoning,' she said. 'It's not listed in the textbooks, anyway. You're a mystery, Barry, an enigma. A special case. I'm going to photograph your chest and also I will scrape off a sliver of one of the lesions so that we can test it down the lab to find out what it's made of.'

'What happens if it is,' I paused, 'notifiable?'

'If it is,' she said, 'we'll be in contact with you right away. In fact it's probably best to stay local.'

'I have a gig tonight. In Whitehaven.'

'Oh yes, the guitar. Well, I wouldn't play the gig, no. Don't do too much for a few days. Stay away from school. Don't get too close to people. I'm just being cautious. I don't want to alarm you. And although you might not *be* a ray of sunshine,' she winked at my mother, '*try* some sunshine. When the weather's nice like it is now after all that rain, it can really help certain skin conditions, like psoriasis, and others.'

'Is it psoriasis?'

'I don't think so. But it might be something from the same group of diseases. So the sun could help.' She smiled. 'Stop worrying! Now Theresa – how's everyone else? Mr Dyer?'

'Hmm. Bill is acting a little odd at the moment, Doctor, if you must know. But that's for another day.'

'And Jenny?'

'Jenny's frightened.'

'Is she?' I said.

'Yes. She thinks she'll catch it, she's – I'm sorry I didn't tell you this, Barry – she's going to stay at Nana's for a while until it's cleared up.'

'What?'

'Yes. She's a girl, Barry. It would be much worse for a girl, this kind of thing. With the sort of clothes they need to wear, and it's summer, and – you know, don't you, Dr Ferguson? She's been so upset about Philomena May, too. It's been very affecting for all of the young girls in the town.'

'I know,' said Dr Ferguson, 'but I'm sure the police will find the culprit soon. People are doing everything they can. Detectives are looking for her handbag at the moment.' She scribbled on her prescription pad as she spoke. 'They're appealing for people to keep an eye out.' She ripped the prescription form off the pad and folded it. 'Brown leatherette. Here.' She handed the green slip to my mother. 'This is for some E45 cream. Might help if it's itchy.'

My mother parked the Allegro outside the chemists and went inside, and while I waited I had a look in her handbag to see if she had any cigarettes I could steal. She was always puffing away secretly unbeknownst to Dad, usually in the downstairs bathroom, where she blew the smoke out of the window.

No fags, but I found a scrunched-up piece of yellow card and I uncurled it to discover it was the torn-off corner of a pack of sweet cigarettes. *Barratt Gold Flake*, it said, above a drawing of two long-haired footballers. On the other side were some handwritten words in my father's handwriting.

I can't stop thinking about you. xxxx

Underneath was a reply, in a different hand, and not my mother's.

Any time, lover boy, in green ink, then a phone number.

The words on the note went through me like something fatal. I saw my parents as a perfect match, a gilded couple who would be together forever.

Marion Crow lying on the counter, her long legs outstretched, my dad filling in the ledger.

When my mother returned to the car, she drove me to Samantha Fry's house and didn't say anything on the way.

'Is Dad OK?' I said, when we pulled in.

'Why do you say that?'

'It's just – he seemed a bit odd at the shop yesterday.'

'Why, what was he doing? Was Marion there? Marion Crow?'

'They were pulling mice out of the traps.'

'Mice. I have no idea, Barry, what is going on in that man's head sometimes, no idea at all.'

She began to cry.

'Mam, what is it?'

'It's, it's everything. Your skin. That poor girl, Philomena May, everything. I'm sorry.' She took a tissue from the glove box and dabbed her cheeks. 'And now your dad is acting strangely.' She turned to look at me. 'But Barry, darling.' Her voice sounded weary. 'This must be horrible for you. This skin thing. You haven't got time to worry about my problems as well.'

'I'm fine, Mam. I'm kind of getting used to it. Don't you worry. Don't you worry about anything.' I squeezed her arm. 'Things will work out.'

'I was thinking. That time in church, what you did at communion, with the host; do you suppose–'

She looked helpless and confused, as if someone had stolen her glasses.

'Don't be so daft, Mam, this is not medieval times. There are no curses.'

'I know. I'm sorry.'

I grabbed my guitar off the back seat and left my mother staring through the windscreen at a line of girls in leotards emerging from the scout hut.

* * *

Samantha Fry opened the door immediately. 'What the fuck happened to you last night?'

'I got lost, crashed into a hedge, then fell asleep.'

'Numbskull. Right. Get in there. I have everything set up.'

I went through to the front room where her Fender Precision was leaning against a Marshal amp, alongside a microphone stand and a fuzzbox.

I strapped on my Eko acoustic, adjusting the guitar carefully in front of me as I was more used to sitting down to play, but Samantha Fry rushed over.

'Stop right there, Val Doonican. Is that how you're going to put your guitar on?'

'Well, I just–'

'Everything is important, Barry. Put it away, sit here, and listen.'

She pressed me down onto the sofa and sat next to me. Her newly bobbed hair, now a deep black colour as she'd got bored with green, swung from side to side as she spoke. 'It's all important. Everything. Everything you do is part of our image. How you walk into the venue. What you wear. How you stand before you go on stage. What you're doing before you go on. What you drink.' Her eyes became bigger and bigger as she grew more animated. 'How you pick up the guitar and how you sling it over your shoulder, and,' she sneered at the big acoustic with its *This machine kills fascists* sticker, 'and what your guitar looks like.'

She picked up my instrument, made her mouth into a downturned urgh and the strings said *whang* when it hit the floor.

'I have this – it belonged to my uncle, who was in a group called the Mysterious Mystery Men.' She went behind the sofa and brought out a strange small electric guitar, the body of which was a tiny plectrum-shaped, curvy lozenge.

'It's a Vox Phantom.'

'But it has no cutaway, so you can't play it sitting down,' I complained.

'Exactly. *Exactly*. Now. Let's go through what we're wearing first, and after we've agreed that, we'll talk about everything else.'

'What about running through the songs?'

She sighed and shook her head. 'Barry, Barry, Barry, Barry, Barry. If we have time, we'll do that. After we've sorted the more important things out. Right. Hair first. I'll get some scissors while you have a go at tearing holes in that T-shirt.'

'How was the disco?' I called after her.

She stopped in the doorway.

'Cancelled,' she said. 'You know – *Philomena May*. It wouldn't have been right.'

'Oh.'

'Barry – is your dad OK?'

'Yes, why?'

'My mother said they were talking about him in Bennett's. Saying he'd been in The Derby Arms that night, too.'

It was then that it came to me in a terrifying surge of awareness; they might think it was my father. They might think my father was the murderer.

* * *

I walked home slowly. But I didn't go inside. Instead, I sat on the scooter and waited for the ghost girl to appear.

It was hot. People were now saying it was the best summer ever. I sweated and boiled on the Defiant's clammy vinyl seat, but the ghost girl didn't come. Maybe she didn't like the heat. I wondered where she went when she wasn't with me and pictured a long dormitory full of sleeping ghosts, their faces grey masks spangled with blood.

I decided to do as the doctor suggested and get a dose of this unusually scorching sun on my skin. Maybe it would help to get rid of the metal lumps. I drove to Ennerdale Water where I knew it would be nice and quiet and no one would be around, parked the scooter, and walked across to the far edge of the lake. I found a hollow of soft grass, took off my shirt, shoes and jeans, and lay down on my back, allowing the fierce rays to lick every inch of me. It was like I was in a secret, private cocoon. All I could see was an empty blue sky and all I could hear was the shishing of ferns in the breeze and, further away, sheep champing at the grass.

The ghost girl kneeled down next to me.

'Hello,' she said into my ear.

'Hello,' I said.

She was still wearing the red wetsuit, the zip a long way down her chest so I could see almost all of her small breasts.

The ghost girl began to feel the metal bumps carefully, one by one, biting her lower lip, and screwing up her little face in concentration.

'Each lump tells its own story,' she said. 'It's very sad.'

'What do they tell you?'

'Oh,' she said, as she fingered one of the bumps. 'Oh no, that's not good.' She fingered another. 'Oh no. That's so sad. That's so awful.'

She went on like that, her voice fading into a distant lullaby, until finally I sat up on my elbows. 'What are they saying?'

'They are telling me what will happen, what will happen with the diver man. Come on. We have to go back there.'

'Is he the man who killed you? This diver?'

'No.'

'Can you tell me who did it?'

'No. I can't.'

'They're looking for your handbag.'

'I don't know where it is.'

'Brown leatherette.'

'I know.'

'I'm sorry this happened to you. I was so frightened of you at first that I forgot to say I was sorry.'

'You don't have to be sorry.'

'Are you OK, now? '

'I don't know if I'm OK. I feel OK. Does that mean I'm OK?'

'I suppose.'

She leaned over and kissed my lips for a long time as if she was drawing life-force from within me and I became erect, but she ignored it. Then she sat still, very still, and just looked. She had a way of gazing at me that went right to my core, making my head tingle.

'We have to go back there,' she said after a time.

'The lake? We can get there on normal roads you know, there's no need to go via a pit of slimy water.'

'His house. We need to go to the diver's house.'

We walked from the edge of the lake to where the Defiant was parked and she got on behind me.

'St Bees,' she said, wrapping her arms about my waist.

'Is that where he lives?'

'No. But your skin is telling me that's the way through.'

At the junction with the main road, she whispered into my ear. 'And take your shirt off again'

'OK,' I said, 'but why?'

'Just looks better,' she said. 'All that shiny metal.'

I undid the lumberjack shirt and tied it about my waist. 'What do I call you? Philo–'

She grimaced and turned her heart-shaped face to the sky. 'Call me Petal. That's what my mother used to say.'

Rasp-rasp went the two-stroke and I flung it into gear, making the front wheel lift up as we tore off down the road. We flew past Cleator Moor Square and across the top of my street, ignoring the junction at Brannan's thermometer factory and the junction for Frizington, then raced down the long mile towards Whitehaven, with me twisting the handgrip harder and harder, leaning into the bends so that the pedals nearly scraped the floor.

We turned off the main road at Keekle and headed towards St Bees' seafront, where we stopped on the concrete promenade next to the beach.

On the sand, two lads were throwing a rugby ball between them – tossing it, catching it, tossing it, catching it – running to fetch it when one of them, usually the shorter one of the two, missed and it rolled off down the strand, and Petal watched them for a time, as if the two men were important. Then she twirled her finger towards the towering sandstone cliffs. 'Up there. That's what your skin is telling me.'

We rode up a steep muddy path, scuds of earth and cow muck flying up behind us, the scooter gaining traction from some sort of magic force, and soon we were on the edge of the cliff, the scooter's front wheel half over. I was beginning to see a pattern. But as well as that, I trusted her. A hundred feet below were razor-edged rocks and pools of snarling spume but when she said 'go', I wasn't afraid. I had every confidence we would fly.

We didn't.

The fall was so quick, there wasn't even time for my fifteen summers to flash before me.

Luckily, we missed the rocks and plunged into a churning, freezing cauldron of Irish Sea and it was only when the scooter surfaced and bobbed about on the waves that I realised Petal had fallen off and was sitting near me on a bony rock pimpled with barnacles nibbling her fingernail and staring at the surf furling white against her feet.

'Sorry,' she said climbing back on the Defiant, 'I lost my, uh, awareness, you know? Let's try again.'

The second time we shot out into the air in a straight line and flew over the sea before rising up and up and eventually entering a cloying curtain of freezing dew. I couldn't see further than a foot in front of my face, but the scooter pootled on, on through this clammy cloud for a few minutes. Petal tapped me and motioned downwards and we descended, slow drop by slow drop, until eventually we were gliding over a row of terraced houses that looked out onto a scrubby piece of wasteland. The grey taxi we had seen at the lake was parked outside and we landed the scooter beside the car and stopped the engine. I was again intrigued by the unusual design of the vehicle, even more so when I saw it close up. The words *Citroën Xsara Picasso* were written on the rear, a model I'd never heard of, and when I looked along the rest of the street, the other parked cars were similarly smooth, shiny and blob-shaped.

The house the man lived in was neither shiny nor smooth. It was a two-up, two-down pebble-dashed cottage in a crammed-together row of a dozen others, and it had peeling and stained walls and broken render. One of the upstairs bedroom windows was splattered with paint. Under the eaves was a rusted curved metal disc that pointed towards the sky. The front door opened right out onto the street and I looked through its glass panel and saw post scrunched up on the mat. The sort of letters no one wanted to open; one was from the Criminal Injuries Compensation Authority, another from a solicitor; another one said HM Revenue & Customs. The postmark on that one was 25 May 2010, which seemed a strange mistake to make, and when I looked at the other letter lying front-side up, it also had a 2010 date.

The diver came from around the corner carrying a carton of milk. He seemed unable to see me and Petal standing in front of him, and I wondered what would happen if he bumped into us.

He didn't.

He passed straight through as if we were made of invisible quicksand, and afterwards he stopped, shivered, then looked behind him.

He opened his front door, picked up the post, and we followed him into the front room.

The room smelled of tobacco and burnt toast and rotting food and damp clothes.

The diver switched on the TV which was the size of a car windscreen and pointed a black device towards it to choose a channel with motorsports on it. People in saloon cars tearing about in mud, making the engines squeal and the tyres spin loudly in the dirt.

Petal sat on a small upholstered chair and pulled her feet up onto the cushion so that the knees of her red wetsuit were at her ears. She looked neither happy nor sad, a serenity in her face like in old paintings of angels.

The diver placed the envelopes on the arm of the sofa then sat down. I sat next to him. I moved my face up close to the man's and stared into it. The diver showed no awareness of my presence at all. It was as though I was examining one of the wax dummies in Madame Tussauds.

From his pocket the man took out a silver lozenge-shaped thing, flipped it open the way they did on *Star Trek*. On the inside were buttons with numbers on. The man tapped a sequence of digits into the device then lifted it to his ear. This was a phone, a portable phone. I could hear toot-tooting from out of its small speaker. As the phone rang out, the man's face began to twitch, his nostrils flaring and unflaring, his breathing becoming loud and heavy.

The phone wasn't answered, but the man spoke to the room.

'Answer,' he said in a soft voice, which had a low, somewhat reedy quality. 'Come on. I need to know about the money. Answer.'

He placed the silver device on his knee and sighed long and deep. He put his hand to his brow.

'That was my money. Answer the bloody phone!'

He looked at the letters on the arm of the sofa. He picked up the one from HM Revenue & Customs, but he didn't open it. He tapped it against his leg and looked at the ceiling.

I stood up so I could look at the diver from above, bending my head and angling it into the man's face.

'What do you think he's talking about?' I said, without turning round.

'I've no idea,' said Petal.

'Why doesn't he open the letters?'

'There's something he doesn't want to know. Once you know something, you know it. That's the end of it. You can't unknow it. He'd rather be in a permanent state of not knowing, because then it can be either bad news or good news, one or the other. Equal chance. He wants to stay forever in an either-or state.'

The diver picked up the letter from the solicitor and pulled a face at it, making his mouth into a pout.

'No, no. Not now,' he said and tossed the letter onto the floor.

On the TV, cars were ripping dirt into plumes of black behind them. The pale vehicles covered in these dark splatters made me think of excrement on porcelain.

I looked at Petal for permission, then placed my hand on the man's head. Petal smiled and I rubbed the diver's scalp with my fingers; I was trying to pass something into the man, trying to calm him, to make him stop. The man seemed to be stuck in a thought loop, riding a wall of death, going faster and faster, round and round, the same thing, over and over.

The man dialled the number again then listened to it ring, tapping his fingers in time to the boop-boops. Again it wasn't answered. 'Come on,' he shouted, 'answer the bloody phone. I know you're there!'

He stabbed the off switch, then pressed a button which made it dial again, pressing hard and deliberately, as if the way he dialled would make a difference to it being answered, and again he listened to it ring and again no one picked up.

'Remember the young men on the beach?' Petal said. 'With the rugby ball? He's ringing the taller one, I think.'

'What?'

'The taller one is his brother.'

'So, this is the future?' I said.

'Yes.'

'It's not much different is it?'

'Not really.'

'Can people like you live in the past as well as the future?'

'It all seems to be the same,' she said. 'Once you're dead, it's like one big house. You can go in any room.'

'Am I...?'

'No. You're tethered to me, that's all.'

The man was dialling. Then he did it again, and again, and again, and when I had counted thirty-two attempts, I said, 'Come on, Petal. We should go. I have my gig with Samantha Fry.'

Petal looked at the diver, manically pressing the buttons on his phone.

'OK. We'll come back. As long as we remember where we were, we can return to the same place in time, I think. That seems to be how it works.'

The diver tossed the phone onto the floor and picked up the long many-buttoned pointing device and the programme on the TV changed.

A topless woman was riding a mechanical bull. The diver made the sound come up. Loud crashing rhythms and ranted words. Then two men in a moving van trying to kill each another with a poisonous syringe. Then another two men fighting acrobatically in slow motion. One fell onto some bags of flour and his face became ghost white as if he was already dead, but he fought on, finally ramming the other man's throat onto a spike in the wall. The water sprinkler on the ceiling started and the winning fighter stood still under it, tilting his head up into the cooling shower of indoor rain, enjoying it pouring onto and off him as it washed away the whiteness.

Things on the screen went quiet and the diver leaned forward to better hear the dialogue.

* * *

'I'm glad I was chosen,' I said, as the scooter glided through the mist over St Bees. 'But why me?'

'I don't know. You're a bit of an outsider, I suppose, and one thing I've gathered so far is that we seem to communicate only with those on the fringes. It's no coincidence that most people who believe in ghosts are considered mad.'

I felt her head loll forward and rest against my back and her face felt warm and cold at the same time, like ice cream that had been baked into a cake.

'Or maybe,' she said, drowsily, into the nape of my neck, 'I made this story happen to you because I knew you'd be able to tell it.'

The scooter dipped, then tilted out of the cloud through thinner wisps into a vivid blue sky over St Bees. The sea had crept nearer the shore but the young men were still playing with their rugby ball in the shrinking margin between the frothing waves and the pebbles. The brother was athletic, could smack the ball hard, nearly knocking the diver over when he made good contact, and each time the diver missed a catch, the brother shook his head and shouted things like, 'Come on, help me out here, I'm training for the match', as the diver trotted after the oval ball bouncing along the smooth, wet sand. From time to time, the diver would lose concentration and gaze up at the high cliffs, or at the whirling seabirds, or at the flat, still sea behind the waves, and on these occasions he seemed completely unconnected to the scene, in another place altogether.

Why doesn't his brother answer the phone? I thought, looking at the taller man, swinging the ball from side to side. I had a sense that something awful would happen to these men and that the unanswered phone call was part of it.

5

Before the gig, Samantha Fry took me to the Three Tuns in Whitehaven where the bikers, the police force, the drugged-up hippies and the arty types drank. She was wearing pink fishnet stockings perforated by bigger rips and holes, giant black boots, a short skirt that looked to be made of fur or some sort of cushion cover, and a leather shirt unbuttoned to the waist exposing a black corset.

The drinkers goggled at her as she peacocked into the bar, defying any of them to say anything with her blank fuck-you stare.

At the bar she pushed a pill into my fist. 'Take this and then we'll drink, er, how many?' She tilted her head up, calculating. 'Five vodkas, yes five. That should do it.'

I stared at the beige capsule in my palm. 'I'm not sure.'

'I get them on prescription. I don't know what they do exactly; something about nerves.'

I swallowed the pill and looked at the ceiling, expecting it to immediately melt into a psychedelic panorama. But nothing happened.

Samantha Fry got the vodkas and we sat in the red-tinged light of the Three Tuns on the velvety banquette seats by the coppery round tables, and she locked her eyes onto mine.

'We're gonna be fucking amazing,' she said, her hands swiping the air as she spoke. 'This gig will go down in history. Just remember the rules. Play everything twice the normal speed and don't sing – shout. And most importantly – rip your shirt off.'

In the dark window, the reflection of Samantha Fry's twirling, swooping hands looked like naked female dancers in the distance.

'Do you believe in ghosts?' I said.

'Yes,' Samantha Fry said. 'I've seen a few, too. My dead grandmother talks to me a lot. And there's an old man I see sometimes in the street beckoning to me, but when I move closer he gets further away and I can never catch him up to see what he's trying telling me. Ghosts,' she went on, 'are people crying out. There are ghosts of living people and ghosts of dead people. We all have a ghost of ourselves. That's what I think. And these ghosts are the,' she took a big breath, 'manifestations of what we really want in life and they go around seeking it out.' She took a slug of her vodka, spilling some on her collar-bone, where it glistened. 'Ghosts are the personifications of our desires.'

'Fuck,' I said. 'Where did you get all those words from?'

'I've been devouring the occult, dear boy. I believe in the Devil and magic spells as well. When my mother thought my dad was seeing this other woman, me and her stole one of the woman's shoes, put a dead mouse in it, covered the whole thing in wax, then buried it at 4.04 in the morning on the fells at a full moon.'

'Did it work?'

'Seemed to, yes. She had a bad experience at the hairdresser the following week – some dyeing process went wrong and all her hair fell out.'

'And then?'

'The hair grew back and now my dad lives with her. She's OK though, really. I quite like her, and I think Mum's happier without him. He was a right miserable bastard – would never pay to park anywhere, didn't agree with it on principle.' She downed another vodka. 'But you can't say the spell didn't work. I cast one about me and you.'

'What?'

'Yes. You. I took one of your fingernails–'

'You said that was for a biology thing.'

'—and I put it in a jar with some of my urine and buried it.'

'What words did you say when you buried it?'

'If I tell you that, I'll break the spell.'

'And is it working?'

She grabbed my face in her hands, both palms on my cheeks, and kissed me. 'What do you think?'

I looked into her grey, swimmy eyes and floated adrift in them. I had two women – a live one and a dead one – and I didn't know which I liked the best.

'What would you say, if I told you I've been hanging out with the ghost of Philomena May and we've travelled into the future together?'

'I would reply,' she said, turning her head on one side and twisting her lips in a curious way, 'that the pill I gave you seems to be working. Come on,' she tossed the last vodka down her throat. 'We have to blast out some tunes.'

At Troubadours, Mr Henderson, the music teacher from the grammar school, was on stage. He was a good fingerpicker and tonight was performing *Dust Storm Disaster* by Woody Guthrie, but the whole thing seemed completely incongruous with his yellow hill-walking anorak, his bike with old-fashioned North Road handlebars, and his semi-detached on the leafy Loop Road. The audience was made up of people in their forties and fifties; bearded, balding men and floaty-bloused, fluffy-haired women, all be-sandalled and love-beaded, a template for an acoustic music crowd. We had been hoping that tonight's gathering would be augmented by the addition of a few kids from our school – the progressive rock grebos maybe, or the bespectacled English Lit girls, both groups often finding themselves in the same oval of a Venn diagram when it came to folk. But in addition to the oldies, there were only two kids; a couple of boys from the year above, the McCauley twins, who had blond feather-cut hair and pointy noses that curved upwards at the tips. The McCauley twins played the working men's club circuit doing

Everly Brothers songs while their dad backed them up on a piano-accordion. Checking out the opposition, clearly.

'Where's everyone else from school?' I asked the boys.

'It's this Philomena May thing,' twin one said. 'No one's going out, especially not the girls.'

'We're getting picked up later by our dad,' added twin two.

The compère looked at me and Samantha Fry.

'Our final act has shown up. Are you ready, guys? What's your name?'

'Boner Juice,' Samantha Fry said, to my surprise.

'Come on, Barry, come on, Samantha!' Mr Henderson called out as we plugged our guitars into the PA with loud phuts, pops and feedback shrieks.

'Give it up,' said the compère, with tangible mock enthusiasm, 'for Boner Juice!'

Samantha Fry began to bang out a two-note riff, jumping around and shaking her hair and, as if I was in the audience not on the stage, I watched her for a time transfixed, wondering which one of my songs would fit this monotonous chugging pattern. Finally, a shape insinuated itself into my fingers on the Vox Phantom and I blasted out a distorted chord, and locked my mouth to the microphone.

'Ain't no marigold,' I shouted, 'pushing its way through the tarmac,' and as soon as I began to sing, the McCauley twins ran to the front and began to jump up and down, twisting their heads on their necks as if heading a football, and holding on to each other like they were in a rugby scrum.

The old people stared.

I refined the words as I went along –

I don't like your tarmac
I don't like your flowers

– and ripped open the front of my T-shirt to reveal my disfigured chest as Samantha Fry had suggested –

I don't like your garden
I don't fucking care
Smash up the house, smash up the house

– and after three so-called 'songs', Samantha Fry hollered, 'Thanks very much, we've been Boner Juice', and we left the stage to raggedy applause and two whoops from the McCauley twins – one each, I assumed.

As we walked through the crowd to the back of the room no one said a thing – no compliments, no criticisms, nothing – and we stood in a silent room staring at the backs of the audience members until the promoter managed to find a way of putting the background tape back on, which was Roy Harper. Ah, the soft strumming of acoustic strings. The room relaxed and everyone began chatting again and it was as if our little punk interlude had never happened. Everyone sang along to *When An Old Cricketer Leaves The Crease* and swayed from side to side in their seats.

* * *

The next morning, I lay in bed and worried about my skin. As far as I could see, the condition was neither better nor worse than when it had first appeared. The night before, I had struck a match and held the flame against one of the metal blisters. It didn't hurt, I felt nothing, but as the blister heated up I felt pain in the skin that surrounded it.

No one else saw the metal blisters. Only me. What others saw, I had no idea. They all seemed to see something different, even the doctors.

I sighed, closed my eyes and turned over, but I couldn't get back to sleep. The house was quiet and I preferred it when there were comforting sounds drifting up from downstairs. My sister was staying at Nana's, still afraid she was going to catch the skin thing off me. I wasn't upset by this. I understood. I might have done the same thing if the situation was reversed. In some ways it was less traumatic to have the condition myself than to be confronted with it in others. I was close to it, somehow in control. I felt the condition gave me something, added a dimension I didn't have before. I felt

I could deal with the lesions. As long as I kept himself covered up, didn't go swimming or anything like that, didn't wear shorts, I could cope. But I was self-conscious about the bits around my face and found myself continually checking mirrors to see how conspicuous they were.

And the mirrors always showed me what *I* perceived, not what others said they saw.

I noticed how different each mirror was, in the quality of the image tossed back, and the level of detail displayed. I liked best my image in the windows of cars, so faint and shadowy I looked almost normal. Yet, in a brightly lit pub toilet, I was horrified by the way the steely blobs around my hairline stood out, sparkling like jewellery. I couldn't decide whether it made me look tough or effeminate.

A man in The Derby Arms stared at me for a long time.

'What happened to your head?' he said finally.

'It's not just my head.'

'What happened, though?'

'Just appeared.'

'Did you get burnt'

'No.'

'Was it a treatment for something?'

People asked these questions all the time and whatever I told them, they were never satisfied.

'So what are they saying it is?'

'They don't know.'

'They'll find a cure, I'm sure,' a woman in the papershop said to me, adding, 'twenty-four men have left Earth's orbit since 1964.'

From my brief dealings with doctors, I realised that most of medical science was based on treatments and procedures no one truly understood. If something worked, then the doctors would continue using it, even if they didn't understand why it was effective. And there were many things that the medical experts just didn't understand it at all.

'The skin,' one consultant elegised, 'is the largest organ in the human body and, as such, is sensitive to all changes, whether mental or physical. This condition you have, Master Dyer, could be caused by environmental fluctuations, pollution, allergies or stress. We simply don't know.'

But if it is caused by stress, other people have stress and yet they don't have this condition. Their stress causes something else to happen in their bodies – stomach problems or hair falling out, or sleeplessness, all kinds of things. The doctors seemed to have no idea why some things happen to some people and not to others. The frightening part of this was that the world appeared to be completely random with no sense or purpose to anything at all. And the people in charge, the adults who ran the system, and were paid lots of money to do so, didn't seem to have a clue either.

Maybe my mother and father's Catholic faith had a function, after all. Maybe all that muttering in crowds and kissing statues and rubbing ashes on your head and telling your sins in a dark box to a man in a dress with his shirt on back to front, all that kneeling down and standing up, singing and shaking each other's hands, going on processions and fiddling with beads; maybe all of that hollow ritual was actually useful. Maybe religion was the way to make sense out of the confusing mess of an average day on Earth.

I thought about the time I had wanked before communion and how later, on the way to church, I had been abruptly oppressed by the thought that masturbation might be like eating and shouldn't be done within an hour of receiving the body of Christ. My stomach had begun to twist because I couldn't tell my mother that I was unable to receive communion because I'd been – what? Intimate with myself, is that what I would say? – and I remembered kneeling against the rails, my brow on the cold brass, and Father Dempsey approaching slowly, swinging the silver chalice containing the hosts. I remembered the murmurings of 'body of Christ', the mutterings of the Amens, the spittly sound of mouths opening and snapping shut on the soft white discs. When the ginger, skinny beanpole Father Dempsey reached me, he held out the embossed medallion of bread, emitting its pungent yeasty smell, and said, 'Body of Christ.'

I croaked 'Amen', poked out an arid tongue, and the dry flesh of Christ was patted onto it.

I closed my mouth. It was so parched in there that I could think only of dried things – dried beans and dried grass and dried oats and dried milk. I had no saliva, the thing wouldn't disintegrate, and I tried to swallow, I really did, but I gagged and spluttered, then expelled the host onto the stone floor, followed by a spun trail of yellowy phlegm.

Father Dempsey swung his skinny body round and levelled his eyes at this demon, this devil who had vomited out Christ's body, Christ's own heart, Christ's own liver, lungs, kidneys and eyes. I remembered tears, the tears you get from throwing up. The church became silent. Father Dempsey rang his bell. Assistants, stewards, official men of St Mary's were called and they made a circle about the host, and the priest decided that the regurgitated mess would have to be cleared up right away and the area of floor blessed. A silver spatula was used to scratch the rolled grey tongue of unleavened bread off the stone and flip it into a special bag, and communion was cancelled for the rest of the day.

I never again received the sacrament and my parents didn't force me, fearing a repeat.

'I don't like the taste.'

'How can you dislike the taste of our Lord's body?'

'It's all dry and makes me want to throw up.'

Maybe these metal marks were my exposed soul, each one representing a time I had entertained a sinful thought.

I rolled over to find a cooler spot on the bed. I thought about my sister, Jenny. I missed her. We weren't close, but we had a sarcastic, mickey-taking relationship that I enjoyed. Jenny liked to watch the *Donny & Marie* show on Friday nights 'because,' she said, 'it's so bad it's good', and although at first I made fun of her, I eventually came to love the sickly-sweet mélange of variety acts, ice-dancing, corny musical numbers and clunky comedy exchanges between the synthetic brother and sister. Sometimes me and Jenny would recreate those creaky skits in broad, Yankee drawls.

'Hey Donny,' Jenny would say.

'Hey Marie,' said I.

'How you been doin'?'

'I've been mighty fine.'

I got out of bed and went downstairs. My mother was sitting in the kitchen staring at the back door. No television, no radio, nothing.

On the kitchen table were two condom wrappers, splayed open, with no condoms inside.

For a moment I wondered if they were mine. But I'd never bought a condom in my life, never mind used one. And as far as my mam and dad were concerned, the Catholic faith didn't allow any kind of contraception but the rhythm method.

'Where's Dad?' I said.

She continued to stare at the door.

'Is he at choir practice? He's still in the choir, isn't he?'

'No. He's gone. He took some things with him. He was upset. He didn't say where he was going. One of his long bus rides, probably, so he can think.'

'Aye lad,' I said, mimicking Dad's warbly tenor tones. 'Ah gets to the end then ah rides it right back again. Tha' ever bin to Cape Wrath, lad? Longest bus journey in the UK.'

My mam smiled at my impersonation, but didn't laugh. She took a packet of cigarettes from under the cushion where it was hidden, slid one out and lit it with a long cooking match.

'This time I'm guessing Newcastle. Based on when he left and the day of the week.'

I put my hand on her shoulder. She didn't move. She didn't seem to feel my hand there at all.

'Has he said anything?'

'No. Nothing. Barry, I don't want it to be true. She, this Marion, she has a husband too, you know?' She cried, a soft cloudy sob. 'I don't want to lose him, Barry.'

'I know,' I said.

She crushed the half-smoked cigarette into a thimble holder on the hearth, then lifted up a cushion, pressed her grey face into it and wept and wept, keening softly, purposefully; getting rid of the tears was like bleeding a radiator to make space for normal emotions to flow again.

* * *

Marion Crow was on a deckchair in a weed-flecked front yard wearing a red bikini top and turquoise shorts. Next to her was husband, Dominic, in a baseball cap and tight cut-off Wranglers, the frayed edges digging in to his large thighs, his chest bare and shiny with oil. His brother Carl, a hulking thug with upper arms like legs of lamb and calves like knots in cables, was there too, wearing a white vest, football shorts and flip-flops. Through gaps in the fence, you could see Crow's distinctive black and gold Ford Capri, in the yard at the back.

I crept into the house through the back door. I looked into the kitchen where Dominic had put up the wall units without permission. I saw wall units which had no permission. I saw a lilac-coloured food mixer and yellow saucepans with orange flowers on the lids

I went up a peeling wooden staircase, halting at the top to look down out of the landing window. At Marion's long brown legs. At the tops of her breasts pressing out of her red bikini. At the silver-painted toenails peeping from green Scholls.

I found the couple's bedroom. Clumps of grey towels all over the floor looked like spawn. The room smelled of flyspray, pillows aged in lager, and the must of unwashed tights.

I opened the top drawer of an age-mottled chest and rummaged through silk, elastic and lace, feeling a frisson of desire which made me ashamed. I continued to search. Something guided me, pulling my hands as though I were a marionette. I discovered a note. On my dad's ledger paper, torn out, and in Dad's writing.

I think I am falling in love with you

I felt sick. Sick at the idea of my mother being betrayed and at the notion of my father having feelings for this young woman; woman? Virtually a girl. Sick at the thought that life was not how it looked on the surface and that everyone was secretive and sinister and plotting.

There was also a photograph with lipstick marks all over it. Dad on holiday in Spain, in an Estartit T-shirt.

I imagined my father on some long bus ride somewhere, wearing his trilby hat, and looking vacantly out at the passing fields, like he wasn't there. Empty. So desperate, so unhappy, so much on his own.

'Dad, Dad, Dad, Dad. You idiot,' I said aloud.

I found something else. Wrapped up in a frilly-topped stocking was a phial of straw-coloured liquid, and, floating in it, a black and grey photo clipped from a newspaper.

It was a picture of my mother, from when she'd been in *The Whitehaven News* after playing the piano for the school concert. I thought about what Samantha Fry had said about spells. Marion would inter this object somewhere remote and incant evil words. I pushed the package into my jeans pocket.

Then something dragged my eyes to the top of the wardrobe. Sticking out from a large Findus Crispy Pancakes box were some leather straps with metal buckles. I stood on the dressing table and lifted the box down. It was a type of body harness. Next to it was a leatherette face-mask with a zip for a mouth. There was also a horse whip, a length of wood with manacles on each end, some steel sprung clips like the ones Frankenstein employed to bring his monster to life, and a pink-stained face-mask. I replaced the box and looked under the bed. Chains and thick rope and a pile of magazines, which I pulled out. One was called *Hogtie*, another was entitled *Bound to Please*, another *Knotty*. I flicked through them. Photographs of tied-up naked girls, some bound like pigs and hanging helplessly from ceiling hooks. Several woman had gags made of what looked like billiard balls. I stopped at one page. The woman in the image, lying on the floor bound up with her hands tied to her feet, looked exactly like Marion Crow. Among all this stuff were some other fancy-dress items; hats and feathers, false beards and moustaches.

Dominic Crow and Carl. Big Carl. Biggish Dominic.

The two men were waiting for me at the bottom of the stairs.

They said nothing. Stared, smiling slightly, blocking my way.

Then Dominic's eye caught the frilly nylon sticking out of my pocket.

'You're a fucking little pervert. We thought it was someone on the rob when we heard you. I always knew you were fucking weird. Thinking you're better than the rest of us.' He laughed. 'You fancy her, do you? Is that what it is? He shook his head. 'In your fucking dreams, my son, in your fucking dreams.'

Carl grabbed my by my throat but then he stopped and recoiled.

'What the fuck?' he said stepping back. 'You're a diseased freak. What is that? Fucking leprosy?'

'Come near me and you'll get it too,' I said, and ran out of the door to the scooter. I could hear the men swearing, but they didn't seem to be in pursuit.

The Defiant started with a luscious *varoom* and I sped away, pulling a wheelie as I did so.

6

I got up early for school and found my mother downstairs in the grey vinyl armchair where I'd left her the night before. The yellow scrap of sweet-cigarette carton she had unearthed from Dad's pocket was scrunched up tightly in her fist and she was staring at the carpet. Her eye make-up was crooked, her lipstick smudged down on to her chin, her powder caked unevenly. She sat there perfectly still, as if asleep with her eyes open, but as soon as she heard me, she leapt out of her trance and darted into the kitchen.

I followed her. 'Mam, I'm–'

She lifted a saucepan from the drainer, took a bottle of milk from the fridge, flipped off the silver foil lid, and dribbled some into the pan. She opened a wall cupboard, took out a box of Co-op cornflakes and tipped them into a bowl. They made a *shush* sound.

She turned the radio on –

Cumbrians are asking for an inquiry into the plan for the new MOX reprocessing plant at Sellafield because of the possible threat to the health of people living nearby – Energy Secretary Tony Benn is

– then snapped it off again and stood looking at the pan of cold milk.

The silenced transistor read *Grundig Party Boy.*

'Mam,' I said, touching her arm. She didn't move. 'You haven't turned on the gas.'

She slid open the drawer, took out a box of matches, twisted the cooker knob, and struck one, the ring lighting up with a *whump*. Blue flames licked the steel base of the pan and she watched the flickering jets for a time. I watched too.

'I don't know what your dad was doing the other night,' she said, as if she had seen his face in the trails of vapour from the gas ring.

'What night?'

'Thursday night. When, you know.'

'Oh.'

She was speaking in small gasping sentences as though she had forgotten how to breathe.

'I asked him. Because I thought he might have been with her. Marion Crow.'

'Mam, I don't think—'

'He said he went to see a bloke about a tip.'

'A what?'

'A betting tip. The horses. It was some feller who worked for the fair. These travelling people, they have horses. They have a history of horses. They know a lot about them. It was a sure thing, your dad told me. He said that he and this feller met in The Derby Arms.'

She breathed in, deep and long.

'Oh,' I said.

'The same place that poor girl was last seen. Then he said to me – you know what he said me?'

The milk sizzled and spat in the pan.

'He said, don't tell anyone I went there. If anyone asks, tell them I met the feller on the Square. Just on the Square. It will make things easier.'

The milk began to roll, foam, then it furled upwards towards the rim, but she didn't touch the stove.

'Makes it easier, your father said. Everyone is under suspicion in the town, he said, every man. Barry, I don't know what to think. I'm worried it will be like in Yorkshire, like what happened there. In Yorkshire, they interviewed every man. Every single one. Some are saying it could be the same bloke, the same man that is doing it over there, he could be coming over from Yorkshire, over the Pennines.

In some way, I hope it is the Yorkshire one. Then at least it wouldn't be one of us.'

The milk surged over the lip of the pan and down onto the cooker where it spread across the surface, bubbling and hissing, turning brown in places as it was scalded by the hot stove top.

I thought about my dad. It couldn't be my dad. But what if he was wrongly accused? It happened. You read about it all the time. Wrongly accused, wrongly arrested, then wrongly convicted. Would my dad have an alibi? He had no regular friends, no deep friends. The whole world was his friend. He spoke to everyone in the same intimate, jokey way as if he'd known them all his life. For Bill, every stranger was a lifelong buddy about whom he knew every surface, edge, crevice, channel and shelf. The only alibi my dad was likely to have would be the Co-op or the betting shop. Or being with Marion Crow. And if that were true, and I didn't think it was, it would be an alibi he'd be unable to use.

'You know it's not Dad, Mam. We know that.'

'I know, love. But it's somebody's father, somebody's brother, somebody's husband, somebody's son. That's what they're saying in Yorkshire.'

She picked at some flecks on her blouse.

'Mary Whitehouse is right. It's that thing.' She looked off into the living room at the TV. 'All those plays and weird documentaries on BBC2. That *Bouquet Of Barbed Wire*. There's too much everywhere.'

She took a packet of cigarettes from under her sleeve, slid one out and bent to light it from the gas jet.

'What if the police find out about this Marion Crow thing?' She pulled in smoke as if it were a life-force, 'and then they link your dad with this, and then find out he was in the same pub and then find out he lied about it? Barry, I'm out of my mind. And with your skin as well.' Her sentences crumbled, melting into tears, and she stopped and gripped my arm. She sobbed for a short time and I held her as if, for that moment, I was the husband.

'Barry, darling,' she said finally. 'What about you? How are you?

With all of this I haven't even asked about your skin. Is it any better? Are there any changes? Do you want to show me?'

'It's the same, Mam, I think it's the same. No worse. Maybe slightly improved.'

'Do you think you should go into school today?'

She twiddled off the gas knob, poured what was left of the hot milk onto the cornflakes and handed the bowl to me.

'Thanks,' I said and sat down with it at the table. 'I'd like to see Finny and everyone. To be ordinary, Mam.'

'I got you some Lucozade. I forgot. It'll make you feel better.'

The bottle stood on top of the fridge, its shiny orange crinkly wrapper like the sheets of cellophane they hang in shop windows to stop things fading.

I wolfed the cereal then stood up and tugged my green blazer out from the tangle of coats hanging in the pantry under the stairs, and pulled it on. In the hall mirror, several metal studs were visible, so I went upstairs and found the straw trilby my dad had bought in Spain and, in Jenny's room, rummaged through a pile of scarves on the floor, coming up with a black and white Spirograph-emblazoned bandana which I wrapped around my throat. Jenny's oval looking-glass tossed back an image that would do.

'When's Dad back?' I called to my mother, who was in her grey vinyl chair, looking at the carpet.

'He's doing Scotland. The long Scottish trip he likes.' She was talking to the floor. 'He told me he needed time to think. He said he would be a few days. The buses up there are slow. The way he likes them.'

* * *

Whitehaven Grammar School was two miles from Cleator Moor and I had to get there on a 17 or 22 from the top of Crossfield Road. I'd been at the grammar for two years, sent there from my secondary modern Catholic school, St Cuthbert's, after I was singled out as having potential. Many of the kids at the grammar were from much grander backgrounds than me, with parents who were solicitors and vets and doctors and nuclear scientists at Sellafield, so I never spoke about my dad managing the Co-op at Moor Row or my mother's job at the infant school. On top of this, because I'd been at a Catholic school, and the grammar school was non-denominational, all the Catholics had to stay behind one night a week to receive religious instruction from Father Dempsey, my parish priest from St Mary's.

When I entered the sports hall for assembly that morning I was surprised to see Father Dempsey sitting on the stage, alongside the school head Mr Heaslip, plus a policewoman and a man I didn't recognise, with long unkempt hair, round metal glasses and tight blue drainpipe jeans, the type of which were not yet de rigueur in West Cumbria, where flares were still embraced.

Everyone on the stage sat as still as a statue, sincerity etched into their grave faces.

Not a single seat in the hall was empty, and those who had been unable to find a plastic chair were standing at the back, in front of the vaulting horses, crash mats, trampoline and heavy medicine balls.

The mood of the pupils was not the usual rumbustious joshing, swearing and play-fighting that went on while they waited for Mr Heaslip's weekly motivational speech; everyone was sitting very still, a heavy blanket of hush lying over them. A few girls were crying, their sharp sobs creating dissonant clusters of notes like the wheezing reeds of a broken harmonium, and you could hear them comforting each other by saying slow things in careful soft voices.

Rosie Whelan and Karen Walsh, the girls who'd been with Philomena May that night, had stayed at home; the rumour was that they had been put on pills by the doctor and that newspaper men had been hanging around their front doors.

Initially, some of the boys fought the mood with bravado and even a few sick jokes, but their forced banter hung stale in the air and now the boys were staring ahead at the stage, some of the younger ones looking as though they might begin mewling like the girls.

My tactic was not to talk about the incident with anyone or to listen when others were speaking about it. I felt close to Philomena, or Petal, closer than anyone else in the room had a right to feel, and it didn't seem right to talk about the crime in that way, or to listen while others presented fantastical theories or speculated about who the murderer was or what exactly had happened on the Grey Stuff late that Thursday night. Petal was within me and no one else knew this. I was unable to think without the sense that my thoughts were being witnessed by Petal, as if Petal was sitting inside my head and watching my mind as it tried to work everything out.

I was sitting next to Finny and in front of Steve Newton who, unlike the other kids, was behaving exactly as he always did, flicking the ear of a girl in front, a wad of chewing gum crackling in his mouth. The McCauley twins were two rows behind, their blond feather cuts and upturned noses somehow inappropriate to the occasion, although, really, what could they do about the happy and innocent way they looked? There sat Samantha Fry near the stage, her arm slung around a smaller girl who was snuffling into a handkerchief, and further down the row from Samantha Fry was my sister Jenny who, from the tilt of her head and the pinched-together look of her shoulder-blades, reminded me of my mother. She must have sensed my eyes on her, because she looked around and gave a little wave, a smile, then a frown as if to say *look at this mess we're in*. Without pause, I did the finger-guns thing at her that I always did, winking and twisting my mouth up, and then regretted it when she didn't return the gesture. I was such an idiot. My insides felt as though they were in turmoil. The whole Philomena May thing was related directly to me, and the metal studs all over my body singled me out as something from elsewhere, from a world of weirdness, of separateness, of alienness, of violence even; of being somehow from a place where the usual civilised rules might not apply.

The metal blisters linked me to the girl, I knew it. That's why her ghost had visited me. They also linked me to the diver man in the future, though I had no idea why or how. My constant state of anxiety, which at first I'd put down to a collection of nameless infantile fears that I would eventually grow out of, had calcified into permanence. I used to imagine the inside of my body as a cartoon factory of pulleys, knobs, chutes, belts, wheels and levers, operated by fourteen men with sewn-up eyes and no mouths. The job of the fourteen men was to feed and water my emotions, calming me or crushing me, stoking me or drowning me, an unceasing roar of activity that made me the twitching wreck I sometimes was on the outside.

A loud electronic *phut* was followed by the thud-thud of Mr Heaslip tapping the microphone before he blew into it, forcing a noise like a hurricane out of the slim Tannoy speakers.

Instead of his usual fawn corduroy jacket and crumpled cream trousers, the headmaster was wearing a black suit that looked a little tight for him, and beneath it a white shirt and a dark blue tie with a gold clip to keep it against his chest. His jagged crown of dazzling white hair that normally he never combed had today been dampened and flattened all over, giving his head the appearance of a sleek wet cat.

There was another stranger at the side of the stage, a man in an orange roll-necked jumper and checked trousers like the ones you wore for golf. He was holding a camera and a notebook and I guessed he was from *The Whitehaven News*.

I looked at the priest, and the policewoman, the man in the drainpipe jeans and the hippy-looking journalist in his orange jumper, and then back to Mr Heaslip; I now anticipated something monumental from my headmaster, some luminous and extraordinary words to calm the pupils, to still our trembling lips.

But Mr Heaslip said nothing for a time, just looked out at the silent pupils with a steady gaze.

Then he went behind the curtain at the side and returned with a chair, which he placed in the centre of the stage.

All eyes looked at the chair, including the rest of the podium party.

Mr Heaslip drew in a long breath which over the loudspeakers sounded like the dying gasp of a large creature.

Then I felt her. I felt her enter me as if she were a bore of cold fog driving upwards and through me, from the soles of my feet to my scalp.

'I expect you are wondering what this chair means. This chair,' Mr Heaslip was saying as he looked at it, 'is Philomena May's chair. She likes to sit near the window.'

Likes? Likes? Mr Heaslip's use of the present tense jarred.

'That's what her form teacher, Mrs Hutchinson, told me.' Mr Heaslip looked at Mrs Hutchinson who had a large handkerchief over her face and was shaking and crying so much that two other teachers had to grip her shoulders at each side to prevent her from collapsing.

But I couldn't focus on the teachers and their emotions. Petal was inhabiting me. I could hardly hear what Mr Heaslip was saying, all I could feel was the mass of her, the cold plasticity of her body, as she pushed out into my extremities until it felt as though she was wearing me like a second skin.

'This is the chair she sat on,' Mr Heaslip went on. Then he disappeared behind the curtains and brought out a desk and put it in front of the chair.

Petal's ears were in my ears, her lips behind my lips, her throat inside my throat. I tried to distract myself and looked around the room. The journalist's pencil was flying from side to side across his oblong pad.

'This is the desk from Philomena's form room,' Mr Heaslip was intoning, his voice crumpled and buried in a fog in my head.

'Inside this desk you know what I found?'

My eyes were filled with grey like I was looking through murky bath water. Petal's breasts were behind my chest, pressing against the inside of my skin, bursting outwards, as if a bubble of gas were trying to escape.

'Her name in Biro.'

In my head came a powerful shushing like the pounding of surf and a rhythmic cheeping like a distant machine. Mr Heaslip's voice crept along the edge of this noise – 'Philly rules, 1975' – as if afraid to be heard.

'Philly is what her friends call her, isn't it?'

Another long pause. More scribbling from the journalist.

'Philomena wasn't a star pupil.'

Wasn't? Isn't? Is? Was? Mr Heaslip seemed to be struggling to define Philomena's state, as if he too knew that Philomena was still here, still walking the Earth.

'She isn't – wasn't – sorry – isn't so bothered about maths and literature and science and geography and history or any of that. But Philomena May is loved by all of us. And I'm sure we will all welcome her back with open arms when – if – when – if – if,' and the headmaster's words became blurred like ink in the rain, a meaningless confusion of murmurs.

I knew she wasn't coming back. Philomena was Petal. Petal was her ghost. She was inside me now – trembling, chilly, afraid, yet in control. And she seemed to have a purpose.

Mr Heaslip regained control and his voice resolved into focus again.

'Many of you live in Cleator Moor where this heinous crime happened,' he said. 'Many of you young girls will be frightened. The police haven't found anyone yet and you'll be worried it might happen again. WPC Cherry here,' he indicated the thin policewoman, who had bits of blonde hair sticking out from under her police cap, and the sort of dry-looking, white skin you'd imagine a person from somewhere dark, like Iceland, would have. 'WPC Cherry is here to talk to the girls about safety and if you young ladies stay behind after this assembly, she will reassure you. She will explain what precautions to take so that you all remain safe and sound. Which I know you will.'

Mr Heaslip paused and looked at the priest and, at this point, like the release of air from a pricked vacuum pack, Petal was suddenly gone from inside me, and I looked all about me to see if I could see this sprite, this elfin vapour, slipping away over my head.

Nothing.

'Father Dempsey will talk to the Catholics, so if all you Catholic boys – and Joan McCricket – could meet him in the music room, he will assist you with religious instruction. This gentleman sitting next to Father Dempsey' – he indicated the man in the drainpipes – 'is a doctor. Dr Moorfield. Dr Moorfield specialises in medical issues relating to the mind. He helps people who are having mental problems and can offer solace in the form of counselling and advice, and I can say myself that when my good wife Mrs Heaslip was experiencing some problems with her nerves, that kind of help really worked. So if any of you are having sleepless nights, or bad dreams, or suffering from nervous exhaustion, or struggling to concentrate, you can see Dr Moorfield, who will be in the small biology lab.'

I wondered whether I should see Dr Moorfield, but only I knew what it was like to live inside my fragile, emotional microclimate; a session with Father Dempsey would be difficult enough.

'There are no words,' said Mr Heaslip. 'No words that I can say that would solve anything or offer any solutions or insight into this event. So I want you to look at this desk and this chair. And I want you to spend one minute in silence thinking about poor Philomena May – praying for her for those of you with religion – and think about how precious we all are to each other, and how much we should value our fellow pupils. How we should cherish each other and–' Mr Heaslip sniffed then jammed his finger and thumb into his eyes, and let out a high-pitched sound. 'I'm sorry,' he said. 'I wanted to say that we should all take care of each other to make sure things like this never happen again.'

And then he walked off the stage and sat down on the front row next to the other teachers.

The silence began. But it wasn't silence, it was worse than silence. It was a room full of breathy whimpering, of the wet spittly sounds of those who have cried too much and were now desperate to stop and breathe normally.

I looked out into the schoolyard. And that's when I saw him.

Marion Crow's husband.

He was standing at the edge of the playground, under a tree, squinting down at a folded newspaper, every now and again glancing up at the assembly hall where he could no doubt see all the pupils and teachers. I was certain that Crow had come to the school see me. The business from the other day at the house was unconcluded. I thought about the things I had seen in Marion Crow's bedroom – the metal clasps, the chains, the pink-stained face-mask, the photographs of the bound, naked girls hanging helplessly from ceilings – and became more and more certain that the reason Crow was here was that he, Crow, had murdered Philomena May and that he, Crow, needed to prevent me from telling anyone what I had seen.

I looked at the stage, at the policewoman and the priest and the psychologist, and then back to the schoolyard. Crow had gone. But I had a feeling that Crow wanted to be seen, and wanted to be seen by me, and I knew that come the end of the day, Crow would be outside waiting for me.

The silence ended but no one said anything. I wondered why we had not sung. The moment felt right to sing a hymn of some sort, but the grammar school was not much of a place for ceremony, or 'pseudo religious paraphernalia' as I once heard Mr Heaslip call it.

The deputy head, Mrs Percival, a plump lady who taught art and French and whose upper arms wobbled when she laughed or, as today, cried, got up on the stage and explained the rest of the morning's sessions. The girls would go to the library to see WPC Cherry, while the boys helped put away the chairs in the sports hall. Then the Catholic boys and Joan McCricket would attend the music room with the priest. After that, anyone worried about their nerves could attend the small biology lab to see Dr Moorfield.

* * *

Later, I headed for the music room with the other Catholics, wondering how I was going to escape from school without Crow intercepting me. On the way, I passed the queue outside the small biology lab, and noticed that Jenny, my sister, was there. Her glasses were crooked like they had fallen off and she hadn't bothered to sort them out.

'Why are you wearing my scarf?' said Jenny.

I put on my American accent. 'Hey, Marie, the guys in Make-up gave it to me. "Try this, Donny," they said, "it'll make you look more rock and roll".'

'I didn't think you'd come in today,' said Jenny, without her Marie Osmond voice, 'with your skin. Is it better?'

'Getting better, yes,' I lied. 'You could come back home.'

'Nana showed me how to make toy soldiers by melting lead in the fire and pouring it into moulds. Granddad used to do it when he was unemployed. Are you going to see Father Dempsey?'

I waved my hands about in the air and incanted in a low voice. 'Hurdy wurdy hurdy wurdy, my son, hurdy wurdy blessed Mary, hurdy wurdy hurdy, go in peace.'

Jenny didn't laugh. At the age of 14 she had, to our mother and father's horror, been bold enough to renounce her Catholic faith and declare herself a Buddhist, so she didn't regard religion as a laughing matter. It was a demonic conspiracy which drained your soul of its vital juices and replaced them with poison.

'Hopefully Father Dempsey will be able to explain why people are evil,' Jenny said, 'and how the Church is planning to put a stop to it.'

The music room had a grand piano in the middle and for some reason Father Dempsey was sitting at the keyboard as if he was about to play. His audience consisted of me, six other boys, plus Joan McCricket, a studious frump from Cleator Moor who arranged flowers in the church and played guitar in the folk mass. She had the sort of small breasts I associated with privilege and, as she sat down next to me, she smiled and I remembered that she had once sent me a card on Valentine's Day that said 'I think you're wild', and immediately lascivious images of her began to roll through my head.

Father Dempsey poked a couple of notes inexpertly on the piano while he stared out of the window. Father Dempsey was a thin man, tall and bony, and he stuck out of his priest's garb like it was fancy dress. He had a grizzly ring of ginger hair around a gleaming bald patch and liked to drink at the Knights of St Columba Club, and in fact had lost his driving licence recently after being caught over the limit driving back to St Mary's, where he lived. Since this conviction, people had to give him lifts everywhere, but it was no problem, he said, because he liked it. It gave him a chance to really catch up with what was going on in the smaller and less-visited corners of his parish. As well as drinking, he liked to smoke and bet on the horses, and would swap stories about horse-racing with my dad when they bumped into each other after mass. My mother knew Father Dempsey very well herself because whenever she had a crisis going on she would go to what she called 'confession', which was in reality a chance to talk over her problems with Father Dempsey without having to see him face to face, the screen in the dark confessional acting to anonymise her, even though Father Dempsey actually knew who everybody was while they were sitting in that box.

I used to wonder why a priest would spend all his time in pubs and betting shops drinking and smoking, but my mother said that it was OK because priests aren't allowed any other pleasures.

In fact, when I was twelve my mother had high hopes of *me* entering the priesthood and one day a special, more senior priest than Father Dempsey visited my old school and interviewed every boy behind a screen to find out if they had a calling, while at home my mother waited excitedly for news. I couldn't remember anything the priest said, only what he looked like; a fat, greasy beachball of a man, lounging back in his chair with his legs apart, cigarette ash speckling his black shirt and globules of his morning egg congealed on his trousers. Alone with him, I had felt exposed and vulnerable. The priest spoke in low, conspiratorial tones, nodding his head all the time; but despite the nods, it turned out that I didn't have a calling to the priesthood, and my mother had to deal with the disappointment, which I sometimes felt she still harboured.

'Boys,' Father Dempsey said, 'and Joan, I'm so sorry to be here to talk to you at this difficult time. But it is at times like this that people turn to their god and their religion. I know that Philomena May's mother is finding the church an enormous help. You know, when I think of this terrible mess, I think of the story of *Little Red Riding Hood*. Little Red Riding Hood was bright, in her red coat. She stood out from everyone else. She was visible and could easily be seen. She commanded attention. And she had lots of good things in her basket. But boys – and Joan – Little Red Riding Hood ended up getting into bed with a wolf.'

'Sir. I mean Father,' said Stuart Bristoe, 'she killed the wolf though, didn't she?'

'Yes, Stuart,' said Father Dempsey. 'But it was a close-run thing. And I for one would rather she had never been in that danger than for her to have to do that. Chop off the head of a wild animal.'

Father Dempsey idly fingered the notes of the piano and made a chord sing out while he thought about his next sentence.

We boys were hot and sweaty after putting away the chairs in the sports hall, and the room smelled like an unclean hamster cage.

I looked out of the window to see if there was any further sign of Crow, but there was nothing out there, only his newspaper curled against a lamppost where the light wind had put it. I wondered whether the newspaper held inside it the full account of what had happened to Philomena May.

'You know, boys – and Joan – a fairy tale is one thing,' Father Dempsey said eventually, 'but this is real.' He swivelled round on the piano seat to face us properly. 'And I want to talk to you about sin and temptation. You'll hear a lot of lurid details about this case. You'll hear people talking in the playground and in the streets and the shops and the coffee bars and the launderettes and the billiard halls, and you won't like what you hear. Doubtless you won't understand some it. For Pete's sake, I don't understand some of the things that people do or the things that drive them to do those things. What happened to Philomena May, well. Whoever found her. Where she was. How she had been. I don't know. She would not have looked a pretty sight.'

The words 'pretty sight' nearly made me laugh. I thought it was a strange thing to say about a horrific murder.

'You'll possibly wonder where God was when this happened.

Why did God allow it?'

Father Dempsey stood up and moved closer to us. 'Well, our Lord, Jesus, God,' he said, looking at each of us in turn, 'God is everywhere, as you know. So yes. God was there, God was on the Grey Stuff that night. There with little Philomena May. But one thing God gave us is free will. He put us on this world to test us. And if God is everywhere, then the Devil is also everywhere. In the form of temptation. You've all been tempted, haven't you, boys? And Joan. Can you give me an example of temptation? Stuart, can you give an example of a time you have been tempted?'

'No, Father Dempsey.'

'Barry, can you?'

'No, Father Dempsey.'

'You might see something another boy has and want to take it from him.' Father Dempsey examined the air above him for examples of things that a boy might want to steal. 'A bicycle maybe? One of those Choppers. Or a—' he looked at his feet, 'or a pop gun. Has that ever happened, boys? Joan?'

'No,' we said together.

'Are you worried about Satan, boys? And Joan?'

'No, Father,' we all said.

'Are you worried about Satan, Joan? I didn't hear your voice or see your lips move.'

'No, Father Dempsey,' said Joan. 'I'm not worried about Satan at all.'

'I killed a baby bird, Father,' said Stuart Bristoe. 'I stoned it to death.'

'And how did you feel about that poor baby bird?'

'I hated it, Father, it chirped all the time.'

'So you, Stuart, were tempted and you fell.'

'I didn't fall, Father. I was standing still, looking down on the bird.'

'To fall is a, a figure of speech. Can any of you explain to Stuart what *to fall* means?'

Joan put up her hand. 'It refers to the fall of man. In Genesis, in the Bible, when Adam and Eve eat from the tree of life and become immortal, they move from a state of innocence to guilt, sin and disobedience. *Peccatum Originale* in Latin. They have to cover their nakedness, Father.'

One boy laughed and Father Dempsey flashed him a look.

'I killed a baby bird, that's all,' said Stuart.

'How did you feel later on when you thought about what you had done?'

Stuart looked at the other boys and Joan. 'All right,' he said.

'That's OK,' said Father Dempsey. 'It's normal to be brave in front of the other boys – and Joan. But sometimes when we are tempted and we fall – which we all do from time to time – we feel bad, we feel ashamed, and we try to cover up those occasions. But what we learn from them, hopefully, is to be stronger and to fight temptation. To look that Devil straight in his yellow eyes and say *no, I won't do it. I am strong.*'

Father Dempsey sat down at the piano again and fingered a sad three-note chord. 'We are all tempted, even myself, as a priest. I am weak and I am tempted.'

He began to vamp the triad over and over, slowly and softly as he spoke. 'I am weak and I am tempted,' he said over the chord, looking past us to some scene he was picturing in the ether. 'But you know what I do when that happens? I pray to God.'

The chord stopped and he moved from the piano and kneeled down in front of us. 'I do this. I get down on my knees. Sometimes when I am all alone. I get down on my knees and I cry out. I cry, *please God give me the strength to fight the urges that I feel within me.* And God answers.' Father Dempsey looked up at the ceiling, at the cracked plaster around a row of fluorescent lighting tubes. 'God answers,' he said to the tubes, 'and he gives me that strength.'

I thought about Father Dempsey's drinking and gambling and smoking, and about the pleasures he wasn't allowed to have. About how close up he emitted a sour, bready smell. The priest's eyes flicked up to look at the row of students looking down at him. Could these be the same eyes that had coveted Philomena May? The same eyes that had moved across her body, the eyes that were last to see her?

No one said anything else and after we had incanted two Hail Marys and a Glory Be, Father Dempsey allowed us to leave.

Outside the music room, Stuart Bristoe sniggered. 'Pop gun,' he said. 'He's round the twist that auld idiot. He's been wanking off in the confession box again. He gets you to tell him your impure thoughts, then he pulls his todger while you're talking. You can feel the confession box rocking and hear him panting.'

I went to art. I went to English literature. I went to biology. I went to French. I went to music, back to the room where Father Dempsey had thrown himself on the floor and admitted his urges. When the time came to leave, I wondered whether I should instead hide somewhere in the school and sleep there until the next day. Anything to avoid the confrontation with Crow. I wondered whether it would be better to get Finny to leave with me. But Finny wasn't a hard case. He'd never had a fight in his life.

I stayed late in the music room, telling the music teacher, Mr Henderson that I wanted to play a guitar in one of the practice rooms, and by the time I'd spent an hour strumming away at my new songs, the school was empty but for the cleaners.

Crow was parked near the bus-stop in his black and gold Ford Capri. He held his hand up towards me and made a come-hither hook with his finger. I went over and stood at the open passenger window. Crow didn't look at me, just held up his hand as if to stop me speaking and stared straight ahead, at the long road that curved down and round the bend towards Cleator Moor. His hand was on the gear-stick and he was rubbing it slowly as if he were polishing an apple, while his other hand flicked the indictor stem up and down, up and down, over and over. He was wearing the fronded leather biker jacket again, and a Hawkwind *Warrior On The Edge Of Time* T-shirt.

'Dyer,' he said finally. 'I have no idea why you were in my house and, whatever yarn you spin me, I won't believe it, so don't bother. Keep out of things. I don't want anyone snooping about my place. What with this Philomena May case. That stuff you saw up there. It's nothing to do with you.'

'OK.'

'Nothing. What do you think you are, son? The Famous Five? You think I'm some greasy-raincoat flasher, doing the not-nice to people? Some sad uncle Ernie? I've got alibis trailing out of my arsehole. It's your dad you should worry about. Things my Marion says. I should have put him on the floor years ago. I think you should watch him. A quiet man. A good man. That's what they say. But they're always the ones aren't they?'

'Don't speak about my dad.'

Crow stopped fidgeting. 'Do you want me to take my jacket off?'

'No,' I said.

'No, you don't.'

The Capri's engine gave a guttural groan followed by a metallic rasp and then settled into a soft *thup-thup-thup* like the beating of large wings, and Crow threw it into gear. But the car didn't move away. Crow changed the angle of his rear view mirror, looking at something behind.

'Don't come near me again,' he said into the glass. 'With that freakoid skin thing, you're a fucking alien, they ought to put you away.'

And with that, the car screamed off and I watched the crouching black and gold coupé disappear round the bend and I knew it was him, knew it was Crow who had killed Philomena May, knew it in the same way I knew my own name.

7

A bus stopped.

A bus went away again.

I didn't move.

A bus stopped.

A bus went away again.

I stared at the empty scrap of wasteland over the road, where a group of teenage girls in the dark blue uniforms of the other school, Overend, were larking about. One of them was demonstrating some dance moves from *Top of the Pops* and the others were copying and failing, then staggering about laughing before beginning the process over again.

I sucked in a deep breath then started to cry, all of a sudden, trembling and sobbing hard, my hands wrapped around my face to block everything out and to hide my misery from the world.

'Barry Dyer, what's wrong?' A girl's voice said.

I looked up and it was Joan McCricket.

'I'm OK.'

She sat down next to me, placing her puce and crimson crocheted bag on top of her bottle-green school skirt.

'How's your Jenny? I notice she's staying at your nana's. That's near mine. I saw her the other day, out of our window. She was in the garden sunbathing, reading her *Judy* annual. Make-up tips, I think. What's she now? Sixteen? My mam says some of the advice in those magazines is too grown-up, but I don't know. Us girls, we need to understand about these things, don't we? Anyway I called down to her.'

I thought about Crow and the images of the girls tied up and the harness I'd found under the bed.

'There's no advice for us on things like that,' I said. 'In *The Hotspur* or football comics.'

'Oh.'

'Or *Sounds* or *New Musical Express*.'

'Oh.'

'The things boys read.'

'Maybe there should be. Maybe that's why you boys don't notice when a girl is, you know, interested.'

'What did she say?'

'Who?'

'Jenny. When you called down to her.'

'KC and the Sunshine Band were screeching out of that wee transistor she has. I was worried she might burn in the sun, 'cos she didn't seem to have any stuff on and she was wearing this really small bikini, so that's why I called down to her. From my window. But she didn't hear me. I have some cream, you know? You shouldn't burn. This summer's bad for burning. There's been so many warnings. It's the hottest yet. Well, hottest since 1914. That's when they started making records.'

'Is it?'

'Yes. '

'So it might have been much hotter before that. Like in 1915, maybe?'

'I doubt it. I think we'd have heard. Why's your Jenny staying there? Are you all OK? At Dyer Towers?'

'Yes, we're all fine.'

'Is it because of Philomena May?'

'I think it might be. Maybe she feels safer in that part of town. More countryfied.'

'In Frizington?'

'Yes.'

'You still writing the songs?'

'Yes.'

'You should write one for Philomena, you thought about that?'

Something shifted inside me and I looked straight at Joan.

'Did you know her? Philomena May?'

'Not really. She wasn't my type. I was scared of her, to be honest. She used to bully me.'

'What are you doing now?'

'What do you mean?'

'Now. This evening.'

'I'm revising for that physics test we have.'

'How long will that take?'

'Well, if a person on Earth took an hour to revise for the test, and his identical twin brother—'

'One of the McCauleys?'

'Maybe. Anyway, if his identical twin brother in a spacecraft orbiting Earth did the same amount of revision, would they take the same amount of time?'

I laughed and Joan McCricket laughed with me.

'I like physics,' she said.

'I can tell.'

'An hour and twenty minutes.'

'Well, let's do something together before that,' I said.

A bus came and we got on and all the way to Cleator Moor Joan didn't stop rattling on about the stories in the girl's magazines that Jenny devoured, and how they were so utterly, utterly puerile.

'I wrote off for a guide, in fact, a guide on how to write stories for girls' magazines. And they sent me a list of what you aren't allowed to write about. Can you guess what was on it?'

'Murder?'

'Oddly enough, no. Under the heading *taboos*, it said the main things to avoid are drunkenness, deformity, illegitimacy, colour, religion and divorce.'

'My life,' I said.

Joan hit me on the leg, laughing and flicking her hair out of her eyes. She angled her throat towards me. 'Can you smell my new perfume? It's Heaven Sent. I used to wear Bonne Bell but my mother says this is more grown-up.'

I noticed that her freckles went all down her neck and wondered if they continued, covering her whole body. I imagined her lying naked on her bed with a tumble of physics textbooks and mathematical instruments all about her.

I inhaled a small pillow of air from around her shoulder-blade.

'Nice,' I said. 'Like strawberry laces.'

'Thanks,' she said. 'To smell like a chemically constructed imitation of fruit was this girl's aim. What's with the hat and scarf anyway? They suit you. You look like a boy with a secret, like an actor.'

I looked at Joan's face. It was roundish and pretty, but not so pretty as to have infected her personality. Her eyes, hidden behind the scratched glass of her bubblegum-coloured specs, were the palest of blue. I decided I quite liked her, with her science and her facts and her serious lips. It was relaxing, I found, to talk to a girl I didn't much fancy. I decided that Joan McCricket's steel trap of a mind might shed some light on my condition.

'I woke up the other day covered in metallic blisters.'

'Oh,' she said. 'That is odd. Have you—'

'Yes. The doctor said to just keep an eye on it.'

Joan McCricket looked to the side for a time. 'In Greek mythology,' she said, 'Artemis, the goddess of the hunt, kept special birds as pets. They were called Stymphalian birds and had bronze beaks and metal feathers. They used the metal feathers and beaks as weapons and it took someone as strong as Hercules to defeat them.'

'That's helpful,' I said. 'Thanks.'

'I'm sorry.'

'They're not like feathers.'

'I said I was sorry.'

She changed the subject and started talking about her old

boyfriend, who she always called by his second name – Malone – and the way she said it, *Maar-loaan*, all long and stretched out, sounded plaintiff and desperate.

'And I said *Maar-loaan? Yes* Joan, says he. *Maar-loaan? You either take me as I am or get lost.*'

'And what did he do?'

'He got lost. *Goodbye, Maar-loaan.*'

A young woman got on the bus at Keekle. She was wearing lime-green elephant-bell trousers, cork platforms and a cheesecloth shirt with several buttons undone, revealing a lot of cleavage. Beads and bangles were all over and her hair was pulled up in a band.

'Do you think she looks good?' said Joan.

'Bit obvious,' I said.

'*Another stupid tart in drip-dry polyester*, my mother would say. The girls in those magazines your Jenny reads all look like that girl. Tiny noses, huge eyes, thick hair. And here's me with glasses and a thousand freckles. That girl,' she said, nodding at the young woman who had sat down near the front, 'she needs to watch it going around looking like that. With what happened to Philomena May. Philomena May used to dress like that.'

'Philomena May always looked interesting to me, sort of otherworldy,' I said, without thinking, and then I wondered why I'd said it because Joan McCricket looked at me, startled.

'The policewoman this morning was very clear,' Joan went on. 'Don't dress provocatively. Don't hang around in pubs or cafes with older men. Don't get into a car, or onto a motorbike or scooter, with a man you don't know. I think that policewoman was a lesbian.' Joan examined her hand in front of her face. 'Short fingernails and lots of loose change in her pockets.'

Joan had nice long nails that tapered to a fine point.

'Why do lesbians have loose change?' I said.

'I don't know. My mother told me they did. Maybe they ring each other up from phone boxes a lot. Maybe that's how they arrange lesbian sex. I can't imagine lesbian sex. I try to, but I just can't. How about you, Barry? Have you ever wondered whether you were a queer? Or a pervert?'

'So the policewoman said it was Philomena's fault?' I said.

'Avoids the question,' said Joan, in a declamatory style. 'We've passed Crossfield Road, by the way. Are you coming home with me?'

We were at the market square and I got up. 'No. *You* are coming with *me*.'

She threw her puce and crimson crocheted bag over her shoulder, incongruous against her sturdy green blazer with its yellow piping, and followed me down the aisle of the bus.

Two old men were sitting on the bench opposite the library, both of them shirtless, their wrinkled chests blazing red with sunburn, pink faces angled up to the scorching rays.

On the civic hall's *Coming Attractions* board the word cancelled had been scrawled over the *Under 18s disco* sign.

Ripples from the Philomena May attack were manifest everywhere in the town. Police cars were parked on every corner, uniformed officers were to be seen walking briskly from shop to shop, home to home, and factory to factory, gripping notepads and looking stern and aloof.

Where normally there were crowds of kids hanging about, there were boys, but no girls. No girls outside Clock Hill Coffee Bar; no girls outside Wilding's Sweets and Papers; no girls outside Meldrum's chip shop; no girls outside St Kevin's youth club. The evening curfew for girls was not official, but it had been agreed silently and complicitly among the town's inhabitants, and, over the last few days between around four and six, the streets had begun to empty of women and, by the time it was dark, no female voices could be heard anywhere.

I set off quickly, Joan McCricket running along behind me as if she were being towed, and we walked past the edge of the fairground, where the Waltzer and the Octopus stood waiting to be reopened that evening, and stopped outside JanWear boutique.

A sign on the door said *Owing to recent circumstances we are closed until further notice.*

'Philomena May bought her clothes here,' Joan said. 'She loved fashion, jewellery, make-up. The policewoman told us that the outfit she'd been wearing that night had been bought here the same day, just a few hours before.'

Tears began to fill Joan's eyes and I put my arm about her and we stood and looked at the clothing in JanWear's window. A bright red suede pea jacket, some long yellow vinyl boots, some purple vinyl shorts, a fur-edged denim coat like my own; every garment a huge, life-affirming scream against the greyness of West Cumbrian life. I turned my back to the shop and Joan followed suit.

We were both crying. Looking in a clothes shop window had made us cry, and we stood there with our backs to the JanWear window and we cried together while staring out over the Grey Stuff where it had happened.

In silent agreement, we crossed the road.

The incident Portakabin was still there, a handwritten sign giving the opening hours and a number to ring with information. A picture of Philomena May had been Sellotaped to the side, a photograph taken when she had been in Cleator Moor Carnival and played the part of Cleopatra on a float to celebrate the Tutankhamun exhibition. You could see behind her the gold-coloured papier-mâché sphinx and a boy wrapped in bandages like a mummy. I stared at Philomena's face, covered in thick brown grease to make her look Egyptian, and couldn't help thinking how inappropriate it was to display this particular image of her, dressed like a famous sexual temptress. I thought of Petal in her wetsuit and began to see Petal as someone different, as a new person, a perfect glistening brand-new thing reborn from the shell of Philomena.

A policeman emerged from the cabin. 'What you up to hanging around here, kids?' he said, removing his notepad from his pocket and licking the tip of a stubby pencil.

'We're looking for rocks,' I said. 'It's a school project.'

'Rocks?'

'We want to find some hematite. There's lots around here, apparently. From the iron ore mines.'

'Kidney ore, we used to call it.'

'That's right, yes,' I said.

'OK.' The policeman looked out over the Grey Stuff.

'Have you two you been questioned yet?'

'Yes,' I said.

'A policewoman come to school this morning,' added Joan. 'WPC Cherry.'

'Mmm,' the policeman said. 'Just watch what you're doing on those stones.'

We walked side by side across the bone-like mound of slag, which at times I fantasised might be a living organism with a level of consciousness which, if it could speak, would tell all about what happened that Thursday night. Now that the blue and white police tape had gone, the site was returning to its normal state as a magnet for fly-tippers and there were several new items of domestic rubbish strewn about – a broken meat grinder, a box of pipe cleaners, a pillowcase with a picture of the Bay City Rollers on it.

'Are you really looking for minerals and crystals?' Joan McCricket said. 'I didn't know you were interested in geology.'

'Finny said he found some quartz here,' I said, speeding up my pace. 'Come on.'

I was heading for the derelict dog kennels that stood on the edge of the Grey Stuff, because it was on the low beam at the entrance to this dilapidated structure that Finny had found the clump of hair.

After spending a short time pretending to look on the ground for rocks, I entered the disused animal shelter and Joan followed me. It was little more than a wooden ceiling propped up by breeze blocks on a bare earth floor and would have been, I supposed, where the dogs slept or sheltered from the rain. It was dark apart from a few long shards of light that came in through holes in the shattered roof and it smelt of damp soil and dog excrement with a whiff of metallic saliva and rotted-down fruit. There was nothing in it, nothing at all.

'I have an ammonite at home,' Joan said, 'and lots of books about natural gems, and fossil-collecting and that sort of thing, if you're interested? Do you know about the Cave of the Crystals in Mexico where there are crystals as tall as pine trees? I didn't know about it until I read this book. I will—'

'Wait,' I said. 'What's that under your foot?'

She lifted her shoe.

Picked out by a rod of light burning in through a roof hole was a triangular torn-off corner of card with handwriting on it. She bent and picked it up and handed it to me, and I took it outside to examine it. The words *Gate Four* were printed on it, above some boxes with dates and times written in them.

A name signed in ink, *P. Dunnery*.

I turned it over and on the back were the words *Royal Frolic* and the numbers *11:2*.

'It's part of a time card from Sellafield,' Joan said. 'For clocking in and out. The staff my dad manages at Sellafield have to use them, but he doesn't because he's scientific. He has a PhD from Oxford in Material Sciences. His subject was fusion, nuclear fusion. He says that once we've cracked fusion rather than fission, which is what they use now at Sellafield, our energy problems will be solved. Fusion is sticking things together and fission is tearing them apart, and tearing them apart is so much more wasteful – it even sounds like it's wasteful, doesn't it, Barry? Sticking things together sounds so much better than ripping things—'

'Shut up for one minute, will you.'

Joan clamped her mouth shut dramatically with the sound of a large fish gulping and made her eyes bulge angrily at me.

'Sorry,' I said. 'Do you know a P. Dunnery?'

'Paul Dunnery is Head of Community Relations at Sellafield.'

'What are all these times?'

'They are the times the shifts start and end. It's to do with the unions. The times used to be two till ten – that's a back shift – but the unions negotiated all kinds of extra time, for things like washing and cleaning, and getting changed, and even extra time for clocking in and out. So you end up with finishing times that are odd numbers. Back shift now starts at 14.11 and ends at 21.47.

'And people work those shifts every day?'

'Usually they are on what they call continentals – three days on, three days off, alternating between earlies, backs and nights. What does *Royal Frolic* mean?'

I put the clock card fragment into the pocket of my blazer.

'That's the name of a racehorse,' I said. 'I've heard my dad mention it.'

I was concerned about the link to the bookies, because it didn't make things look good for my dad. But my dad would definitely not own a piece of a clock card from Sellafield.

Father Dempsey likes a bet
Priests are not allowed any other pleasures
Look that Devil right in his yellow eyes and say no

'Do you think he attacked her here?' said Joan.

'Yes.'

'Who can know?' said Joan McCricket. 'Let's just hope she comes out of it soon. Then she can tell us what happened herself. Tell the police what this creep looks like. If she remembers, that is. Sometimes people block everything out.'

'What?'

'When she comes round.'

'I thought she was—'

'She's in a coma, Barry. Been like that since it happened. But they think she'll come out of it.'

'So she's alive? Philomena May is alive?'

The hooter from Brannan's thermometer factory sounded mournfully for the end of the day.

'Yes. Didn't you know?'

I felt the universe rearrange itself around me.

'No. I thought… why was everyone saying she was—?'

'Just lying there without a flicker. Vegetative state is the technical name. They don't know what might happen.'

I realised that I hadn't seen a newspaper or watched *Border News and Lookaround* for days. So maybe Petal wasn't her. Maybe Petal wasn't Philomena May. Maybe Petal wasn't even a ghost. But she – it – looked exactly like her. Exactly like Philomena May. Can you be a ghost when you're in a coma? I remembered a ghost story by Dennis

Wheatley called *The Ka of Gifford Hillary*. A man is buried alive and while he's in a coma his spirit – his Ka – prowls the Earth for revenge. At least that's how I remembered it. Dennis Wheatley must have got the idea from somewhere; everything must have a root in truth. I stood staring at Joan McCricket for a long time, stewing in the melancholy knowledge that maybe there is no truth, no reality. Maybe all you ever know about the world is whatever is right in front of you at any particular time. You have to deal with things as they appear to be, regardless that later you might find out everything was actually something completely different, that an entirely unexpected set of truths was unfolding and you'd been looking at the whole thing from the wrong angle.

'Joan,' I said, but as I began to speak, Joan McCricket let out a long slow moan, her eyes slid upwards in their sockets, exposing the whites, her lips seemed to buckle, and her mouth listed to the side. She began to drool a grey milky fluid, and her face looked as though it was melting. I didn't know what to do. Joan grabbed the door frame tightly as if a strong wind were trying to gust her away, then she fell heavily onto her back inside the kennel, her skirt riding up and exposing mushroom-coloured legs and more freckles.

I kneeled down and gripped her arm,

'Joan what is it? Should I call someone?'

A voice from her lips spoke. 'I'm cold.'

It wasn't Joan McCricket speaking. It was Petal.

'I'm shivering.'

'Petal, where are you?' I said.

'It's cold in here. Dirty.'

She spoke ponderously –

'No, I don't want to. No.'

– enunciating each word like she was trying to imitate an accent.

'Not on the floor. No.'

'Petal–'

'Let me stand up. Please.'

Joan's lips moved robotically as if she were being operated by a ventriloquist.

'We need to go. Right away. My tether.'

Bubbles of saliva leaked from Joan McCricket's mouth, her hands and feet were electric with twitches. I looked at the soles of Joan's shoes, pointing up towards the kennel's roof like two long, sad faces, and all of a sudden I worried that Joan would die and I grabbed her shoulders and shook her roughly. A creaking sound came from her mouth like the noise of a giant vault door opening, then the floor shuddered slightly, and Joan's face clarified and her twisted body straightened. She sat up, brushed crumbs of earth off her uniform then stood, tottering and dazed.

'Hey Dyer,' she said, 'what happened to me? Did I faint?'

Outside the kennel, I could hear the *phut-phut-phut* of the Defiant's motor and I saw Petal parked outside JanWear and, under Petal's watchful eye, I walked Joan slowly to the Square and waited for a bus to put her on.

Joan and I agreed to meet up and do something else together soon. I was not to worry. She would be fine. I was not to take her all the way home, there was no need. She probably just hadn't had enough to eat that day.

8

Petal's wetsuit was zipped up high, but I could see the bulges of her small breasts against the fabric, and her anthracite hair was wilder than before, bristling with energy, and going off in all directions. I jumped on the back of the Defiant this time and Petal drove as if she knew every inch of the terrain, looping through back lanes, lonnings and tracks, hurtling through yards, back gardens and front gardens, soaring over walls and hedges, skimming over rivers and streams, all the way through Keekle, Moresby, Whitehaven, Lowca, Harrington and finally to Workington, where we stopped at the gate to the Moss Bay steelworks and, with a few rapid twirls and swoops of her fingers, Petal described the way we had to go.

Once inside the plant, all you could hear was the constant rush of gas escaping from coke ovens, men shouting, the enormous clangs of metal against metal, and everywhere bright flares reflected in steam and smoke. We drove near a blast furnace being tapped, hot coke being pushed, soaking pits being charged. Coke oven carts trundled by, filled with flames. Then she spotted what she was looking for. A giant steel egg-shaped monster on two legs which was being tilted down so that men could pour molten iron into it. Once filled, it was swung back to a vertical position and a blast of air was blown through the base, making a fountain of fire shoot out of the top; a mini volcanic eruption.

The men tilted the furnace again and as the melted iron went in,

Petal twisted the handgrip and the scooter shot inside. I felt a rush of heat all around me, but just as when we had been underwater, my body seemed impervious. We waited inside the cocoon of molten steel, hot iron rolling and swirling around us like syrup, until we were shot out of the top in a long plume of sparks and into the end of a Workington afternoon in 2010.

We were in a broad grey carpark surrounded by big shops. Asda, B&Q, Halfords, and the diver was sitting in his taxi, so we parked behind him and watched.

'Someone told me that you're not dead,' I said, watching Petal's little face screwed up in concentration as she studied the diver in his car.

'How could I be a ghost if I was alive?'

'I don't know,' I said. 'Did you see my gig?'

'Music doesn't sound the same when you're like I am. It sounds like science. It's annoying. A lot of things happening at the same time for no reason when all you want to do is hear the individual bits.'

'So you didn't enjoy it?'

'We have important things to do, you and I. My tether.'

A suited man with bushy white hair came out of B&Q carrying a leafy plant in a pot, and the diver leapt out of his car and called over to him. The white-haired man stopped and scoured the area, before glancing down at the potted plant as if he was considering whether it would make a useful weapon to protect him. Then he smiled uncertainly, walked briskly over to the diver and thrust out his hand for shaking.

The diver seemed already weary with looking at the man, as if he had been chasing him all day and was exhausted with the futility of it, and he ignored the hand and began to speak loudly into the man's face.

The man listened but didn't reply.

'There are things underlying,' I heard the diver say.

The white-haired man shoved back his sleeve and looked at a heavy silver watch.

'I have to complete on a barn conversion for a dentist in Keswick,' the white-haired man said. 'But I'm free tomorrow?'

'You're here now buying bloody flowers.'

'It's a tree fern.'

'You're good at pointing out when I'm wrong, aren't you?'

'Did you get the email?'

'I'm no good at that. Some of them just seem to vanish.'

'It said what you thought.'

'They just disappear.'

The man with the white hair looked around the nearly empty carpark, then at the road, then up at the sky, then at the tree fern, then at his watch again, then over to a black car that said BMW on the back.

'OK. I'll follow you,' the man said.

'No,' said the diver. 'I'll follow you.'

We drove off, the diver's taxi hugging the bumper of the man's black BMW, me and Petal at the rear of the diver's Xsara Picasso.

At the diver's house, the white-haired man parked up, took a large square-shaped briefcase out of his car, and went inside.

Petal and I followed. The diver pulled a Fray Bentos Steak & Ale Pie out of a carrier bag.

'The single man's dinner,' he said, and sliced the lid off with an old-fashioned steel claw tin-opener, leaving dangerous-looking jagged edges.

He put the saw-toothed tin lid down on the table and the white-haired man looked at the lethal blade.

The diver followed his gaze. 'Watch yourself on that,' he said.

'Why don't you get a modern tin-opener?' the white-haired man said.

'I like to be close to nature,' the diver said, as he put the pie in the oven. 'Don't like anything new-fangled.'

The giant TV had been left playing and a programme about the Second World War was on, black and white images of soldiers walking about, the words *History Channel* in the corner.

The diver had laid out a large pile of paperwork on the table. Next to it was a crowbar.

The white-haired man sat down on the sofa and looked at the monochrome soldiers walking through the rubble of a bombed city.

'I don't like watching programmes about the war.'

'Sometimes it's the only way to solve something,' said the diver. 'It had to be done.'

'There are always other ways.'

'Not that time.'

'That's why I like the law. The law is advanced civilisation's alternative to violence. I'm an optimist. We can even sort out your tax if we put our mind to it.'

'I'm going to prison. It's fine. I'm resigned.'

'You're not going to prison.'

'It will be fine,' said the diver, deadpanning it. 'I'll break out, like in that film.'

'If you did go to prison – and you won't, of course – but if you did, it's all open prisons now. You'll be put with all the other white collars and get to go home at weekends.'

The diver stood up. 'What the hell are you talking about?'

'There's no chance of you going to prison, of course,' said the solicitor. 'I am just explaining that if there was the tiniest sliver of doubt, it would be a nominal sentence of a couple of months and you would serve only half of it, and you'd serve it in low security. It's my job as your solicitor to point out all possible outcomes, even if it's not likely.'

The diver's face was on fire. 'You can stick your bloody advice up your bloody arse.'

The two men sat quietly for a while looking at the soldiers rounding up Germans from the bombed-out buildings. An old man came on the screen, this time in colour.

'I asked my general what we should do in the next town because we were collecting too many prisoners. "Waste them," the general said. "Waste them all." I had never heard the term "waste them" before,' the old man said.

The white-haired solicitor took out some papers from his briefcase and laid them out in a fan shape on the floor. 'Basically what HMRC are saying is that the amount you've spent on diesel doesn't tally with the amount you've got coming in. That amount of diesel would equate to this many trips and you've got income down for less.'

The smell of the tinned pie warming up in the oven was sickly, like old wallpaper paste.

'I don't know anything about accounts or tax.'

'They use a special ratio for taxi drivers. That amount of diesel on your receipts, take that back six years, which is as far as they can go, and that's where they've got the figures from.'

The diver picked up the crowbar. 'Let me show you something.'

He took the solicitor over to a corner of the room, and Petal and I followed. He knelt down, levered up a floorboard, reached down into the hole, and pulled out several fat wads of money, which he stacked up next to the solicitor's who had knelt down next to him.

'How much is there?' said the solicitor.

'About ten grand,' said the diver.

Petal lay on the floor next to the diver, resting her chin on her fists and looking straight into his eyes, as if she were reading some code that would tell her what the man was planning to do.

I looked at Petal's bottom in the tight wetsuit, smooth and curvy like the flank of a seal, and thought about all the things we could do together if she ever came out of hospital.

'So you don't trust banks?' the solicitor said.

'I'm like Ken Dodd.'

'Oh.'

'But without the Diddy Men. He got off, didn't he?'

'He's a comedian.'

'Don't you think I'm funny?'

'Bank this money and use it to pay them off.'

'Look at it.'

The diver slipped one of the notes out from under the elastic band that held the wad together and put it in front of the solicitor's face. Petal followed the note with her eyes the way a cat would watch the tip of a moving pencil.

'It's an old note. You don't see those much any more.'

'Dead on, chummy. It's as useless as a rusty can of nineteen-seventies Spam.'

'You can't spend them, it's true, but you can cash them in at the Bank of England.'

'That would leave a record.'

'What do you want to be? A ghost who makes no marks? Has no reflection?'

'They would know I'd been hiding it.'

'It was for your pension, your future. Something for the kids.'

'Other people don't think like me.'

'It's not a crime to be...' the solicitor looked away towards the window, 'to find life complicated.'

A burst of gunfire and shouting came from the television.

'You know what I'm going to do with it?'

The diver gathered up a pile of the notes and went off into the bathroom. The sound of flushing filled the terraced house and the solicitor remained kneeling on the floor gazing at the piles and piles of useless money.

In the kitchen, the diver took his Fray Bentos pie out of the oven and put it onto a tray, which pictured a hairy russet-coloured bull with long horns. He grabbed a spoon from the draining board and put that on the tray then brought them into the living room.

The solicitor looked at the crowbar. He looked at the money, he looked at the fan of papers on the carpet.

The diver began to dig in to the pie, mechanically, without looking at it.

'Do you want some?' he said after a time.

'I had a salad at work,' said the solicitor, getting up off the floor and scraping dust off his knees. 'Have to watch the old ticker at my age.'

'You're no age, feller. You're the same age as me. We'll both die at the same time, regardless of what we eat.'

I went into the kitchen. A newspaper on the table said:

Witch doctors, poison plots, and a young internet bride – the downfall of Britain's greatest drummer

I looked out of the back window. In the yard, there was a small raised pond, half-empty of water, its algae-smeared black lining exposed around the edges, and a ginger cat was drinking from it, but when it looked up at me, it leapt in the air and scarpered.

A gnome with a fishing rod sat next to the pool, and I remembered the diver placing one at the bottom of the lake.

Next to the pool was a disintegrating kitchen unit, a rain-warped wooden table and a folding metal director's chair with a burst cushion on it, the filling splurging out like road-kill intestines. An electrical extension lead was snaking out from under the shed door and up to the table, and there was a sun-lounger too, some squat green beer bottles, and hundreds of cigarette stubs.

The leaves on a birch tree behind the yard shuddered in the breeze.

Petal came over and stood next to me and we looked out of the window together.

'Do you see the same things as I do?' I said. 'Or do you see everything? All things, at all times, in all places, all happening all at once?'

'I see what you see,' she said. 'A tumbledown yard. Somewhere for a man to sit on his own and drink beer and smoke. Somewhere for him to think. I sense that too much thinking has gone on out there.'

I looked at her. Her face looked luminous, like some deep-sea glowing creature, and she turned her coppery, agate eyes to me and kissed me long and deep, and the kiss felt like falling into a pool of cool, still water.

When we left, the solicitor was picking up the papers from the floor, and the diver was sitting at the table in the kitchen, his head lowered so close to his portable phone it looked as if he were trying to eat it, the light from the device making a Pierrot mask of his face.

* * *

Petal got on the Defiant and I got on the back and as we flew, I gripped her tightly, leaning hard against her back as if I were holding on to life itself.

Over the town of Seascale, near Sellafield, the scooter stalled in the air and we began to descend slowly like a plane whose engines had failed, and neither I nor Petal knew why.

When we came out of the low cloud, it was raining heavily and there on the beach below were dozens of people standing under umbrellas listening to a priest. All around were television cameras and large vans with white dishes on the roofs and the names of television companies on the side.

We could hear what the priest was saying because he had an amplifier. It was a mass to remember the dead. Words about the ones who had died and how they will be missed. How it was a senseless tragedy. The priest's grey head was uncovered and the rain was pouring down over it, but he focused only on reading out the names of the people. I couldn't make out the names, but as each was spoken, a different one of the metal studs in my body pulsated the way a slug cringes when sprinkled with salt.

We glided back up through the clouds then down again into Cleator Moor and for the first time I noticed how the area had changed in thirty-four years. I saw that the market square had been enclosed with decorative metallic fencing and the once bustling Co-op was shut, its wrought-iron canopy buckled and rusted. Several pubs had closed down too, and there was a multitude of take-away food places – Chinese, curry, burgers, kebabs, pizza – whereas back in 1976, there had been only chip shops. A fluorescent cardboard star in an off-licence window offered cheap lager from Poland. Opposite the market square, the Grey Stuff had gone, and had been replaced by a park with trees. A playground stood where the derelict kennels had been, and I noticed Petal slowing down to look at the space where she had been found all those years ago, with an expression on her face not of horror, as I expected, but more of fascination.

She put the scooter down there, on a children's roundabout, and when she started the engine again, the roundabout spun faster and faster and faster, and moments later, as it slowed, I could see that I was on the roundabout at the fair in 1976, and the fairground men were shouting at me to get off, while slowing the ride down with their hands.

Finny was leaning on the rail at the side of the Waltzer, watching the whirling cars flying by, and as soon as he saw me, he smiled big and broad and thumped me hard on the arm. I nodded and took up a position next to him, and we watched the spinning metal cradles and listened to the pounding, distorted music as the disco lights rippled, flickered and pulsed all around us. Mesmerised by the sensory overload, we didn't say anything to each other for a while. The DJ played records and, between the tunes, the rolling wooden floor of the fairground ride creaked and rumbled, and the engine that drove it wheezed with the effort.

The fair wasn't exactly busy, but it wasn't empty, and a few souls were enjoying the rides. But it felt very different with no girls. No screaming, no shrieking, no hooting, no laughter. The few boys who had tonight decided they wanted to be spun around on the Waltzer (a strangely unmasculine thing to do, I thought) were sitting solemnly in the metal carts, looking ahead and avoiding the stares of the fairground man who leapt recklessly from car to car, his rubber-soled feet adhering magically to the sides as they careered around the circuit. Every now and again, the fairground man would spin each individual car to make the ride more exhilarating and, usually, when there were girls on the rides, he would ask them if they wanted it faster. But the man didn't say anything to the boys; just gave them long hard stares as he flung their cradles around, as though he despised these idiots who could sit there motionless, silent and effeminate and allow a man to toss them around in steel carousels like they were dolls.

I turned to Finny and looked at him as he stared blankly at the rolling Waltzer cars. The grease in Finny's long locks of black hair glinted each time a spinning beam of light licked over him.

'I need your help, mate,' I said. 'I found something else at the old kennels on the Grey Stuff.'

Finny looked at me with a curious what-are-you-talking-about expression.

'I think I know who did it.'

'What?' said Finny.

'Crow.'

'What?'

'Marion Crow's husband.'

The pulsing reds and greens of the disco lights made Finny's skin look bruised and shiny.

'What?'

'Marion Crow's husband!' I shouted ever more loudly, but this time the music had dropped out for a few seconds and the words echoed about the wooden Waltzer hall and everyone seemed to look over.

A strobe came on, making Finny's long lugubrious face as white as the inside of a radish.

'Come on,' he said, with a jerk of his head, and clomped off outside with me following.

The grass around the rides had been churned to mud by a hundred shoes and we walked through this sucking sludge to a line of wooden duck-boards which led to a private dark space behind the attractions, among coils of thick black electricity cables. Here, away from the dissonant clatter of overlapping music from several different music systems, all you could hear was the sound of the generators chugging and purring as they drove the power into the rides.

'What's this all about?' said Finny.

'I found this.' I took out the scrap of clock card. 'Where you found that other thing.'

'You didn't tell anyone about that thing, did you?'

'Who could I tell? I don't see anyone.'

'Maybe I shouldn't have taken that thing. I definitely shouldn't have kept it.'

The shadow of a fairground worker, enlarged by a low-angled light and looking like a stretched-out goblin, crept along the walls of the tent behind us.

'Look at it.'

I held out the scrap of clock card on my palm for Finny to see. The times and the gate number – four – and the name, *P. Dunnery*. Turned it over and showed him the name of the racehorse.

Royal Frolic.

The giant Golem on the tent wall stopped still as if it were listening to us, and we lowered our voices.

'The only reason anyone would tear something up is if they wanted to hide what it said. Who is P. Dunnery?'

'Well, the point is not what it is, or what it says. The point is where it was. It was in the place where it must have happened.'

'We don't even know if that thing I found is anything to do with it.'

We stood and looked at each other for a time. We didn't want go back to watch the Waltzer, we didn't want to go to the Clock Hill Coffee Bar, we didn't want to go to The Derby Arms to play pool.

I looked down at the black electricity cables, the shining mud, the dirty wooden walkways. The flickering lights from the rides made everything look like an image from a broken-down film projector.

* * *

I had never been so close to the Sellafield nuclear complex before and I looked in wonder at its towers and globes, so large and gleaming in the hard stare of the sun, they seemed to be figments.

Gate Four was at the back near the sea, so Finny and I found a field which had nothing in it but a huddle of mud-splattered black and white cows in a corner, sat down on a hillock with a pair of binoculars, and waited.

It wasn't long before a tractor appeared in the field and, after dropping off some bales of food for the beasts, the farmer, a large man in a baggy beige jumper and grey wellingtons, got back in, drove towards us along a set of ruts in the earth, stopped nearby, switched off the engine, and jumped down from the cab.

'Bird-watching, lads?' he said, as he walked over.

'He lost his kestrel,' said Finny.

'Lot of raptors round here,' the farmer said, stopping next to me as I looked through the binoculars, 'despite that place.' He jabbed his thumb towards the plant.

'With two beaks, three legs and ten eyes,' said Finny.

Neither us nor the farmer said anything for a time. All you could hear was the soft wind, the low rumble of machinery from inside the site, the dull *clop-clop* of an axe against a tree in the distance.

'See that cow over there,' the farmer said, nodding his wind-bronzed face towards his herd, 'the one on the far edge? Born without a single hair on any of his legs. Last year a calf was born with his tongue shaped like an hourglass. Another had ears that hung down like long thin straws.'

'And you think it's that place causing it?'

'Funny isn't it,' he said, 'no one can say. British Nuclear Fuels Limited say there is,' he put on a posh robotic voice, *'no demonstrable causal link*. But strange that it all happened after a leak of radioactive iodine gas.'

The farmer stood with his hands on his hips, his wellington boots far apart, and stared at the nuclear plant. He said nothing else for a while and I continued to look through my binoculars as a line of cars crept through security at Gate Four.

'Any sign of it?' the farmer said after a while.

'Of what?' I said.

'Your kestrel?'

'He's elusive that one,' I said. 'I used to have two. Mike and Bernie Winters. Now it's just Bernie.'

'A million gallons of waste is pumped into the sea every day from that place. A million gallons. They have a building in there called B30 – *dirty thirty*, the process workers call it. It's not a building, it's a pond where they store the spent fuel. Birds land on it and then fly off. And every time they land on it they take a small amount of radioactivity away with them. Who knows where they end up. Birds can go anywhere. Your kestrel could land on it. Bernie, was it? They told me not to worry. They would build what they called a confinement wall in case of, wait for it, earthquakes. You ever heard of earthquakes round here?'

'No,' said Finny.

'Exactly,' said the farmer, who then went silent again for a time, a silence us boys were not inclined to break.

'There's algae on top of it now,' he said.

'On top of what?' said Finny.

'The pond I was telling you about. So now they can't even see in. People at the plant say there's a thousand kilograms of plutonium in that pond and loads of it has sunk into the mud at the bottom. Some of this stuff is from all over the world. Places like Japan. Why are we taking their shit? The radiation levels around that pool get so high that staff are not allowed to stand near it for more than two minutes. And to make matters worse, it's not even watertight any more because the bad weather round here has cracked the concrete and poisoned water can leak out all over. Ravenglass,' he waved his hand towards the coast, 'over yonder, has a hundred times higher than normal background radioactivity. And my friend's sheep graze there.' He went on like this for about twenty minutes, his words mounting in bitterness as he spoke. Then he stood for a time in silence, staring at the plant.

'I've got a cassette player in the cab now,' he said. 'Christmas present from the wife. Funny that we were talking about raptors, because you know what I've been listening to?'

Silence.

'In the cab?' the farmer clarified.

Silence.

'The Eagles.'

'Funny,' I said.

'Do you like The Eagles, lads?'

'We like punk,' said Finny.

'Well, lads, I've got to get on. Watch yourselves now. And I hope you find your kestrel, young man.'

The tractor trundled away down the tramline ruts made by its own tyres, just as I spotted the black Ford Capri with its gold-edged wheel hubs in the line of incoming traffic.

On our way out of the field, we were stopped by two BNFL policemen with guns around their necks.

'Lads, can we have a word?'

I looked at the guns, then at the men's thick black canvas uniforms with loops, pockets and pouches all over, then at the puzzled smiles on the men's faces, and I hoped that the men would not have cause to point their weapons at me.

'What's your business here with those binoculars?' said one.

'We're doing a project for school,' said Finny. 'About the effect of the nuclear industry on health.'

The policemen looked at each other. 'You from Greenpeace?'

'No. We have an appointment with Paul Dunnery, the community feller. At three o'clock. We spoke to his secretary.'

The men escorted us out onto the road and down towards the main gates. Finny and I didn't say anything to each other on the way and the men did not make small talk.

A high-tension fence of diamond-shaped apertures surrounded the site, punctuated at various points by sets of heavy gates, and we went through one of these, and soon we were inside the plant and the men began to march us more briskly through the complex.

A sign shakily written in big capitals with two different pens said:

ALL PERSONNEL WHO HAVE VISITED PILE ONE OR POND AREA MUST REPORT TO B34 CHANGEROOM FOR MONITORING

Steel cylinders the size and shape of jet engines were being rolled about on trucks. A freight train rumbled into the site carrying massive silos in concrete casings. There were long thin chimneys with square filters on the end and everything was concrete and grey except for the yellow warning signs – one, on a strip of plastic wrapped around a green steel structure, said:

RADIATION LEVEL ABOVE 25 MR/HR DO NOT LOITER

Steam gushed out of every orifice and I tried to avoid walking near it.

The men led us into the entrance of a low building that said B56 on the side. Men in white coats stood in front of panels out of Dr Who's Tardis. There were dials and indicators everywhere, their needles flicking this way and that, and a constant reptilian clicking sound.

We had to wait in a small reception area until Paul Dunnery came out and shook both of our hands hard, squeezing them as if he were trying out a wrestling grip. He was about sixty years old with thick brown wavy hair and a tanned wrinkled face that looked as though he didn't smile much.

He didn't smile then. 'I'm Paul Dunnery,' he said. 'Head of Community Relations here at Windscale. And I'm happy to help you with your project.' He laughed mirthlessly, with no glimmer of joy in his eyes.

We followed him into his office where there was a desk piled high with papers and cardboard folders, pens in a pot, and, in the corner, a small green TV screen with a typewriter under it. A packet on the table said:

POTASSIUM IODATE TABLETS
TO BE USED ONLY IN CASE OF A NUCLEAR ACCIDENT

'Sit, sit,' Paul Dunnery said. 'Sit down, boys.' He lowered himself into a leather revolving chair behind the desk while Finny and I perched on plastic stackers in front of him.

Mr Dunnery's joyless smile pulled his lips up at the sides, but his eyes remained narrow slots. 'My brother has boys, but I never any had kids. Sometimes I'm glad, what with the world as it is.' He paused and looked towards the door, 'With what happened last Thursday night, for example.'

I looked at Paul Dunnery's hands and wondered if they were the hands that had touched Philomena May. He didn't seem a likely candidate, but his name was on the clock card. His name, his signature.

'Now,' Paul Dunnery said, 'the first thing I want you to do is blindfold me,' and he handed me a strip of dark cloth with two ribbon ties at either end.

I looked at the cloth and back at Paul Dunnery, then at Finny, and then back at Paul Dunnery.

'Don't worry, don't worry, it's a scientific experiment that will be most helpful for your project.'

He turned round in his chair so his back was to us and I put the blindfold over the man's eyes and tied it at the back.

'Now hand me some paper-clips,' he said.

I found a blue ceramic pot shaped like a clamshell which was full of paper-clips, and handed it to Paul Dunnery.

'You two boys move to the sides of the room and watch this.'

In a series of abrupt jabbing gestures, Paul Dunnery pulled paper-clips one at a time out of the blue ceramic clam and began to toss the metal fasteners backwards over his shoulder so that they landed on the carpet. He did this dozens of times so that eventually the carpet had a large amount of paper-clips all over it.

He removed the blindfold. 'Now, to make it fair,' he said. 'I want you two to both do the same thing.'

First me, then Finny, put on the blindfold and sat on the revolving leather chair and tossed paper-clips backwards over our shoulders.

'That's it. More, more,' he said whenever we paused, and soon the blue ceramic clamshell was empty.

'Take off the blindfold,' he said to Finny when he'd finished, 'and come up and stand on this desk with me.'

We all climbed onto the desk, me and Finny standing either side of Paul Dunnery, and looked down at the paper-clip-strewn carpet.

'You'll agree that we threw those paper-clips randomly with no idea how they would fall?'

'Yes,' said Finny.

'Yet, look at how the paper-clips have landed. See over there, where there is a cluster of them all together? And see this part of the room where there are very few?'

'Yes.'

'That's what happens when you do something randomly. Things won't end up evenly spread out over the carpet. They will cluster in some cases, and in some areas there will be none at all.'

Paul Dunnery climbed down off the table and sat in his chair and we returned to our seats.

'And that,' he said, leaning back, 'that explains why you might find clusters of certain diseases around the Windscale nuclear plant. Or Sellafield, as you locals call it. Clusters can be random. Just because radioactivity causes certain cancers and more of those cancers appear in a cluster around a nuclear plant is no proof that the cluster is caused by the nuclear plant. It might be, it might well be. But also it might not. I believe that it is not,' said Paul Dunnery. 'Because the doses received by people living around here are not high enough. Jungle drums tell me that some locals think we have fountains of green fluorescent stuff spurting out of holes and it's all held together with Plasticine and Gloy. But look at how carefully we monitor the health of our staff. This is an incident sheet. Every single incident of contamination is recorded here. All mishaps on the site. You have mishaps in any industry. But as long as you record them and learn from your mistakes, that's all fine and normal.'

I looked at the sheet. The left-hand column said the date and next to it a description of what had happened: *Plutonium spillage, whole body exposure, explosion in fume hood, glove box pressurisation, fire in Drigg trench, overexposure in Magnox ponds, personal alpha contamination, spillage scrubber circuit, release of airborne activity, high film dose, high by head dose, loss of Windscale suit exhaust*; and next to each incident the name of the person and a digit saying how much radiation they had received. The highest said 1,000-13,000 rems.

I remembered a story on the news about a Sellafield worker who developed bone cancer and his wife saying *his bones kept jumping out.*

I didn't know what this meant but the idea sent shudders through me.

His bones kept jumping out.

'Since the 1957 fire at Number One Pile, radiation has escaped from the site only fourteen times. Fourteen times in twenty-odd years. Not bad eh? And yes, it's true we've paid out compensation. We've been generous. Twenty-two thousand in one case, sixty-seven in another. A nuclear laundry, they are calling us, or worse, the world's nuclear dustbin. And the media. Well.' A big weight of defeat hung over him as he explained how the BBC and the left-wing papers continually misunderstood his innocent industry. 'The two of you know as well as I do that this place brings valuable jobs to the area. Over ten thousand workers. Many of your friends' fathers work here, I'm sure.' He stopped. He was staring intently at me. 'What are those marks on your neck?'

My scarf had slipped and I pulled it back up to cover the lesions.

'It's just some thing that happened to me.'

He looked at my wrist where another lesion was showing under my cuff.

'All over your body?'

'Yes.'

Paul Dunnery pushed his lips into a frown, lifted a large notebook from the top of his out-tray, raised a fountain pen from the desk, and wrote something.

'I'm sorry. I hope they find a way to help you.'

Underneath the notebook, in the out-tray, was a big batch of clock cards tied in an elastic band; each, as far as I could see, with the signature *P. Dunnery* on the bottom. In that batch of cards, I was certain, would be a card with the name Crow on the top. Now I had no doubt.

He saw me looking.

'Yes, I'm personnel, really. I check a lot of clock cards. But the community relations part of my job is becoming much busier. And, I have to say, it's more rewarding somehow.'

He asked us if we needed to be driven back to Cleator Moor, and we lied, saying that Finny's dad would pick us up.

So a member of BNFL's private police force drove us down the long wide empty road away from the plant and dropped us at the roundabout on the dual carriageway.

When the policeman had gone, I looked at Finny.

'What are we going to do now?'

Phut-phut-phut

I felt electricity branching though me.

There was the Defiant and on it sat Petal, the same pale pixie face, the same wistful, empty eyes, the same sullen pout, and still wearing the red wetsuit, this time the zip halfway down her chest. At first her face looked distant and sleepy, then her head jolted back and she stared at me, furrowing her brow in puzzlement, as if I was the dead one, the ghost.

What about Finny? I mimed at her.

She got off the scooter and walked up to Finny and looked into his face, the way you would examine a horse you were about to buy. Then she breathed into his mouth, hard, as if expelling fire. Finny's head tilted to one side and his face took on a ecstatic look, transforming him for a moment into an angel. His eyelids quivered and closed very slowly, then he fell over into the hedge where he lay peacefully, an empty expression on his face.

Petal beckoned me over.

'Tether. My tether,' she said. 'Bad things are building up. They were born at the same time, from the same mother, but one looks at the other and feels no love. Tether me, Barry.'

And then I felt her lips like icy waves of bitter water and her long tongue like some deep sea tendril coaxing me into her mouth of melting snow.

10

Petal twisted the throttle hard and we sped off, hovering a few inches off the ground and slipping along so quickly that everything blurred into a whipped-up cream of colours. Eventually we jerked higher into the air, swivelled about abruptly, and then we were headed skywards. A clear day, no mist this time, and the higher we went, the better I felt. I began to forget about Crow, my skin, my dad and my mother, and Marion. I liked being able to fly. Better than all the drugs I had read about in the Hell's Angels paperbacks and *Go Ask Alice*.

Soon we were alone on the fells and I could see the lower peaks below us and the higher hills like Scafell Pike and Haystacks looming up above. An RAF jet plane shot by underneath, the driver's face a smudge of pale grey, the roar of its engine following later, and I wondered what would have happened if we had collided. Petal turned the bike again and we climbed even higher. Now, there were no trees, only bare rocks. A buzzard circled below. Higher and higher we went until eventually she stopped the scooter on a pile of rocks on the top of what seemed to be one of highest mountains, judging by the way so many other peaks fell away below us. Petal dismounted and, shading her eyes with her hand, she scoured the area, everything sitting down there like objects on a blanket. She squeezed her face small, focusing on the dozens of villages and towns; the houses, the fields, the roads, the paths, all teeming with people, cars, dogs, cats, mice and insects.

'There. He's at the brother's house. Come on.'

We accelerated towards the edge and it was just like what had happened on St Bees Head; the scooter didn't hang or float, it plummeted, tumbling off the mountainside with all the grace of a grand piano tossed out of a plane, twisting in the air with us both holding on, me shrieking and crying in a mixture of fear and joy, and Petal placidly gripping one handgrip, concentrating hard. She regained control above a cluster of symmetrically planted pine trees, the wheels of the scooter brushing the canopy and making the pine-tops flick forward and back. Up, up, up again, then a sharp swerve, before zooming off towards Cleator Moor.

At the village of Lamplugh we hovered, Petal searching the streets, the gardens, the house fronts, then soon she pointed out two men standing on the drive outside a smart-looking converted barn, and we swooped down and parked next to them.

One of the men was the diver. His face was pink and he was sweating and shouting at the other man, who was the brother – I recognised him from his rugby-playing younger version on the beach. The diver was flailing his arms about, while the brother – the taller one – tried to calm him, touching him on the shoulder, pleading, making 'I understand' faces, serious faces, nodding.

Yes, of course

It will be OK

Don't worry, yes

Of course I see

Yes, I know. I understand why you're upset

Yes, that's exactly what will happen

No, it's not what you think

I have to reassure you as a brother that would never happen

We have your welfare at heart

We are your family, we would never allow that to happen

You are getting things all out of proportion, out of proportion, out of all proportion

That's not how it is, it might look like that, but things are not how they appear

Mountains and molehills, mountains and molehills

– and so on and so on and further on and further on and more like that and like that even more.

But the diver pushed him away, stamped off down the drive, got into his Xsara Picasso, and tore off along the road to Whitehaven.

Petal and I followed fast behind, trailing in the wake of the car, like a tender dragging behind its yacht.

In Whitehaven, the diver whizzed around the one-way system, pulled up at the taxi rank and jumped out. A long line of cabs, but not much work going on. No one in Whitehaven seemed to be looking for a lift anywhere. A handful of cabbies were leaning against their cars, chatting. One of them said hello and slapped the diver on the back. Another of the taxi drivers had a black and green Guinness hat he must have found months ago, on St Patrick's Day, and the cabbies began to mess about with it, each of them putting it on and strutting up and down in it, singing. They were laughing a lot, but the diver merely watched them, and didn't join in. One of them, a happy-looking feller who had glittering eyes and seemed to vibrate with exuberance, handed the diver the hat, and urged him to put it on too. But the diver wouldn't. He shrugged the man away. The same one grabbed him and plonked it on his head and then they all laughed. One shouted something and the diver ripped the hat off his head and chucked it on to the pavement, shouting something back.

The diver looked as though he wanted to throw these men down a pit shaft and then pull off his own skin. He jumped in his car and the tyres squealed as he disappeared up the road out of town.

Petal and I followed on the Defiant.

At a small house in Cleator Moor, the diver stopped and we parked behind him. The diver sat for a time in his car and I got off the scooter, opened the passenger door to the taxi, and climbed into a warm stuffy interior with the sour smell of rotten milk. A girl on the radio wanted everyone to try sleeping with a broken heart.

The diver's hand was on the steering wheel and I placed my palm on top of it and squeezed. The diver looked in my direction but nothing flickered in his eyes. He moved his gaze onto the house we were parked outside, then looked ahead again and sighed.

The song on the radio changed to an American man shouting poetry over pounding beats, punctuated by the words *not afraid, not afraid*, and the diver grimaced and switched it off.

The diver opened the glove compartment where there was an envelope stuffed full of something. He took out the envelope and placed it on his lap. He pressed his hand on his brow as if taking his own temperature. He pulled down the sun visor, flipped open the mirror, and looked at his face, frowning. He adjusted a few hairs on the top of his head, and rubbed some marks – food stains possibly – from the skin around his mouth.

Petal got in the back of the car.

'Whose house is this?' I said.

'I don't know,' she said.

'Is he going to do something bad in there?'

'I don't know, I don't think so. Not today. I'm getting tomorrow more strongly.'

The diver took out the silver portable phone flipped it open and stared at a photograph.

A photograph on a phone.

The image was of an Oriental-looking woman. She had eyelashes like a camel's and a river of dark hair flowed around her shoulders. Big satiny lips. The diver gazed at the woman's face for a long time. Then he used his thumb to clear the picture away and bring in another photo. This one was full length, the same girl sitting at a bar, one long leg jutting through a split in a shiny blue dress trimmed with fur. She looked like a dancer, the sort of dancer you might see in Pan's People on *Top of the Pops*. Another photo showed her in a white bikini and long black boots with a sign behind her that said, in luminous orange letters, *Spicy Girls a Go-Go*.

The diver pressed a button and the words *Are you sure you want to delete this photo?* came up. He clicked yes and the photo disappeared and he did the same with the others as well. The diver looked at the envelope then at the house again. He opened the envelope. It was full of some kind of currency – not the notes that had been hidden under the floor – and he counted it carefully. He wrote on the envelope *For my dearest grandson*, then sealed it up.

He sniffed the air, wrinkled his brow, then rubbed his hand under his armpit and snuffled at it. His expression didn't change. He blew breath into his cupped palm and inhaled it back. His expression didn't change. He sat back in his seat and began to tap on the steering wheel, fast, faster, faster and faster, drumming all five of his fingers, one after the other, in a rippling motion, a rolling rhythm that got louder and louder with his thumb slamming heavier and heavier at the end of each sequence.

He grabbed the envelope of money, jumped out of the car and ran up to the door and knocked. A young man answered and the diver went inside.

Petal motioned me back to the scooter, and I got on the pillion, then we headed back to Rowrah, to the diver's house.

Round the back this time, through a hallway full of diving gear and plastic bags and wellington boots and faded waterproof coats, and then into the kitchen.

Each time I went into the diver's house, I noticed different things. A single bowl and a spoon waited on the drainer. A calendar pinned to the back of the door showed pictures of Thailand and was open at the correct month. Letters had been scribbled near certain dates. On the floor was linoleum the colour of dirty ice, covered with ridges that looked as though they had a gripping function. On the lino, a stacking chair, faded red, like a disappearing scar, next to a small, fungal-white table patterned with pale blue speckles. The surface of the table had long straight scratches on it like someone had been using a craft knife. Letters and documents had been laid out neatly in piles, and I picked a few sheets off the top. One pile related to the man's house – the deeds were there, along with an old waxy map showing the terrace marooned in a carpet of green fields. The original estate agent's description was there too. Another pile related to his bank accounts; a third pile was of correspondence between him and the tax office; a fourth was of electric, gas and phone bills; a fifth was of greetings cards, and there was also a heap of letters from a firm of solicitors.

One letter had been torn up and scraps were lying on the mouldering linoleum.

In the living room, we stood and looked about.

'Behind the sofa,' said Petal.

I looked. On the carpet, wrapped in a stripy winceyette bed sheet, was a long rifle with sights, next to a chunky double-barrelled shotgun, the type I imagined farmers using. A rucksack next to the guns said *Rohan*; imaginary lands, fictional maps.

I lifted the bag. It surprised me that sometimes I could touch things – even move things – because more often than not my invisible quicksand fingers went straight through.

I tipped out its contents to reveal dozens of cartridges I recognised would fit the shotgun, several cardboard cartons containing rounds for the rifle, and some small functional-looking accoutrements like screwdrivers. Next to all this was a can of fluid called Hoppe's Number 9, a carton of something called Rem Oil and two oil-blackened yellow towels. Peaks of grease on the dark metal gun parts glinted. Everything smelled of fish, of crushed match heads, of Banana Toffos.

'Is he a farmer? Could be for shooting foxes?'

'I don't think so,' said Petal. 'Barry, I'm scared.'

I wondered how a ghost could be scared and what could she be scared of that was worse than what had already happened to her.

I returned the ammunition to the bag.

'If he's going to shoot someone, can we stop him?'

'I don't know,' said Petal, biting her lip. 'But we'll try.'

'Can't we dump this stuff in the lake?'

'You can't move things. They reappear.'

Hopelessness opened up in me like a sinkhole. We stood and looked at the guns and the ammunition for a long time, until the front door clicked open and the diver entered, breathing heavily. We watched him furtling through the piles of papers on the kitchen table, picking up a couple and moving them further away from his face so he could read the small type, then he came into the lounge, picked up the shotgun and took it over to a wood-rimmed oval mirror that hung above the gas fire.

He pointed the gun at his reflection. 'Nice round here, isn't it?' he said, in his soft reedy voice. 'But you can't eat scenery.'

He jerked the gun back and made an explosive sound with his mouth.

'No. You can't eat scenery.'

He turned and looked directly at me.

'You,' he said. 'Yes, you. Come here. What time is it?'

I went over and stood right in front of the man, right in front of the gun barrel.

'Come here. Yes, you,' the diver said, now staring through me at a space by the sofa. 'What time is it?'

He paused as if listening to an answer.

'No, that's wrong. It's my time. That's what time it is. Your time and my time together. This time. This time, this time now, will be the time that binds us together forever. It's the same time, you see. Exactly the same time, so it will be an anniversary. Every year the same date and time will come round and everyone will remember me and you. And all the others too.'

He looked to the side and was silent for a long time. He sighed. 'What does it take to change the essence of a man?' he said and looked at me again. 'What does it take? You don't know? I do.'

Then he seemed to become a different character and stood to the side of the mirror and pointed at his own reflection, speaking as if he were delivering a lecture to himself.

'In you, I have seen a great spirit.'

A pause.

'Yes, you.' he said. 'Are you willing to discover the nature of that spirit?' He paused as if he was listening to a reply from himself, then said, in a low muttering voice which was hardly audible, 'I see what man has done to the world. Deep sadness and suffering. I have chosen you to go forth.'

The diver went close to the mirror, so close that his breath began to mist it over.

'And you must teach them to fear,' he said softly.

He turned away and tossed the shotgun onto the floor, then he went round the back of the sofa and began to sort all the equipment into bags he could easily carry.

When he had everything ready, he looked down at his tools.

'You will fight the most difficult battle,' he said towards the Rohan bag, 'but you will find your way back. I will see you on the water when the task is done.'

Petal left the room, went through the kitchen, and disappeared out of the back door.

I followed.

It was raining heavily, gushing down from the sky like grey soup, and Petal stood in it, thinking, while it ran over her, through her, and off her like she was something inanimate. She fiddled with the zip on her wetsuit.

'Where now?' I said.

'There's something else,' she said. 'Something about when he was younger. Your skin is telling me.'

We drove, or rather flew, through the watery air to Cleator, to St Mary's Church, and Petal led me inside.

I looked at the glossy brass altar rail, at the red sandstone walls, at the stone floor, at the curtained tabernacle where they keep the hosts, at the door which Father Dempsey always came out from.

But it wasn't about any of that.

Petal led me to the side aisle, where the confession boxes were.

'In here,' she said, and pushed open a door.

I was not surprised she'd led me into one of these. St Mary's was reputedly haunted by an old priest who died of the drink, and a few people claimed they had given their confession to a person on the other side of the curtain on an evening when it turned out that all the living priests had been away doing other things.

Inside there was a strong smell of wood shavings and polish.

From somewhere, the squeal of steel cutting through timber.

The door of the confessional closed behind us, then opened and we were somewhere else.

A workshop full of stacked sheets of uncut lumber and carpentry tools hanging off the walls.

An electric circular saw was at the back of the room and there was a half-finished coffin in the middle. Through the back of the workshop was a smaller space, plush and quiet, nicely wallpapered and clean looking, and in it was standing a young man, not much older than me. The young man was recognisable as the diver, even though he was slimmer and had more hair. The same pleasantly round and friendly face that looked as though it could be easily embarrassed.

He was wearing brown overalls with lots of pockets and an apron which held tools. A chisel was in his hand. In front of the diver, a dead body was laid out. The body was dressed in a dark double-breasted suit and long shiny shoes with price stickers on the soles. The room smelt bitter, of chemicals, astringents, a little like a women's hairdressers. The diver was staring at the body. Not moving, just staring at it. The dead man's face had thick make-up all over it and the hair was long and grey and had been carefully combed. The comb was next to the man's head in a vanity case with all kinds of scissors and brushes and clippers. A safety razor with wet soap on its blade lay next to the corpse's head.

A moaning fan stirred the air.

I hadn't seen a dead body before. I was surprised that the dead man's face didn't look peaceful; it looked more like it was impatient.

The diver lifted his hand and touched the cadaver's cheek. He bent his head to stare at the man's face from a different angle. Then there was a noise outside, a car parking up, and he fled out of the back room and began to plane away furiously at the unfinished coffin, at the long edges that waited for the lid, narrowing his eyes as he tried to make it level and smooth.

On a shelf behind the diver, there were glass bottles with floral-patterned pink and blue labels that said *Introfiant Arterial Chemical*. They looked like the Pernod bottle in Finny's mother's cocktail cabinet.

A brochure lying open on a low table offered a full couch

mahogany casket with satin lining in muted gold.

An older man came in to the workshop, wearing a suit mottled by the rain, a checked trilby, and a white flower in his lapel. He smelled of aftershave.

'Hi Stan,' said the diver.

'Hello lad,' the older man said, smacking the side of the box hard. 'This box. Good joints. Well done. You have a fine touch. Are you liking it here OK?'

The diver smiled. 'I like it. I like working with wood.'

'So you *do* like it here, then? I wasn't sure. You're a bit quiet a lot of the time. I mean, each to his own. Everyone doesn't have to be always chatting away.'

'I like making things. I've never worked with these tools before. I like that there's a certain tool for every job, with special blades. The awls, the rasps, the spokeshave. I like how you keep them really sharp.'

Stan's trilby hat had begun to drip rain and he took it off and banged it against his leg.

'So why Sellafield?'

'Oh.'

'Yes. They've been in touch for a reference.'

'I don't know. This place. Like I said, I like the work. Making things. With the wood. And using the tools.' The diver clasped and unclasped his hands as he spoke. 'But you know, the thing we do here. With people dying. and the people who come in, the people who have, you know, lost people. I don't understand how you can talk to people every day who have just had someone die. Every day.'

'Death. It's part of life, lad. This is a good way to learn how to enjoy the world.' Stan began to dart about the room as he spoke, tidying and shuffling and putting things away. 'That's what the funeral business has taught me. To love being alive. To cherish what you have and look after the people around you.'

The diver turned to face him. 'I make it. I make it beautifully, I think. I think I do the best I can with it. I work at it until it's perfect, smooth. Balanced. And then what? Then it's buried, and no one ever sees it again. How can you work like that? Everything you produce, that you've worked on all day, ends up under ten tons of earth.'

Stan stopped still. 'Or burned.'

'Yes. Or burned.'

'Well, it's up to you lad. I have to go and see a family in Egremont now. Do you want to come? Help them choose the finish? The style?'

'No, I'll get this one done.'

Stan headed to the door, then stopped.

'I'll give you a good reference, don't worry.'

'I know, Stan. Thanks.'

When Stan left the workshop, the diver began planing the wood of the coffin vigorously until he was sure Stan had gone. Then he stopped and looked about him. After his encounter with Stan, the diver's body seemed to have wilted; his head down, his shoulders sloped, his posture full of apology. Deep within the young man's eyes, I felt I could see the half-crushed sensitivity in his soul.

The diver stood still for a long time. Then he went over to a wooden chest and plucked a yellow square of dusty cloth out of a drawer. He went over to the workbench, picked up some of the smaller tools, folded them inside the cloth and put them in the pocket of his outdoor coat, which was hanging on the wall. After this, he returned to the room at the back, where the corpse lay. He stood and looked again at the dead man's face. He couldn't stop looking at it.

The diver began to murmur to himself, a whispered prayer.

'Nail set, sliding bevel, caliper, jig.

'Feather board, rip fence, miter gauge, jig and dado, compound miter.

'Router, drill press, surface planer, jointer, awl, rasp, spokeshave.'

* * *

Outside the undertakers, Petal looked suddenly pensive, distracted.

From the docks behind the undertakers you could hear the *chink-plonk-chink* of halyards slapping against masts in the breeze.

'Sometimes I feel I can't hold on to it. Like I'm fading. Something seems to pull me back, like I have to recharge.'

We headed up, up into the sky high over Whitehaven where the coastline curved around to Scotland in the north and to the south you could see Morecambe Bay and Blackpool Tower, and we climbed into the mountains again and then somehow, after a shaky descent through a pine forest, we landed with a bump back in Cleator Moor 1976, and, when I looked behind me, Petal was gone.

11

'There is no God,' Dad said as he pulled his thick gardening trousers on over his suit pants. 'Not if he lets things like this happen. That poor girl. Barry's skin. I can't see the God in that.' He nodded at Jenny, who was now back from Nana's and had her ear glued to a transistor with *I'm Mandy Fly Me* blaring out. 'I'm going to join our Jenny in the Buddhists.'

Then he went into the garden to do something with his chrysanthemums and my mother and I left for mass, my dad's Brylcreemed head bobbing up over the privet hedge to watch us leave.

In St Mary's, I noticed how little difference there was between the church now and the one I'd been in with Petal in the future, and thought about how unfair it was that material things like stone and wood and glass stay virtually the same, while human beings crumble away before your eyes.

Hanging from the roof of the church was a steel corona shaped like a crown set on top of its mirror image and I always looked at this sculpture closely as I sat through the tedium of mass. It floated above the congregation like a funnel attached to a spout, as if it was sucking human souls up from the bottom and shooting them out through the top towards heaven.

The church was packed and the atmosphere tense because this mass was special; it was offered up for Philomena May, and a picture of her was standing on an easel in the centre of the altar. Not the photo where she was dressed as Cleopatra, but one of her school ones, one where her mother clearly hadn't known it was photograph day because Philomena's black hair hung crooked and unwashed and she had a red pimple on her chin. She was pulling a funny face.

Several non-Catholics had come along to show solidarity and even Samantha Fry was there, the black helmet of her bob and her fuzzy black and red jumper standing out among the white-shirted men and pastel-frocked ladies.

Joan McCricket was performing in the folk group and, after everyone had settled down, she scratched out a chord on her acoustic guitar, Peter Richardson's electric bass went *plod-plod-plod*, a tambourine rattled, Maureen Riley from the sixth form scraped an intro on her violin, and then the chorus of St Cuthbert's juniors came in mournfully and pleasantly out of tune.

Maaur-ning hars broh-ken

This mass, the 5.30 on a Sunday, was usually full of all the kids who were forced to go, but hated it, and many would hover in the vestibule, chatting and laughing. Sometimes Michael Kennedy would have a transistor and he would play the Radio 1 chart show, Tom Browne counting down the Top Twenty. When Donna Summer's *Love To Love You Baby* was played (before it was banned for its heavy breathing), we all thought that was hilarious.

The commotion started after communion was over and the priest had begun his closing remarks. People in the church began to murmur, a growing soft roar of muttering, and when I turned round I saw that a piece of vitally important information was being passed from person to person, travelling like a wave through the congregation. Until the wave reached my mother, that is, because that's when it abruptly stopped. My mother stood up, clutched at her breast, and cried out loudly.

The church fell silent. Father Dempsey stopped mid-incantation, pushed his bony hand through his grizzly ginger hair and made a motion with his head at one of the stewards, who happened to be Joan McCricket's father, a thin man with blue-tinted oval spectacles and hair that was short and spiky on the top and long at the back. It was he who helped my mother out of the church.

The cacophony of whispering in the church grew louder and Father Dempsey had to rap his knuckles against the lectern several times.

'We are all going through difficult times,' he said. 'Let's close this mass now and go in peace. Can the folk group please play us out?'

The congregation pressed towards the back of the church and the choir sang glassily.

Sweet the rain's neeeew faall
Surnlit from hea-eh-eh-vern

I located my mother in the carpark where she looked a bedraggled, desperate figure, and was lurching forward in spasms, buckling and wobbling as if she was about to fall on her face. By the time I reached her, she was leaning against the car, the door open, panting and holding her throat.

'I can't breathe,' she said. 'Everything's gone blurred.'

'What's happened?'

'Everything is tilting.'

From inside the church –

Praise for the sweeeet-nehrss
Of the wet gar ah ah den

Samantha Fry appeared. 'It's your dad,' she said. 'The police have taken him in for questioning.'

My uncle Charlie came over and helped my mother into the car and drove her home, and I was left standing next to Samantha Fry. I looked at her and couldn't tell if she was real or something I had imagined. I didn't know what month it was, what year. I couldn't remember my name and was suddenly gripped by a feeling of emptiness, an exhaustion so enormous, so relentless, that I had to lean against a gravestone to stop myself from fainting. I felt as though my head was expanding with gas and about to explode. Rows of headstones before me made me think that I was dead and that one of them would have my name already inscribed on it.

I thought through the situation in my head. What could I do? My mind landed on several options, but none of them seemed possible or achievable. All I knew was that I had to act, had to do something, but when I considered some of the options, I felt everything go black inside me, as if my soul had gone gangrenous. I thought about my skin. The metal blisters had not changed. They surely marked me out as damned, damned to perform some nauseating evil act in an effort to clear my father's name, or put someone else in the frame – or what? I had no idea.

I thought about Crow, and tried to imagine what had happened.

I spotted her in The Derby Arms, laughing and flicking her hair about, and I wanted to do to her what I pretend to do to Marion.

Samantha Fry helped me to stagger into The Brook Inn, a pub opposite the church, and settled me into a corner. She got us drinks, and we drank one, then another, then another, then another. The landlord had a record player behind the bar and kept playing *Next* by The Sensational Alex Harvey Band.

Nerkst! Said Alex Harvey.

I flicked my cigarette into a puddle and pulled the girl close to me. She kissed me back. The cigarette hissed in the water.

Samantha and I sat in The Brook for several hours. Father Dempsey came in for a pint of Guinness and a natter to the barman about Cartmel Races.

Nerkst!

She was willing at first but suddenly she wanted me to stop. She kept saying she was cold and that annoyed me because, in fact, it was one of the hottest nights ever in history, so that's when I first hit her.

Samantha suggested we run away. We could hitch-hike our way down the country to Bristol where Samantha had an unconventional auntie we could stay with.

Nerkst!

Then she started to scream so I took her over to the old kennels and that's where I needed to shut her up for good otherwise the place would have been crawling.

I agreed to the Bristol idea. I had a sudden urge to test myself, to take risks, to rush towards the edges of things. And I couldn't think of anything else to do.

Nerkst!

Afterwards I felt sick and terrified and so I tried to hide her, but not very well, it turns out, and the next day I went to confession at St Mary's.

I couldn't face home and I didn't want to go into the future again with Petal. I was becoming terrified of the metal studs all over my body which were showing no signs of disappearing.

Nerkst!

Did I tell Father Dempsey what I'd done? No, I told the priest that I kept thinking about doing bad things to women and asked how I could stop myself thinking these things because I was worried I would really do them, what with what happened to that poor girl. Father Dempsey said that I should pray to God for strength.

Samantha Fry and I staggered out of the pub and stood by the road with our thumbs out.

Nerkst!

* * *

The van door slid open and the two of us jumped in. The driver was short and round with tiny features set deeply in a pale, plump face, making him look like a biscuit. He was wearing a red satin shirt, a bootlace tie, a white suit covered with pale brown stains, and ornately carved leather cowboy boots.

He indicated his clothes with a downwards tilt of the head.

'I just finished a spot at the Working Men's on the Moor. I'm a drummer,' he said. 'You have to, like, dress up a bit.' He spoke in high yelpy tones. 'It was the hardest set too – the one before the bingo, and most of them only go for the bingo, so they don't care. Charity do, so just expenses, but that's all right. I was backing up a guitar vocalist called Randy Lee Moon. You know him? he does all the crowd-pleasers – *Come On Over To My Place, Armarillo, One Man Band.* Where you two heading?'

'Uh...' I said.

'Cockermouth,' said Samantha.

The man threw the van into gear and drove off more quickly than we had expected.

'I know a joke about Cockermouth,' he said. 'But I can't tell you 'cos you're too young.' He laughed, a high-pitched *hee-hee-hee-hee* sound, somehow false, like a bird imitating a human voice.

'I don't like jokes,' Samantha Fry said.

'I have to go and pick up my spare drum kit from the social club at Broughton Moor dump. Lent it to the resident drummer there. I can take you on to Cockermouth after that, if you like? Wouldn't want you out late in the middle of nowhere on your own.' He put his hand out towards me. 'I'm Gary Glass by the way. But people call me Animal 'cos of the way I play the drums. Off *The Muppets*? You got relatives in Cockermouth?'

'Yes,' said Samantha. 'My mother's brother's second cousin's hamster lives there.'

The man looked across at her, and made his squeaky laugh again. His lips were glossy and the colour of raspberry pulp and his small lashless eyes were shiny as though he had been crying. I was glad I was sitting between the weird man and Samantha Fry.

The town petered out and was replaced with fields of sheep. Large grey rocks covered in bleached lichen were dotted about, half-buried in the earth. The van went past the open cast and off into the empty, nowhere lands between Workington and Cockermouth. We saw signs to the steelworks at Moss Lane, the shoe factories in Maryport, the ice-pop works near Flimby, the dartboard factory in Broughton Moor.

'Are you a full-time drummer?' I said.

Gary Glass gave a catarrhal wheeze. 'Semi-professional. I work days at Sellafield. Walk around with an empty box all day chatting to people. Nobody seems to mind. I think they've forgotten they took me on. But I clock in every day and put in the shifts and the pay packet arrives. Nobody does anything there.' Gary Glass laughed his hee-hee-hee. 'The people on nights – they sleep upright in cupboards. They take it in turns while someone keeps a lookout and they get away with it despite it being as tight as Colditz.'

He looked past me at Samantha Fry.

'You're a mature-looking lass. What age would you be? Nineteen? Twenty? Do you mind me asking? '

'Yes I do mind.'

'Sorry. Does your mum know you go out looking like that?'

'Does yours?'

He sniggered breathily. 'You've got a point.'

'My mum's a prostitute,' said Samantha, 'she doesn't care. She's on the game down at the docks and she's always getting the clap. You probably know her.'

Gary Glass didn't say anything for a time, just watched the long road rolling out in front, the white lines disappearing under the van.

'Feisty,' he said after a time. 'Isn't she feisty? I like feisty kids.'

I was beginning to regret getting into a van with this small fat man.

'This thing can really move, you know,' squeaked Gary Glass, nodding at the dashboard. 'Observe,' and the engine whined horribly before he slammed it into a lower gear making the vehicle surge forward violently as if rockets had been shot out of the back.

We pelted recklessly round the bends, overtaking every car that got in our way, never once slackening the pace, regardless of what might be coming from the other direction, and I worried we would fly off a bridge and land in a river and be trapped for hours in an air pocket and have to eat our own hair.

Soon the sun began to disappear and I looked out of the window at the dark fields and dark hills and beady lights from houses on the fells and thought about how lonely the towns of West Cumbria were at night, with nothing joining them together but thick belts of blackness and inky roads winding around empty fields where sheep contemplated the starry bowl of the sky.

Eventually we turned off the dual carriageway and the road got twistier and the van got slower and soon we arrived at a set of high metal gates operated by men in security uniforms. One of the men came over and Gary Glass spoke to him through the window, and they allowed him to drive in. The sign outside said RNAD – Royal Naval Armaments Depot, Broughton Moor.

Behind the gates was a set of fields and yards dotted all over with the indigo outlines of sinister low buildings and corrugated huts. The complex went back a long, long way, with no visible limits, and Gary Glass drove us along a tarmacked road for a while, as we penetrated the centre. Lots of low reddish-coloured buildings. Piles of earth that looked like shooting ranges. Warning signs saying things like:

CAUTION EXPLOSIVES STORE 400 LB, 200 LB, 100 LB

'This is the ammo dump,' said Gary Glass. 'You not heard of this place? Run by the Navy. There's a special train line just for this site that comes out of Workington. They store all kinds of bombs and explosives here and they used to test things here, too. Chemical weapons, gas, that sort of stuff. Fifties, sixties. Back when your dad was pulling down your mother's knickers behind the fish factory. Hee hee hee.'

The social club was a low concrete building in the middle and when we pulled up outside I saw in the yellow light from the windows two men playing billiards and another man standing at a long empty bar, polishing a glass. It reminded me of the prison officers' leisure lounge in the sitcom *Porridge*.

At this point, Gary Glass's pale face became blank and illegible, his mouth a dark slot.

'Stay here,' he said. 'And don't move. This is a high-security site and you shouldn't really be around.'

Once Gary Glass was outside, he locked the driver's door and then the passenger door as well and we watched his squat fat figure roll off into the club.

'We've got to get out of here,' I said.

'Why?' said Samantha. 'Once we get to Cockermouth we can nab another lift to Penrith where the M6 starts.'

'I don't trust this feller.'

'He's just some daft old berk.'

'Nope. I've got a bad feeling.'

I turned and pushed at the wooden board that separated the front seats from the back of the van. It didn't move at first, but after shoving a little harder, I was able to dislodge it and it popped out and fell into the back of the van.

We climbed over and tried the van's back doors which were unlocked, but before we escaped, Samantha insisted on having a look around. The van's floor was covered with empty dog biscuit bags and silver-coloured fittings for drums. There was a thick mattress that smelt of sweat, a radio, some empty vodka bottles, and an upturned ashtray that had spilled its stubs and ash all over. A box that said *Cadbury's Smash* on the side turned out to be stuffed with dirty magazines – *Razzle, Mayfair, Penthouse*. At one point someone had stapled grey fur around the interior walls of the van, but now there were only a few patches left, making it look like the skin of a sick and exhausted animal. The fur on the walls confirmed it and we fled out of the back doors and into a dark warm evening and, without halting to look behind, headed towards a cluster of small unlit buildings.

'In here,' said Samantha. 'We'll wait till he drives off. He's just some lonely nutter, I expect.'

Inside the building, we found a wide ledge above the ground where we could lie out of sight and watch through a horizontal narrow slot in the wall which looked like it was meant for guns to poke through. We could see Gary Glass's van lit up by the lights from the social club and we watched him come out of the club carrying a floor tom, and when he saw the empty front seats he stopped still as if he'd walked into a pane of glass, dropping the drum to the ground.

He went round the back of the van, and saw the doors swinging open. He looked around him, towards the building we were hiding in, and then over it and beyond, shading his eyes as if there was too much sunshine, even though it was now dark.

He rubbed his chin, then went inside the social club and returned with one of the security men. He pointed to the van and then waved his hands to indicate the expanse of buildings and fields all around them. The security guard switched on a torch and walked off in the opposite direction to where Samantha and I were hiding. We heard him calling – 'Hey, hey, hey. Anyone there?' – but he didn't search very hard. He came back to the van and spoke for a while with Gary Glass. Then Gary Glass put the rest of the drums into his van and drove away.

'Do you think there are unexploded mines? said Samantha Fry. 'There are drawings of bombs everywhere.'

'Let's just stay here until it gets light.'

I took off my jacket and made a pillow of it and Samantha Fry did the same and we lay still and looked through the slot at a dark, starry sky. We watched the few drinkers leave the social club, and saw the place being locked up by the security man, who looked about him for a short time before getting into a car and driving off, leaving the ammunition dump silent and empty.

As we lay there, close together, I could feel Samantha's breasts pressing against the side of my arm, and I became erect and wondered whether I should do anything about it. But Samantha must have sensed it because she moved away, lay on her back, and spoke towards the dark roof space.

'Have you seen that ghost again? The one you told me about?'

'I think I imagined it.'

'Ghosts are recordings,' she said. 'That's what I think. As we go through life, at certain points we leave behind impressions of ourselves, as if our bodies and faces have been pressed into wax. Sometimes, if you concentrate and look hard, you can see them, see them through the mist of your past, like films of yourself at all your different ages, and other people can see them too, and that's what I think ghosts are.'

I thought about this and imagined the air about me brimming with life and death and memories, the future and the past plaited around each other like strands of DNA.

'Can I tell you something if you promise you'll never tell anyone else?' Samantha Fry said.

'Yes,' I said.

'I think I like girls more than boys.'

It took a while for me to understand what she meant. Then I said, 'That's OK.'

'In case you were getting any ideas,' she added.

A metal sign rattled in the wind.

'I was,' I said.

'Well, I'm sorry but you'll have to wipe it.'

'I'll record something over it,' I said, then felt callous to have implied that I could simply move my feelings of attraction to another person so easily, like changing a coat. In fact, I felt destroyed inside.

'That spell I told you I cast over me and you?' she said.

'Yes?'

'I was trying to see if I could change the way I felt. About girls. And the way I *couldn't* feel about boys. But it didn't work. So here I am, the same.'

I put my arm about her and we lay together in a warm non-sexual embrace, which I enjoyed more than anything I'd experienced for a long time. I heard the dim clank of metal on metal from somewhere far away. I watched a halo of flies spinning around an orange lamp and wondered if the flies knew anything about where they were or what they were doing. Was their understanding of the world and their place in it any clearer than mine? Just outside, through the door, hidden in the dark tessellation of leaves and branches, I conjured the desperate contorted faces of soldiers suffocating from the poisonous gas and chemicals they had tested. After a time, I slept, fitfully, waking up every few minutes with a start, listening for noises, for signs of security men, or worse, Gary Glass. But neither security nor Gary Glass ever came. At one point I was sure I heard German voices, but came to believe I had imagined it.

We were collecting too many prisoners
Waste them, the general told him. Waste them all
The old man on the television had never heard the term 'waste them' before

When I woke up, I felt desperate, as low as I had ever felt I could be. Even though it was day, I felt as if the night had seeped in through my pores and I would live forever in darkness. I stared at things. For a long time I stared at a bush that had grown around the shape of a wall and wondered if that's how people were too, growing around the shapes of the things and the people that were nearest them, becoming the same shape as the problems they had to face.

When it was completely light, about 5.45 in the morning, we went straight to the social club where we found the security man sitting with a big mug of tea and some toast. After he had rang each of our parents, who were out of their minds with worry, especially Samantha's (the police had been called and were searching), the security man made us tea and toast which we had while we waited for our lift. The man told us the history of the ammunition dump and how it was now mainly used by West Germany to store old munitions.

* * *

My mother was so distressed about Dad being questioned by the police that she hardly had the energy to tell me off for causing so much trouble. My father didn't even speak to me, just stayed in the back room all day, distracting himself with the *Daily Express* racing page. The police were concerned that he'd lied about being in The Derby Arms, but there was nothing else to link him with the case, so after a few hours they had let him go. Nevertheless, he'd been told not to travel far.

I had to do something to remove any element of doubt about my father once and for all. Only I had the knowledge and the means to change things.

Later, I was sitting with my mother watching Ronnie Barker stuttering through *Open All Hours*, when I caught her looking again at the scrap of sweet-cigarette carton with the note from Marion

Crow on it. None of that had been resolved, none of it, and she and Dad were not speaking, the subject standing like a slab between them.

I switched the television over and the screen filled with gurning faces in stacks of cubes piled on top of each other.

Celebrity Squares.

I snapped the set off altogether and my mother didn't even notice the sudden silence, just continued to stare at the blank green screen.

I looked out of the window into the Cumbria perma-dusk and saw the vapour trail of a jet heading north towards Scotland, where it would turn left and out over the Atlantic, bound for America.

* * *

The street outside Finny's house was edged with thoughtful trees. Clumps of shrubbery drooped over the garden walls, bobbing like the heads of friendly donkeys.

I looked at the envelope I had taken from Finny's room, the scrap of hair and scalp sealed up inside it, and set off towards Crow's house.

I was in my bedroom listening to *Chant of The Ever Circling Skeletal Family* from Bowie's *Diamond Dogs* when I heard the phone in the hall and ran down.

'Barry Dyer?' An older male voice with a London accent.

'Who is this?' I said.

'Your mate's in a bit of a pickle, isn't he?'

'What mate?'

'What's he like? As a person? He's got stuff from the scene, that's what we hear.'

'Who is this?'

'We heard they couldn't slip a fag paper between you two.'

I put down the phone and went in to see my mother. She was sitting on the floor with her eyes closed. Her favourite misery tune, Distant Drums by Jim Reeves, was playing on the stereogram, the unbrushed stylus making a crackling sound nearly as loud as the singing.

I hear the sound of distant drums
Far away, far away

Her face was wet from crying. A dank fruity smell came from an empty sherry glass and a half-empty bottle stood in the grate, the cork next to it. My mother didn't usually drink but I noted that she'd used the correctly shaped glass, not just any vessel.

And if they call for me to come

Then I must go, and you must stay

On the rug was the torn-off scrap of sweet-cigarette carton, note side down, the footballers mid-tackle on a yellow background.

I hear the sound of bugles blow
Far away, far away

I looked at the footballers' heads with their collar-length hair, the grim expressions on their faces, the words *Barratt Gold Flake sweet cig–* above them.

And if they call, then I must go
Across the sea, so wild and grey

She didn't notice me looking at her, and she didn't notice me leave the house, and when I was outside I looked in at her through the window for a short time and it was like looking at a doll that had been glued to the floor as part of a museum exhibit.

* * *

A policeman was standing at the front door of Finny's house, and vans and cars were parked higgledy-piggledy all over the verges. A bloke in a leather jacket had a camera with a long lens balanced on a fence post and focused on the door.

I took the Defiant down a lonning and left it by a gate. I climbed though a hedge, went through the back field where I'd first ridden the scooter, and easily got into Finny's back garden.

All the curtains were drawn, the windows opaque with condensation, but the back door was unlocked and I went in.

They didn't see me at first. Finny's mother Angie was with a policeman in the kitchen and she was showing him kung fu moves, performing them very, very slowly, as if she were suspended in jelly. He was following her, mirroring every flourish and gesture with a solemn expression on his face. Normally, Angie was a noisy, brittle, edgy, shrill sort of woman, fidgeting and fussing over everything. Now, today, she looked to be drained of all life's forces, an empty expression on her face, and she didn't seem to register me when I said hello. But as soon as the policeman saw me, he stopped kung fu-ing, and pulled a serious face.

'Who's this, Mrs Finn?'

'Just Barry,' she said, in a slurred drawn-out mumble. 'Barry is Finny's friend. He's all right.'

'OK,' the policeman said. 'You been interviewed yet, lad?'

'Yes,' I said.

'Good. All in order then,' the policeman said, and turned back to Angie. 'Do you want to show me some more?'

'Yes,' she said. 'This is a good one.' And she lifted one leg and stood still, and the policeman followed suit, the two of them standing there teetering like flamingos, looking at each other.

Finny was at the dining table staring at the carmine bee-eater, the hummingbird, the bearded parrotbill and the three unknown South American birds.

He jumped up and pushed his long greasy black fringe out of his eyes. 'They took me in and questioned me. They found the thing I had. Must have searched the house. I told them. I told them I found it by the old kennels.'

How could the police have linked this to Finny? It should have been Crow. Crow should now be safely behind bars.

From the kitchen:

Snick, crackle, blare—

You've got the sound of summer!

Finny's hair was back down over his eyes so he pushed it away again and kept pushing it and pulling all the while he talked.

'The papers got hold of it even though I'm a fucking minor, a kid, and although they didn't use my name, they said it was a boy from the school.'

Snick, crackle, blare—

The happy sound—

It's national—

Finny paused and looked at the window with its curtains drawn tight, allowing no light in at all.

Snick, crackle, blare—

Heaven—

Must be missin'—

An angel—

'Known to be a bit of a loner and not well liked.'

'That's not you.'

'But with an unhealthy interest in girls. A girl from the school – they spoke to a girl from our school – said that the boy, this boy, stared at her a lot in class, stared in a weird way. She said she could definitely imagine him doing something like that. Me. Of course I stare at girls at school. I'm a fucking teenage boy. Loner. Not well liked. So this loner, this not-well-liked boy, has been questioned and released on the condition I don't go far away. So everyone round here knows it's me. And I've had the fucking parents, her parents, driving past. We have to keep the curtains shut and stay in, and then the phone goes and either it's just a breathing sound or it's some threat. Like this bloke said to my dad, "You should watch your back. Your family, your whole family needs to watch their backs. All of you." The police say they don't have enough concrete evidence to charge me at the moment. But they keep saying, meaningfully, that they have no other suspects.'

'Christ. I'm sorry, mate,' I said. 'Once they find the bloke it will all be over. They'll find him. It's a small town.'

'It's a fucking nightmare. What the fuck did I do except find some of her hair and skin? They put the shits up me, man, the fucking shits. They said I could be tried as an adult and go to adult prison. They said that although I'm only 15, they could wait and try me as a 16 year old. They said that wasn't a problem, it was usual.'

Heaven—

Finny pushed his long black fringe up off his forehead again and kept doing it, the way an animal rubs itself against a particular bar of its cage repeatedly, and each time he did it, the hair fell back and he did it again.

'They asked about you. And I told them about the metal.'

'What?'

'Where have you been, man? I need you around. Why are you looking at me like that? I had to say something about the metal things. They were baffled by that, but they wrote it down.'

Must be missin'–

An angel–

Missin' one angel, child–

'I met this girl,' I said. 'But it's a secret. I can't tell anyone.'

'Is this to do with the five pounds?'

'No. I'm not going to go through with that now.'

'Me neither – obviously.'

'It's her. You know – her. I think I can feel her near me. Philomena May. Like she's a ghost. She appears to me. She speaks to me. Can that happen?'

'What the fuck are you talking about?'

'Honestly, Finny. That's what's happening. That's where I've been.'

Finny's face flushed pink. 'OK, fuckhead. Ask this ghost, this spectre of Philomena May, this shade, ask her from me, from this boy, ask her if it was me who attacked her. And ask her to float down the chimney at the fucking police station and tell them the truth too. You fucking dickhead. How could she be a fucking ghost – idiot.'

The hooter from Brannan's thermometer factory sounded dolefully for the one o'clock dinner break.

Finny pushed his fringe up again, this time holding it for a few moments, keeping his fingers buried in the greasy locks for some sort of comfort. 'This is no time for secrets. This is not Enid fucking Blyton,' he said.

His hand fell out of his hair. The hair flopped down again and again he pushed it back up.

'Why did you tell them that I thought my skin condition was metal?' I said.

'They wanted detail about where I'd been and who with. Detail proves you're telling the truth, doesn't it? I have to work harder to make the truth sound like the truth. When I was telling them real stuff, it didn't sound like the truth. It sounded made up. So I had to make some things up to help it sound more true. The alibi, you see, what I was doing at the time she was – you know – I was with Moggsy at the fair, so I told them all the rides we'd been on and they checked them out and it turned out that these particular rides didn't exist or weren't at that fair. And I didn't know how much they cost or where I'd got the money from to pay for it all.'

'But why lie?'

'I couldn't just say we stood at the side of the Waltzer looking at girls for four hours. It doesn't sound true that you could do that for four hours. Plus, looking at girls for four hours makes us sound weird – exactly like we might murder someone.'

'But if that's what you did, Finny – stand about on the Waltzer – tell them the truth. I don't remember seeing you there, I have to admit.'

'I was with Moggsy, You weren't near the Waltzer. You were round the Octopus.'

'I know. Well, Moggsy can vouch for you. Where's Moggsy now?'

'He's on a two-week package holiday in fucking Spain. The Costa-Fucking-Blanca. He flew out the next day. They'll interview him when he comes back. There's no rush, the Chief Detective says. I don't know. Maybe I did do it. Maybe I blacked out and lost my memory. Moggsy's my only alibi.'

Finny's fringe was down again, nearly covering his eyes and nose, but he didn't move it.

'It's battering my mum's nerves, zombied out on Valium. Might need one meself.'

An angel—

I stood up and lifted the scooter helmet off the table, then stopped.

'There's something else I need to do. Then I'm all yours.' I grabbed Finny's shoulder and squeezed it. 'All yours then. Hang on. Let's just hope she comes out of it soon. That's my only hope. Then she can tell the police what this sick bastard looks like, what diabolical name he has, what slime-pit he took her to, what the twisted fucker did to her, everything.'

Heaven–

'My cousin Siobhan works on the intensive care ward in Carlisle, where they've got her.'

Must be missin'–

'Siobhan says she's just lying there – not a twitch, not a squeak, not a whisper. They don't know what might happen.'

I looked at the plates on the wall that depicted the nuns herding cattle, and wondered why Finny's nervous mother had found these images important enough to collect the set and display them.

Angel, must be missin' an angel–

The happy sound–

You've got the sound of summer!

Worp, crackle, snick–

Kindness to animals and believing in God.

13

I went to the pub and drank on my own. I drank a lot. I thought about what I had done to Finny. The envelope that the curl of hair was wrapped in linked it to him. But wasn't I implicated too? Wouldn't Crow have told the police about me sneaking in that time? Or was he worried that I would speak about the violent sex magazines the couple enjoyed–

Hogtie, Knotty, Bound To Please.

I thought about my mother sitting on the carpet absorbing her miserable music like it was poisonous gas. I thought about Marion Crow and my father and wondered whether any of it was true. I continued to drink.

Next to the pub's urinals I felt a hand on my arm and discovered her standing beside me. Her red wetsuit looked dusty as if she'd been sleeping under floorboards. She was staring at the orange tiles in front of her face, squinting at the patterns and moving her lips, as if within the cracked glaze she could make out the hieroglyphs of a hidden puzzle, a secret language of the dead, encrypted messages left by ghosts for other ghosts to read, the way dogs leave codes on lampposts or gypsies mark the way with sticks.

I saw a row of ceramic squares.

'So you ran away from home with Samantha Fry.'

'She brings me out of myself, as my mother would say.'

'Like a ghost of yourself. You become a ghost of yourself when she's around.'

'But which one is the ghost? This me? Or the other me?'

'Samantha Fry never spoke to me at school because I wasn't cool. Just some thicko who's gonna leave at sixteen to smile at fat people across a till.'

'She's all right.'

Petal beckoned me into the cubicle and she sat down on the rim of the toilet.

'Take your shirt off.'

I did as she asked, and she began to finger the metal bumps, pausing every now and again to sigh and shake her head, moving all over my chest and arms and throat, until finally she halted at a particular stud, one that lay just under my left nipple, and pondered. She pressed her lips to it and I felt her tongue flicking and then she began to suck at it softly, like a kitten feeding, her little face tilted up to mine, her eyes filling up with something, something like ecstasy. When she stopped, she seemed delirious; a saint in a trance.

'We have things to do. You and I. My tether.'

'Oh.'

'Yes. You have to come with me right away.'

'I don't want to.'

'What?'

'I don't want to.'

'Oh.'

'I'm worried about my mam. I need to know what's going on with Dad and Marion Crow.'

I followed Petal out of the toilets and into the bar, into the back saloon where there was a door to a cellar.

'Your skin says underneath,' Petal said, and led me down the steps in pitch dark until we came to a fireplace.

'Openings like this link to other openings. That's how things are joined up in my world.'

We clambered into the fireplace and she began to slither up the chimney and I followed her. Soot and dust rose up, filling my mouth and my nose and my eyes until I felt as though I was being buried in grit, and we emerged from the fireplace in the Co-op at Moor Row.

Marion Crow was in the stock-room amid the sacks of cereal and tubs of pet food, standing in front of a long mirror with a sign above it that said *This is what the Co-op customer sees.*

The sickly-sweet smell of the raw meat. The sharp tools for cutting it.

She was holding herself in different poses like a model, and the bottom of her Co-op overall was unbuttoned to the top of her thigh, revealing black stockings. White high-heeled shoes were on her feet and she lifted her leg to eye one of these shiny stilettos, and smiled.

'My mam buys my shoes, Miss,' she said to the empty room, 'and you're not my mam.'

She went over to the desk in the corner of the stock-room.

'That poor family, they've never had two pennies to rub together,' she said, sitting down and unbuttoning the top of the overall to expose a black lacy bra. 'It's not like they don't love her, though.'

She slid her hand in the left cup and took out the scrap of sweet-cigarette carton.

'Cheap plastic sandals,' she said, 'dropping to bits.'

She laid the scrap of carton out in front of her.

'But my mam buys my shoes, Miss. And you're not my mam.'

She picked up a black Biro and wrote carefully and slowly on the back of the carton. She smiled at what she had written.

'Look at your little toes, your tights,' she said. 'Darling, they're soaking.'

Then she wrote the reply in green pen and scrunched up the piece of card tightly and looked about the desk. Her eyes fell on a pile of papers ready for the bin, and she took one, put the scrap of carton inside it and squashed them together.

She stood up and glared into the tall mirror, intently, like she was outstaring an enemy.

'My mam buys my shoes, Miss,' she said. 'And you're not my mam.'

She looked over to the door where my dad's work trousers were hanging.

'Poppet, you look so thin, so cold,' she said as she stalked over. 'And the Catholic Aid Fund have some lovely things, pet, they really do.'

She stuffed the package into Dad's trouser pocket.

'Like I said, Miss, my mam buys my shoes. And you're not my mam.'

Then she sat down on the edge of the chair, put her head on the desk and began to cry, snuffling and whimpering softly to herself, while she ran the fingers of one hand up and down her nylon-sheathed leg.

'I don't understand,' I said, once we were outside.

'Neither do I,' said Petal.

'What can I do?'

'Do everything you can to keep them together. Things will be OK. That's what I sense.'

'Are my parents still there, in 2010, in the future? Do they still live in Cleator Moor, in West Cumbria?'

'Yes,' she said.

'Am I still in Cleator Moor?'

'I don't think it's a good idea to see yourself in the future.'

'Why not?'

'I could show you everything if you wanted me to. All the people you'll ever know, all the places you'll ever live. But it seems wrong. It seems to me that if I did that you might begin to doubt all of your decisions. Maybe you'd say, actually I don't want to do that. I don't want to go there, to that place, to marry that person, to get that job, to father that child. You would always be worrying about whether something is the right thing to do, and then you will never know which future is the right one.'

'I guess,' I said.

'The knowledge that you are going to do something in the future you don't want to do is strange; kind of the opposite of regret.'

'But where am I in 2010?'

Petal said nothing.

'I'll come with you, I'll help, I will. But please tell me something about my future.'

'You are in Manchester. At this very moment you have just left your daughter's degree ceremony.'

'God.'

'You had been watching it on a video link in a lecture hall.'

'Oh.'

'You weren't invited to the post-ceremony lunch because it would have been awkward with your ex-wife's mother being there and everything.'

'Oh.'

'Is this too much?'

'I don't know. Where do I live?'

'You live in a flat in Ancoats, a regenerated part of the city.'

'Alone?'

'Yes.'

'Why?'

'I don't know.'

'Where am I going now?'

'You are on your way to Durham. You have a ticket in your pocket to Durham station and you are heading to Manchester Piccadilly. You have a return stub valid in four days' time.'

'Who's at Durham?'

'Do you want to see?'

We went outside, and there was the Defiant, waiting, and Petal fired it up and took off eastwards. In less then five minutes we were above Durham Cathedral and the flat slow river that wound around it, and I could see the railway station high above the town.

We landed on the platform next to a bench where a young woman, somewhere in her early thirties, I guessed, was sitting, looking impatiently at her watch. She had long straight ginger hair, creamy, blemish-free skin and a well-sculpted pointy nose. Small, and abrupt in manner, she was dressed in smart brown clothes as though she had come from a high-powered office job. Chunky platform sandals were on her feet. I went up close to her and, as I did so, she glanced at her portable telephone and there was a message on it. From me. From Barry Dyer. From the future Barry Dyer. On the phone there and then.

Train's running late, see you in the bar? it said, followed by three kisses.

The red-haired girl frowned at these words, rammed the phone into her handbag, and hurried out of the station in a bustling, business-like way.

I looked at the bench, at the space where the young woman had been, and then at the station exit out of which she had disappeared, then back at the bench.

Petal jumped down off the pillion and looked out towards the west, her hand shading her eyes. 'We have to go. Now. The diver is moving.'

Florence Mine was a partly flooded chasm deep under Egremont town. A steel-barred gate prevented anyone wandering in to explore, but when Petal and I were riding the Defiant, we were able to melt through barriers and we soon found ourselves hurtling down a dark shaft that smelled of treacle and hair, our passage making a whistling sound like a plummeting cartoon boulder.

When we landed, I flicked on the headlamp. The walls were divided into sections by ribs of rough wood and patterned by the shadows of the flumes and cradles that lay about them. A set of rails on the floor led into a low opening in the wall which must have been where they pulled the carts of ore. Everything was cloaked in crimson, like being inside a human body, surrounded by pulsating blood.

'We need to go in there,' said Petal, pointing at the tunnel.

'There's hardly room for this,' I said, nodding at the scooter.

'Your skin says that way. I think he's setting off. We need to be quick.'

I twisted the throttle and we entered the dark tunnel, the Defiant's handlebars scraping against the ochre rock, the headlamp picking out rusted metal fixings, hooks, and small crevices where possibly cigarettes or lamps were rested. Every now and again a name etched into the stone loomed out of the darkness then fell away, and I thought about poor Jimmy Connolly, humming to himself as he died.

Soon we came to another cave, and everything wasn't red, it was black. Seams of glistening wet coal were all around us, and at this point there was another shaft so I accelerated and began to climb up the sides, wall-of-death style, and to my surprise, the bike stuck tightly to this trajectory and rose higher and higher, corkscrewing up like a bullet along the barrel of a gun until the Defiant roared out of the hole and was in the open air again.

We had emerged from Haig Pit, the colliery and were on the low headland overlooking the twinkling port of Whitehaven.

I switched off the engine and looked at the view. It was dark, but the streetlights marked the town's grid of buildings with rows of smudged orange halos. The clock on the market square said it was ten past three in the morning.

I listened to the sounds. A gull crying out; a truck changing down a gear as it climbed the hill out of the town; the distant chuckle of an electricity generator from a row of sheds.

I looked at the docks. The sea was the same dark grey as the sky and hardly moving, just rolling with the tide a little every now and again, groaning against the piers, slipping up and down the hem of coal-blackened sand, lapping around the soft sandstone rocks that went off round the head towards St Bees. The night was still, there was no breeze, but the air had a sprung quality as if everything was about to change.

Then I saw the grey Xsara Picasso. It was parked outside the place where the undertakers had been, which was now a branch of Barclays bank. The diver was standing on the pavement staring hard at the low beige building, hard into the past. Maybe he could see himself working on the coffins, just as Petal and I had. Something in his posture was different. He looked more graceful, a little like when he had been floating underwater.

The diver looked at his watch, then at the sky, then down the road towards the taxi rank, then he got into the car and drove away, and

Petal and I followed. We left Whitehaven and drove along the A5086 through Cleator Moor and Frizington and ended up at Lamplugh, at the diver's brother's house which was called High Trees Farm. The diver parked the car outside, opened the boot and took out something long and dark. He went inside through an unlocked door and we followed.

We found the diver in a small bedroom at the top of the house.

He was wearing a black fleece and black trousers and pointing a rifle at his brother, who was lying asleep in a single bed. Being a warm evening, his brother was only half-covered by the sheet so you could see that he was wearing work overalls.

Work overalls in bed.

The brother's hand lay in front of his lips as if he had been sucking his thumb.

The diver stood very still. He stared at his sleeping brother for a long time. The trigger of the gun was pulled back in the leathery loop of his finger. There was a sound modulator on the end of the barrel.

I went up to the diver and squeezed his shoulder. His flesh gave a little, and he twitched. But he continued to point the gun.

I tried to move the weapon away, but it wouldn't budge.

'Don't do it,' I said. 'Please.'

The diver took his hand away from the gun barrel and rubbed his ear roughly with his fist.

On the wall there was a photograph of the brother with his wife and children in front of a lake. On the bedside table was a pipe, a tin of Golden Virginia tobacco, and an ashtray with a picture of a stag on it and the words *Visit Lowther Wildlife Park*.

The diver reached down.

Petal grabbed my arm.

'My mother's here.'

'What?'

'My mother is in the room. I can hear my mother's voice, talking about my handbag.'

The diver was reaching down.

'My mother's voice,' Petal said, 'as if she is next to me.'

The diver pulled the sheet away.

'She is talking about the handbag. Telling them what it is made of.'

The diver was reaching down and pulling the sheet away.

14

A silver thread. Imagine a silver thread. The silver thread emerges from the centre of your forehead and on the end–

slap

I was sitting cross-legged on the sofa with the forefinger and thumbs of both hands pinched together.

My mother was slapping my face.

– and on the end of it –

'Barry, Barry, Barry! What are you talking about? Stop it. The men are here.'

slap

– on the end of this silver thread –

slap

– on the end of it is your mind.

I opened my eyes and saw through the window two men in dark suits getting out of a long black chauffeur-driven Daimler.

My mother let in the men and, although she seemed to have been expecting them, looked flustered as they showed their identification cards. One card said Ministry of Defence Royal Naval Armaments Depot, Broughton Moor, the other said British Nuclear Fuels Limited, Health and Safety Monitoring.

My mother's breath smelt of sherry and it was 11.30 in the morning.

'He's in here,' she said, bustling the men down the hall.

I looked at my clothes. Smart school trousers, a clean white shirt, and the horrible pus-coloured tie from Burton Nana got me for Christmas. I was sitting in what Samantha Fry had described as the lotus position, practising my meditation to see if I could get high like she did and maybe make contact with Petal somehow. When my mother saw me, she widened her eyes; I should sit on the chair properly because we had discussed this and it wasn't a good thing to look hippy or punk or bohemian in front of establishment figures. 'As far as they know,' she'd said, 'you're just a normal boy.' And she smelt of sherry at 11.30 in the morning.

My mother left us alone and each man took a clipboard out of his briefcase, attached an A4 form to it, and then, in perfect unison, clicked the nibs out of their ballpoint pens and began.

The click of the pens.

My mind flipped back.

Wearing a black fleece and black trousers
His leathery finger looped round the trigger
The sound modulator on the end of the barrel
The brother in bed, still in his overalls

Focus on the room, focus on now. The men.

'It's just, er,' said MOD.

'A few questions,' said BNFL.

'Mr Dyer,' said MOD.

'Regarding, er, safety,' said BNFL.

'And, for us, it's a bit about, er, security,' said MOD.

My mother returned with tea and Battenberg cake, and – somewhat coquettishly, I thought – said, 'Well, two smart young men in my sitting room', and laughed, putting her curled hand over her mouth as she did so and emitting more sherry smell. A dense quality had infected her speech.

'Well,' said BNFL, 'We try.'

'Yes,' said MOD.

'Do use the cake, it will go stale otherwise,' she said, and then she left, giving, I thought, an unnecessary swirl of her skirt and moving her feet in a forced, happy-go-lucky manner.

The men looked big on the sofa, like upright hippos in a miniature house, and I became aware of the oddness of some of the things in the room: the cut-crystal woodland animals on the mantelpiece; the black and white photograph of my sister at Blackpool awkwardly holding a drugged-looking chimpanzee, and, dotted about all over the place, the handwritten signs Dad made out of torn bits of cardboard. Next to the gas fire – *hold button in and count to ten, don't put it up higher than medium*; the one Sellotaped next to the door that said knock off the lights!; the one next to the TV that said, *BBC 1 = 3, BBC 2 = 7, Border = 1* – and the pliers you had to use to switch the set on because the real knob had broken off. Years ago.

The men were looking at these things.

'So Mr Dyer,' said MOD. 'Let's start with school. Are you happy there?'

'Yes.'

'Have you ever been to Eastern Europe?'

'Er, I'm 15 years old. Is that like, Spain?'

'Czechoslovakia, Poland, Romania. Eastern Germany? You been anywhere like that?'

'No.'

'How long were you in Russia?'

'I haven't been to Russia.'

'They didn't tell you it was Russia?'

'What was Russia?'

'Where you were. When they made the skin thing happen. That was Russia. The place you were at.'

'Oh. When?'

'When you were last there. The last visit. Your last visit.'

'OK,' I said

Scrat-scrat-scrat went the pens.

'What was the radio station called that they asked you to listen to?'

'I don't know. Luxembourg? Caroline?'

'No, that wasn't it. The woman who says the numbers and the poetry.'

'I don't know that one.'

'Magdeburg Annie?' The MOD man then adopted a high-pitched robotic voice. *'Dreiundzwanzig... sieben... elf... elf... elf... vierzehn... drei... drei... zwanzig. Ich weiß nicht, was soll es bedeuten, Daß ich so traurig bin.'*

He looked hopefully at me, with his eyebrows raised, then after getting no reaction, continued in a louder register.

'Vierzehn... drei... drei...'

'It's German,' said BNFL. 'He's talking in German.'

'Ein Märchen aus uralten Zeiten, das kommt mir nicht aus dem Sinn. Siebenunddreißig.'

The man stopped and waited. Long silent seconds yawned between us.

'I'm afraid that if you had the misfortune to cut yourself on *my* knowledge of German poetry,' BNFL said finally, 'you'd need a tetanus injection.'

The MOD man looked at his notes then at the BNFL man and they shook their heads.

'Have you been noticing anything odd around you?' the man from BNFL said. 'Seeing strange things or hearing voices that aren't there?'

Flip back.

Looking like he'd been sucking his thumb

The ashtray with a picture of a stag – the words Visit Lowther Wildlife Park

The family in front of the lake, smiling

The diver pulling the sheet away

The room, the now, the men.

'I've been feeling fine,' I said. 'No voices, no apparitions, nothing.'

'Apparitions? What do you mean?' said BNFL.

'I meant hallucinations,' I said.

'What's the difference between the two?'

'What do you mean?'

'I'm interested.'

'I don't know. Is an apparition, maybe, a person?'

'Yes. I'd say so. So you have had hallucinations of other things, but not people?'

'No.'

'OK,' said the man and wrote something down.

I saw on the wall the reflection of a flashing light from outside. It was blue.

'Looks like they're here,' said BNFL, and both men resheathed the nibs of their pens and put away their clipboards.

'That's fine, Mr Dyer. Thanks for your time. It's just so everyone, all of the authorities involved in a case like this, has a clear picture.'

An ambulance and a police car were outside and four people were coming up the steps.

The men hadn't eaten any of the cake.

* * *

Cumberland Infirmary was in Carlisle, just out of town on the ring road, an old building that had the look and feel of a castle. The white-sheeted metal beds and the drip stands looked incongruous against the red stone walls, and I wondered how they cleaned it properly and decided they probably didn't.

My first day was spent having tests – my temperature, my reflexes, my heart, my blood pressure – then on the second day my treatment began in earnest. They had decided to approach the condition as if it was psoriasis, and for psoriasis there was a standard daily programme of treatment which lasted three weeks. First, a session under a sunlamp for which I had to wear dark green plastic goggles like you have for swimming. When this was over, I was taken to another room in which a nurse was waiting next to a large tub of dark viscous matter and several rolls of bandages.

'Everything off, down to your pants,' the nurse said, smiling at me in a slightly crooked way. She was a short girl in her early twenties, with rose-water coloured spectacles, blonde hair jerked back into a ponytail, and a pink face and throat that looked as though she was constantly blushing.

When I was down to my pants, the nurse ignored the erection that was making a tent of my Y-fronts and began to slather the greenish-black goo over every inch of me, moving her hands vigorously as if she were greasing a baking tin.

She communicated mainly through pulling faces. A face for come over here, a face for sit down, a face for lift it up, a face for drop it, a face for that's done now, you can go, all achieved through various permutations of her crooked little mouth, which she would twist this way and that. At first I wondered if she was deaf, but it transpired that she just preferred peace and quiet.

I followed her face obediently, lifting my limbs up and down, turning round and about, moving to the side, tilting back, then forwards. There was no sound in the room other than the slick, wet slaps of the tar.

Once the sludge had been thickly applied over every inch of me, she picked up a roll of bandage and pursed her lips, nodding towards my leg. I lifted it and, beginning at my foot, she bound up the whole limb in pale beige fabric. Then the other, and then my arms, and finally my torso, so that eventually I was wrapped and sealed like the mummy in the photograph of Philomena May playing Cleopatra.

Pyjamas and dressing gown back on, the nurse sent me to the ward with two sullen porters by my sides (ostensibly to stop me getting lost, but more probably to prevent me from running away). Every time I moved, a dribbly slick of black stuff oozed out from somewhere. I felt like a sticky stinking walking poultice, and wanted more than anything to escape through the nearest exit and go home.

The porters checked me back into my ward and I was sent to a day-room where I was told to sit and listen to the radio until lunchtime when food would be delivered on a tray with my name on it.

There were two wards on the skin unit; a male one and a female one, but the day-room was shared. It was not a place for quiet contemplation.

'What you in for?' said a middle-aged man with an earring and wiry black sideburns, who was also covered in seeping stinky bandages. 'Psoriasis? Me too. Don't worry. You'll always get girlfriends, I've never had a problem and I've had this my whole life. I'm on my third wife. Got five kids. But when I first got it, I did worry. I've got it on my cock too, have you got it on your cock?'

'No,' I said.

'If you have,' the man said, 'then the nurse will put a bit of that magic black stuff on there for you too, if you ask. That's something to look forward to every day.' He leaned in close to me. 'Sometimes, if she's the only one in the room, she keeps going. You know what I mean? Keeps going.'

Two women came into the day-room, one with a knuckle-sized ebony lump on her forehead, the other a weeping emerald abscess on her shin. A boy in there was about my age. He was tall with a thin pointy face, and also covered in tar and bandages. In a low singsong voice, he asked me about my hobbies and when I told him I played guitar, he said, 'Do you ever just freak out, like just freak out?'

'What do you mean?' I said.

'Do you ever get your guitar and just freak out?'

'No,' I said. 'I mean I could do, but I never do.'

'I would,' said the boy, 'I would just freak out every day if I could play the guitar. I live in a caravan. They are saying that's why I've got this skin thing, because I live in a caravan, but I can't see why that would be true. I've always lived in a caravan, my whole family has; we're travellers. No one ever had this though,' he nodded down to his body. 'No one in the family has ever had anything like this. I'm a mutant, that's what my mother says.'

Most of the patients, like the thin-faced boy, were in there because of psoriasis, a condition which consisted of red patches on your skin with dry white scales on top; nobody seemed to know what it was or what caused it, and as it didn't itch and wasn't sore, the sufferers seemed fairly relaxed about it.

In hospital, in limbo; a place where neither the past nor the future had any purpose. A loud radio played all morning, mainly the Carpenters and twangy instrumentals by The Shadows. It was switched off at lunchtime and, after lunch had been eaten, a colour television came on, also loud, and tuned as default to Border. There were no volume or channel controls available to the patients, and requests for particular programmes had to be made via the staff. The television stayed on until 3.15 when it was turned off for tea and biscuits and not switched on again until six o'clock for the news, being finally extinguished at 10.30, when, after the removal of the bandages and the showering off of the tar, everyone was forced to go to bed. You were woken at six – because that's when the shift changed – with a cup of tea on a saucer and turfed out of bed at 6.20 after drinking it. Breakfast appeared dead on 8.28 and, at 8.50, after eating that, the radio was fired up again.

The ward was on the fifth floor and my bed was next to the window, so I had a good view. After some discussion with the other patients and the staff, I managed to find out that over on the other side of the quad, a floor below us, was the intensive care ward, where electricity, oxygen and intravenous feeding were keeping poor young Philomena May alive.

'It's the ward with the red lights blinking on and off,' the nurse said, as she slathered my hip with that day's dose. 'You can see them at night. Like little spaceships. I don't like doing shifts there,' she added. 'The noise is stressful to me. The ventilators blowing, the monitors beeping, the alarms going off, and people, you know, not staying alive.'

Not staying alive. It was an odd way to put it.

In hospital, everything seemed to be slowed down and speeded up at the same time. The day, as you lived it, was unbearably long. Then, looking back on it from the vantage point of the evening, impossibly short, because nothing had happened to punctuate the hours other than the same treatments, the same chat, the same meal times, the same cups of tea on the same saucers.

The same words.

If I had a guitar, I would freak out

She'll rub it with tar and keep going. Keep going, if you know what I mean

They think it's because I live in a caravan

I thought about the words the nurse had said about intensive care.

People not staying alive. People not staying alive

Flip back—

Wearing a black fleece and black trousers
His leathery finger looped round the trigger
The sound modulator on the end of the barrel
The brother in bed, still in his overalls

One evening I confided in the long skinny boy that I believed that my skin was covered in metal lumps which were only visible to myself and ghosts, and the next day the thin-faced boy told everybody else. Anxiety spread throughout the ward. Whatever was wrong with me was obviously more exotic, more rare, and thus more deadly than anything they had. They began to shun me in the day-room. They refused to use the toilet after me. They wouldn't touch anything – a towel, a plate, or even a chair – before asking whether it had been used by the metal boy, as I heard them calling me. In the end, one of them had a word with the head nurse and I was moved into a private room.

This suited me perfectly. No more, 'If I had a guitar, I would freak out', no more, 'She'll rub it with tar and keep going', and far away from the shrieking laughter of the nurses and the constant Stylophone rasp of the reception buzzer.

The room I was given had an old sash window that was an arm's stretch away from a rusted steel fire escape. On my first day in this secluded retreat, I looked out of the window for a long time, across the quad, to the intensive care unit where Philomena May was lying on her tubular metal bed with the winking lights and the sighing ventilators around her.

Not staying alive
Looking like he'd been sucking his thumb
The ashtray with a picture of a stag and the words Visit Lowther Wildlife Park
The family in front of the lake, smiling

The diver pulling the sheet away

The next day, I located the cupboard where they kept the patients' clothes and while the porters were busy unloading boxes – more tubs of tar and rolls of bandages – I sneaked in. On a wooden rack of shelves, there was a set of plastic trays labelled with the names and birthdates of every patient on the ward, and they were full of each person's possessions. Mine weren't there – presumably taken as 'evidence' – but I found the one belonging to the thin-faced boy and took out some jeans, a T-shirt and shoes, stuffed them inside my dressing gown, and scurried back to my room.

I laid the clothes out on my bed in the shape of a person. The jeans were white, with wide, flapping flares – the sort of trousers I'd seen worn by Northern Soul dancers on *Top of the Pops*. The shoes were small black pumps like you use for school gym. The T-shirt had a picture of a bowtie and frilly dress shirt on the front.

I hid the clothes under my mattress, checked who was on duty that evening and it was perfect; the quietest, least intrusive of the night nurses, a plump, sorrowful-looking woman, who buried her face in fat science fiction books and rarely wandered about to check on the patients.

Pretending I was nipping out to the toilet, I took a look at her. The top of her dark hair was peeping over a book called *Marauders of Gor*, the cover showing a half-naked man fighting with a giant fanged gorilla wearing armour. She wouldn't look up until it, or her shift, was over.

I dragged up the heavy sash window but it wouldn't stay open, so I took the clipboard from the end of my bed – the one that held a daily record of my temperature and pulse, and a row of ticked boxes showing when I'd emptied my bowels – and used that as a prop.

Outside, it was warm and dark with no moon and no wind. There was a swampy, soupy texture to the air and the sounds and smells of the night swept in on it. I leaned on the ledge and drank it in. I could hear a car tooting its horn, distant male laughter, the rasping *caw-caw* of a crow, the cardboard *whump* of a bass drum from a juke-box. I could smell chip shop fat, cigarette smoke, the sweet stench of vegetables rotting in the bins.

I was thinking about how differently this world smelled and sounded to the world of 2010 as I reached out of the window and swung myself on to the fire escape. Once I was on the metal steps, I went down one floor and looked across at a narrow ledge that encircled the quad. It was quite wide, certainly wide enough to stand on, and if you could stand on it, you could walk on it. I stepped out and as I did so, heard a clunk from above my head and watched as my clipboard tumbled down into the quad and landed in a clump of hydrangeas. Looking at the ground made me feel queasy. I stood still for a few moments and breathed. Don't look down again. I used my feet to work out whether there was enough space on the ledge to manoeuvre safely. There was, and the black pumps were nice and small, and gave me a good grip, like you could use them on a tightrope. Three feet above me was the window frame, and when I stood erect, the flat wooden edging provided a gripping surface for my fingertips. Right hand, left hand, right hand, left hand, I slowly shifted my fingertips from the window's edging to an indent between the row of sandstone bricks, and used this leverage to take a shuffling step. My first target was to reach a drainpipe on the next block, using the windows above as regular points of safety to punctuate my journey. Without stopping to think, because thinking would have sent me crawling back inside the hospital, I continued to creep along towards the drainpipe, my fingers sliding along the lumpy, jutting-out tops of the sandstone bricks, my black-canvassed feet on the ledge below floating one over the other in slow motion, like Finny's mother's graceful kung fu. I could hear the *click-click* of the metallic blisters on my bare arms scraping along the rough stone, and once or twice I felt one of them catch and tug at a fissure in the wall's surface.

I moved along the ledge. I kept moving along the ledge. I didn't look down. Eventually, when I reached the drainpipe, I grabbed it and held it, caressed it almost, the metal feeling pleasantly cold against my cheek. I stared at the red wall, at the dizzying grid of mortared cracks between the stones, and then I began to quiver, then to tremble, and soon my whole frame became convulsed with intense shuddering. I tried shutting my eyes to stop it but, after a few seconds, a wave of dizziness gushed through me and I had to open them again. Fear surged up inside me and solidified. I couldn't move. I couldn't go forwards, I couldn't go back. I clung on to the drainpipe as if it were part of my own body that I was about to be separated from. I waited for the enormous monster in my chest to die, and it must been after several minutes when I heard it.

A squeaking sound like the *peep-peep* of a baby bird. It went on repeating like that for a few seconds, but then it changed into a loud scraping of metal against brick and I felt the drainpipe sway slightly, then lurch outwards. It didn't completely tear away from the building, but hung in mid-air with me clinging on to it, and I couldn't see how I would be able to climb back to safety. I heard footsteps from the yard and saw beams of torchlights strafing the building.

I aimed my feet at the hydrangeas and slipped my fingers away from the pipe. Warm air rushed around me.

I fell and kept falling for a long time, much longer than the distance to the hydrangeas could have been, and because my eyes were tightly closed, I had no idea where I was.

Perhaps death was like falling forever.

His hand lay in front of his lips as if he had been sucking his thumb

I sensed her with me, falling with me. She wasn't touching me, but she was with me, and we were falling fast together, tumbling down a long chute.

The trigger of the gun was pulled back in the leathery loop of his finger

There was a sound modulator on the end of the barrel

She was humming as we fell, I could hear her voice moving closer and closer to me, and after a time I felt safe enough to open my eyes and there she was, in her red wetsuit, floating next to me, her arms and legs outstretched as if they were wings.

On the wall there was a photograph of the brother with his wife and children in front of a lake

She stared at me long and hard as she hummed and I hummed along with her as, like free-falling parachutists, we moved closer and held hands.

On the bedside table was a pipe, a tin of Golden Virginia tobacco, and an ashtray with a picture of a stag on it and the words Visit Lowther Wildlife Park

We fell as we hummed, and hummed as we fell, and the diver

reached down and pulled the sheet away from the man.

His brother's hand went up. 'Hey, what the... no!'

There was a clunk like the sound of an expensive car door opening and the tip of the gun spurted gold and apricot.

His brother pawed the air, waving away the bullets.

I turned to look out of the door, at the landing, at the top of the stairs. I counted eleven shots. Eleven creaks of the trigger, eleven clicks, eleven explosions, eleven whooshes of air, eleven rattles of cartridges hitting the laminate floor, eleven convulsions of the body, and eleven eruptions of blood on the wallpaper and pillows and bed sheets and duvet. A scud of displaced wind hit my face after every round, *whup-whup-whup*, on and on, driving home a stubborn nail, ensuring it was flush, and, each time he was hit, the brother cried out and it was only after the tenth that he ceased to make any sound. Maybe that's why the diver kept on shooting. Maybe he was thinking, *If only he would stop shouting, I could stop pulling the trigger.*

Afterwards, the diver's face was sprayed with pink mist, the corner of his lip curled up, quivering, his mouth drooping open, showing his tongue.

He walked out of the bedroom and stood on the landing, looking down the stairs into the hall, as if he was waiting for his brother to arrive home so he could show him what he had done, as if the thing he had shot in the bed was something else, not a person, but a cipher, a symbol, something to demonstrate the diver's power.

The diver went down the stairs and out of the front door and we followed him. He looked tired. He drove home and sat in his car outside his house. He didn't go in. He kept looking at his face in the vanity mirror. He watched the sky slowly filling with a dim grey light, the morning mist pooling white on the fields. He looked at the door of his house as if he expected to see a different version of himself emerge; a man who would get into another Citroën Xsara Picasso, stop at Calvert's Cornershop and pay a pound for an 85p carton of milk and say, 'Keep the change', and go to work at the rank, have a laugh with the fellers – always with their jokes and jibes and pranks, but all good humoured – and have himself a normal day. He stared at the front door for a long time. That other version of himself never appeared. The only version of the diver was here, sitting in the car. And this version had a different day stretched out before him.

'Can we stop him?' I said.

'I don't know,' said Petal. 'Maybe we can stop some. Maybe we can warn some. Maybe we can help some. We can do our best.'

The Xsara Picasso went roar and the diver slammed his foot down, did a sharp U-turn in the road without looking, and went off towards Frizington,

At a place called Mowbray Farm, he parked skew-whiff at the bottom of a long drive that led up to a large house. It was about ten o'clock in the morning now. The Xsara Picasso was blocking the way to anyone who wanted to get past, and he sat in the car and stared at the door of the house.

Petal and I got into the back of the car and waited with him.

We waited for a long time.

Eventually, the white-haired solicitor in his smart suit came driving down to his grand front gates and found his way blocked. He smiled at the diver. Then he looked concerned, and went to open his car door. The diver fired the shotgun out of the window twice, one bullet shattering the man's windscreen, the other bouncing off the roof, leaving a deep crease in the metal.

The solicitor jumped out, holding his shoulder where the fabric of his jacket was darkening with blood, and ran back towards the house. On the doorstep, he fumbled for his keys before taking an anguished look towards his car where he must have left them.

He collapsed on the step. The diver put down the shotgun, picked up the long .22 rifle with the sound modulator, lifted it to his shoulder and aimed through the sights while leaning on the open car door.

The man's body jolted as if an electric bolt had passed through it. The diver went over and looked at him, lying on the floor. The man wasn't moving. The diver pushed the man's body with his foot, lifted the rifle and, *whup*, another shot rang out and the man's head jerked sideways. The diver sighed. It was as though he was disappointed in his victim. The man had not properly played his part in this piece of theatre.

The diver returned to his car and got in. But this time he didn't sit and think; this time he worked quickly. Whatever grievances had been stowed away in the shuttered halls of his furtive past had been loosed.

The huddle of taxi drivers didn't notice when the Citroën Xsara Picasso pulled up next to the line of queuing vehicles. Petal and I stopped the Defiant behind it.

The diver's electric window duzzed as it slid down. He put his head out and called one of the taxi drivers over. The man made a 'what now?' shrug at his friends, wandered over to the diver's car, and bent his head in at the window.

The diver lifted the shotgun and pointed the ends of the barrels into the cabby's face. The man smiled for a moment, then a thought seemed to pass across his features like a breeze making a ripple across a pond, and his smile melted. He had begun to turn his head away as if leaving a conversation he was uninterested in, when the diver pulled the trigger. The man's head and upper body whipped about, turning at the waist violently as if he were swivelling hard as part of some vigorous exercise regime. But instead of swinging back again, his body kept moving in the same direction and soon his balance was lost and he toppled over onto the kerb. The diver pointed the shotgun at him again and a burst of lemon and crimson sparks came out and the man's stomach jerked inwards, as if to disguise his paunch for a photograph.

I looked away from the explosions. I saw the parade of shops near the rank: Gents Hair Stylist, The Absolute Beauty Co, Oriental House Chinese takeaway, Retro Hair Design, Shakers Cocktail Bar; and on the opposite side of the road: Brooks Music Shop, The Bed Co, Riva Design and Gifts, Winstons Hairdressing, Seville barbers, X-Tensions, La'al Tattie Bar.

Seconds trickled past.

Seagulls plunged and screamed.

There was a strong smell of rust and salt.

Everything seemed frozen as if we were locked in a diorama of the diver's making.

I noticed that my view of this future world was now odd, distorted. I saw everything as if through an insect's eye, through the myriad lenses of a crystal, as if I was a human panopticon. At times I was inside the diver's head, the diver's thoughts running beneath everything like a stream of ticker-tape.

I went over and looked at the cabby on the ground. His chin and most of the left half of his face had gone and his neck was ripped away like an animal had torn at it.

I felt sick.

I looked up and saw that the diver had driven a few yards along to the other end of the rank and was pointing his gun out of the window at another man.

Petal ran over and put herself between them.

Wop, said the gun, and the round went harmlessly through Petal's chest and hit the man in the back as he fled, flicking up a triangle of T-shirt fabric, speckles of blood spritzing out.

Petal followed the man and pushed him so that he fell down behind the row of taxis, then he crawled over to where the first man was lying and Petal followed. She grabbed the door handle of an empty taxi and opened it. The fleeing man got behind it, using it as a shield, but quickly the diver was there.

The diver stared at the trembling man on the floor, next to the blooded corpse of his third victim, but this time, as he lifted the gun, he shook his head slowly.

I spoke. 'Stop. Don't shoot,' and the diver flinched as if he'd heard the words, and lowered the gun towards the ground.

The diver watched the man crawling away in the dirt, with his T-shirt flushed crimson with blood, then looked again at the man on the floor with his jaw gone and his throat holed, and he turned away.

A woman came running out of Absolute Beauty and when she saw what had happened she tapped numbers into her portable phone. As she spoke into it, the diver lifted his rifle and aimed at her.

Petal ran up behind him. She wrapped her arms about the diver's body as though hugging a tree, and she squeezed.

The diver stood still for a few moments as the ghost girl in the red wetsuit hugged him.

He didn't shoot.

Another woman came out of the La'al Tattie Bar and laid two towels over the dead man.

The diver turned away and walked towards his car, Petal remaining attached to him like they were playing piggyback. She slid off and watched as he opened the door and got in.

The diver drove away from the rank and we jumped on the Defiant and followed. Past the police station, where the calls would be coming in about the first shots and the policemen, the rural policemen with no guns and no armoured suits and no Kevlar-coated helmets or knife-resistant vests, would finish off their cups of tea and run out towards the van that always waited by the gates. Past the civic hall where posters advertised The Whitehaven Male Voice Choir's summer concert, Status Quo with support from local bands, The Cowper School of Dancing's annual show with 100 dancers, The Big O Blue Bayou Roy Orbison Theatre Extravaganza. A children's event called *The Singing Kettle* was due on at two o'clock and audiences had been encouraged to dress up in their favourite colour. Outside the library, there was a queue of children – some sort of half-term activity club, I assumed.

The diver ignored the civic hall and the library and the children. But he didn't leave town. Instead, he turned and roared pell-mell round the ring road, past *The Whitehaven News* office, where they would soon be measuring the words they would write about him in yards, skirting the edges of the town centre, past the John Paul Jones pub, Chattanooga Pizzas & Kebabs, Strandz 9, Shooz 'n' Sox and Slik, and back up to the taxi rank where a crowd had formed around the fallen men while they waited for the ambulance.

Police had arrived. One of them had taken off his fluorescent yellow jacket, and covered the dead man's head with it. The diver slowed down, put his gun out of the window, and fired – once, then once again – the first shot lifting a chunk of brick out of the wall of Gents Hair Stylist and the second removing a shard of guttering from Shakers Cocktail Bar. Then he speeded up and went off again and I wondered whether he was going to drive round and round the one-way system like this, taking shots at random people and buildings. But as he slowed down for the lights at the junction of Scotch Street and Lowther Street, he caught sight of a man, someone he must have known, walking along the pavement towards the taxi rank. I recognised the man as another taxi driver from the day before.

The diver stopped the car and called the man over by his name.

'Hey,' he said. 'What time is it? Come over here.'

I stopped the Defiant, jumped off and ran over to the man. I grabbed the man's arm but it felt as if I were clutching at fog, or not exactly fog but something half there, and the man touched the point on his arm where my hand had been, then approached the diver's car and leaned in at the passenger window. He immediately saw the gun and began to move, and I tried to help, tried to push him as hard as I could, and it seemed to have an effect. The diver lifted the gun and pulled the trigger and the man was a few inches further to the side than he might have been if I hadn't shoved him, meaning the man took the shot on the side of his face. His hand flew up to staunch the blood that was pittering out and he staggered to the side of the road where he leaned against the wall, panting and jerking.

A passing man pressed buttons on his portable phone.

As the diver was pulling away, a policeman appeared from out of the police station and jumped into a car driven by a man who'd been watching the incident unfold and who pointed out the diver's car to the policeman.

'Follow him,' the policeman said.

They did, but the diver didn't seem to mind that he was being followed by a policeman.

He spotted another taxi driver in a car that said *Whiteline* on the side, pulled alongside, and sent a blast into it.

Whop! The pellets shattered the windscreen, but this cabby must have been able to see the cluster of shot flying towards him because he put up his hand to stop it and the slugs were deflected, taking away his little finger and his thumb and smashing out several of his teeth, before peppering a young female passenger in the back. At this point, the diver tried to turn his car around and return to the taxi rank. But the policeman in the civilian's car and the police van and the car belonging to the recently shot taxi driver were blocking his way.

The diver got out of his car. He raised his gun and pointed it at the policeman and the civilian, and they ducked down behind the dashboard and waited for the shots to fly over their heads.

No shots came.

The diver jumped back into his car and headed up Lowther Street to where it turned into Flatt Walks, and the police van followed. But the heavier vehicle couldn't keep up. According to the Defiant's speedometer, the diver hit seventy as we followed him up the steep hill out of town.

He screamed through the red lights at the top of the hill and pointed his car towards the Western Lakes.

He didn't, however, stay on the main road. Out of sight of the police van, he turned to the right towards Sandwith, onto a quiet, little-used back road, and headed off that on to a single-tracker that hugged the coast.

Petal didn't say anything. She held on to me tightly as we followed the diver and I hoped that the diver was escaping the scene, that he had killed all he had to kill, because, in the end, what could the ghost of a murdered girl and a half-metal teenage boy do to stop him? I had a bad feeling. I had been inside the diver's head. The *whump-whump-whump* of bullets hitting heads seemed to have intoxicated the man and now all he seemed to want was more.

Near a short row of houses, a woman was walking a large yellowy dog. It was a big dog, too big for the woman, really, a dog that dragged her along rather than vice versa.

The diver pulled up alongside her.

'Hey,' he said. 'Can you help me? What time is it?'

The woman approached the car.

I got off the scooter.

The woman was getting closer. She could see through the diver's car window now; she could see everything.

'Do you know what time it is?' the diver said.

Something changed in her face, and I called out to her, and the yellowy dog, the big tugging yellowy dog, turned and looked right at me. The yellow hairs on its body went stiff and it lurched and pulled at the lead, and the woman was jerked away. She walked fast, then faster and faster, as the terrified dog pulled her to safety.

The diver didn't follow. He stared ahead of him, and I stared where he was staring, at a sign attached to a lamppost about a show of local artists that weekend at the Lowes Court Gallery in Egremont. I wondered if this was relevant, and decided not; the diver appeared to be looking right through everything, as if he was in a different dimension.

The diver drove on.

A small woman with two plastic carrier bags was coming along the road and the diver braked hard, tyres squawking, thrust the gun out of the window, and sent two clouds of shot towards her. Her shopping fell to the ground and she lifted her hand to the upper left side of her chest. She looked down at her Co-op plastic bags, and a tin of oxtail soup, an apple and a carton of cream rolled out. She looked at her hand, which was red, and then at the car, and began to trot awkwardly towards a row of mouse-coloured bungalows, tilting to one side as she moved. Petal jumped off the scooter and tried to help her go faster, pushing at her and pulling at her, screaming into her face.

I watched the staggering woman and wondered how all this could be happening while normal life was going on everywhere else. I thought about the Lowes Court Gallery show, which featured local artists Deborah Madell, Mu Putnam, Liz Redmayne, Madeleine Warren, and others. Life-drawing workshops had been held.

The diver rubbed his shoulder where the recoil from the gun must have bruised him. He looked at the woman lumbering away, then put the car into gear. The glove compartment fell open and from a tangle of crisp packets and receipt books, a small card fell into the footwell. A line of dark-haired Oriental women in white bikinis and long black boots and the words, in a luminous orange font, *Spicy Girls a Go-Go*.

He switched off the engine, picked the rifle off the passenger seat, and walked over to the tottering woman. When he reached her, she was gasping and holding her side. He put one arm about her shoulder as if he were helping her, or about to have a drunken singsong. She struggled, but he pulled her closer. He was trying to force her onto the ground. Petal attempted to get between them. I stood behind the diver saying 'no, no, no' into his ear loudly, but the diver gripped the woman even harder and although she struggled against him, he worked her body down towards the floor as if he were using a wrestling move, and soon she was partly on the road, partly leaning against the diver's legs. Then the diver lifted the rifle, placed it to the back of her head, and fired. Her body relaxed, her full weight sagging against the diver's legs making him tilt backwards and windmill his arms for a moment to rebalance.

The woman lay flat on the tarmac.

I guessed that the diver didn't know her. This was the first person he'd killed who he didn't know. Maybe he liked it better, killing people he didn't know. Maybe it was easier. What did it matter to him? He knew nothing about them, or their lives. If the real diver had been there, the one who didn't shoot people, he'd have said, *At least shoot people who you don't know. At least have the courtesy to do that.*

I got back on the Defiant and beckoned to Petal, and she got on behind me.

'We aren't doing any good here,' I said. 'Unless you can find a way that we can stop him, it will continue, it will go on and on. Have you seen how much ammunition he has in the back?'

The diver was back in the Xsara Picasso and had started it up, and we followed him along a high-hedged single-track road which he sped down with no care as to what might be approaching the other way.

A man was walking along the road with a Border terrier. He was carrying a folded *North West Evening Mail* and used it to signal hello at the diver. The diver crossed the road in his car and pulled up next to him.

We were too late to distract the terrier.

'What time is it?' the diver called out and the man leaned into the window.

Whump, said the man's face as the bullet hit it. Scull crumbs and stray shot sounded like hailstones against the wall.

The terrier skated and whimpered down the road and the diver watched its diminishing form until it had disappeared around the corner and its yelping faded. The animal had not harmed the diver. It was not even a member of the same species who had harmed the diver.

The dead man's newspaper lay next to him. Its headline said:

A LIFE ON THE OCEAN WAVE

Engineers installing wind turbines off the Furness coast are living in a luxurious floating hotel

The diver looked at this headline for a short time and I wondered if he was thinking about the luxurious floating hotel and wishing he was there.

The diver put the car into gear and headed towards another man, this time on the other side of the street, who he called over and said something about the time. I ran as hard as I could towards the man and felt my body pass through him like vapour. But the man moved, he really seemed to move, so much so that only part of the shot from the gun hit his face, and he managed to turn away from the diver altogether. *Whump*, the diver shot him again, this time in the back, but because the man's coat was thick, he was able to stagger away.

Down the empty windswept ribbon of road the diver went, sirens at his back, helicopter above, past long scrubby fields dappled with the pale flanks of cows, past sheep with their faces shoved into the grass, and at this point I thought that now he must stop, now he has done enough. But the diver had not completed his task, not by a long way. He turned onto an estate of sixties houses and saw a young girl whose dark hair was held back with a headband and a clip. A black and white scarf was round her neck and she was carrying an A4 folder with primary-coloured printed flowers on it and a white textbook called *Human Geography: People and the Human Environment*.

The diver stopped and gave her a curdled smile.

'What time is it, love?' he said.

The girl came over to tell him and Petal leapt off the back of the Defiant and called out.

Whether she, as a teenaged girl, was more open to receiving messages from dead people, or whether she was super-observant, I didn't know. But for whatever reason, in a microsecond she spotted the gun, clocked the sweaty blood-speckled face, diagnosed the hopeless void in the diver's eyes, noted the shattered windscreen, witnessed the trembling hands, felt the fear in the air, heard the sirens in the distance, and put her hands over her ears and ducked her small frame down low so that the diver's bullet whisked over her head and ricocheted off a house.

The diver drove on and Petal and I followed.

He was heading towards Cleator Moor, there was no doubt about it. Police and ambulances were everywhere; one even passed the diver going in the opposite direction, but none of the police cars seemed able to stop him. He passed the market square, then went towards Crossfield Road, spraying shots randomly out of his window as he went, hitting buildings and trees and cars. As he turned down Crossfield Road, I began to worry. Sums in my head told me my parents would be eighty-odd years old. But would they still be in the same house? The diver appeared to be heading directly there.

This is happening,

This is real.

This is happening.

The diver pulled up outside our house and pressed the heel of his hand on the centre of his steering wheel, sounding his horn loudly. He sounded it for a long time but there was no reaction from inside the house. Then, a twitch of curtain upstairs from my mam and dad's bedroom.

I jumped off the Defiant, but as I did so, Petal slid off the pillion behind me in a drowsy, drunken manner, and landed on the pavement at my feet. She looked up at me vacantly, from a trance.

'What's wrong?' I said.

'I feel strange,' she said. 'We have to go back.'

'We can't go back now!' I shouted. 'This is my house!'

'All I know,' she said, lolling against my legs as if she had been injected with a giant dose of Valium, 'is that something is pulling me home.'

Her eyelids became slack, drooping and quivering, and her neck was no longer able to support the weight of her head. She began to talk in a murmuring, blurry voice, as if someone else were speaking through her.

Was the strap made of the same material as the main body of the bag?

The body of the bag?

The bag part. The part which contains things

I don't know. It was brown. Made of leatherette

How many compartments?

I don't know. It was very normal. A very normal bag. That's what she was like. Normal

I'm sorry, Mrs May, but every detail helps. How did it fasten? Was it clasps or zips?

I left it in the pub, I think. Or at the fair

The diver sounded his horn again, and again the curtains moved, but the diver didn't seem to want to leave his car.

The man doesn't have it. The man didn't take it, nothing was taken from me

The sirens were getting nearer and the helicopter was transmitting a warning, a male voice, repeating and repeating, telling Cumbria to stay indoors, telling Cumbria it was an emergency, telling Cumbria it was dangerous.

The diver sounded his horn again; the curtains twitched again.

What was inside the bag? Was there a purse? Was the purse made of the same material as the bag?

I don't know

Everything went black.

16

The hydrangeas gulped shut on me. Low male voices swore and tutted, a torch beam rippled across the leaves.

I hunkered down in the bush and waited till everything was quiet.

On the ring road, I thumbed a lift from a van that said *Superior Lady's Attire* on the side. It was five in the morning and the driver was heading for Whitehaven Market.

'Nighties and aprons,' the man said, jerking his head towards the back. 'First rule of retail: always sell a product for women, because men buy diddly-squat.'

The apron salesman didn't say anything else for the full hour's drive, just kept giving me sidelong glances and chuckling to himself.

At Whitehaven bus station I got a 17 to Cleator Moor and went straight home to find my mother in the front room, polishing the cut-glass woodland animals using Windolene and an old sock. She was wearing her camel-coloured trews and her blue pussy-bow diaphanous chiffon blouse she kept for parties and sometimes church. Loud violins were blaring out from the music-centre – her Strauss album, which she played when she and my dad would waltz together in the kitchen, like they used to at the Empress Ballroom in Blackpool Winter Gardens.

I twiddled down the volume.

'Mam, you have to leave. You have to go. Leave Cumbria.'

My mother looked at me for a long time. 'How did you get from

Carlisle to here?'

'I hitched a lift.'

'What have I told you about that, Barry?'

'Mam, you have to leave this house, this town. Both of you. Get Dad away from Marion Crow. It's all true. She's leading him on. She has a picture of him in her drawer with lipstick all over it. She's obsessed.'

'What are you wearing?'

I looked down.

The bowtie T-shirt, the flapping jeans, the black pumps.

'The hospital gave me them.'

My mother continued to polish a cut-glass squirrel as she stared.

'Please Mam, listen. You have to go. Both of you. And never come back. You can live in another place, a long way away.'

I spilled all. Told her about Marion's way of sitting on the counter. About how she climbed the high ladders to show off her thighs. About everything, everything I knew, stirring in the information about hiding the note in her bra before stowing it where my mother would find it.

My dad came in from the back room, holding the racing paper, his face filled with toast.

'What's going on?'

My mother replaced the squirrel on the mantelpiece, angling it carefully so it was facing the same way as the other animals. 'Barry, you have to know,' my mother said. 'Marion wasn't well. Marion Crow. She was having some problems. Your dad didn't write that note – it was her. She copied his handwriting from the ledger. I went to see her and she broke down.'

'I've had to let her go,' said my dad.

'Apparently, she had a grudge against me. For years. Hated the fact that when I was her teacher in the infants, I offered her some shoes from a charity. Marion Crow brooded about this all her life. She wanted me to know what it felt like to be *last*. Well, she succeeded. For a short time, I knew what it felt like to be last. So, well done, Marion Crow. She made herself ill with it, though. The husband is mortified.'

'But at least we're all right now – thank God,' said my dad.

'But Mam. Her husband put up units without permission. Wall units. He could do anything. You have to leave this house!'

'Son, we love this house,' my dad said. 'What are you talking about?' My father's face was all of a sudden quivering with rage. 'I'll be leaving this house in a box. There's no better part of Cleator Moor to live. It's quiet. Nothing ever happens.'

* * *

Dad dropped me off at the hospital, the anger disappearing as quickly as it had flared, and I managed to persuade him not to come inside.

I marched into reception and told the lady on the desk I was here with a message for Siobhan on Intensive Care.

'From her cousin. Is she on? Or I could leave it with one of the others?'

'OK.' The receptionist smiled and looked down at a long list of names. 'Yes. Siobhan is there now.' She looked up at me. 'You been somewhere nice?'

My mud-stained comedy T-shirt, my ridiculous billowing jeans.

'Fancy dress,' I said. 'It's a comic book character from *Whizzer and Chips.*'

She laughed, 'OK lad.'

The lift doors hissed open and I got in and pressed the button for Intensive Care.

Petal was lying on ghost-white sheets surrounded by clicking, whistling, beeping machinery. Wires and tubes climbed over each other to get inside and out of her. I looked at her face, at the rosebud cheeks, scuffed and scraped, and grubby with impacted dirt. Her eyes shuddered behind their lids, her tongue slurred in her mouth, her fingers curled and reached into the air at nothing. I touched her arm and then, as if I had some sort of magical power, her back arched, her head reared up, and she emitted a loud roar like a heavy creature impaled. It was a noise I was unable to connect to the frail body before me.

She looked at me through the half-lidded slack of her eyes. Her fingers moved over her body as if she had been punctured and was trying to stem a loss. One hand clasped at her throat to loosen an invisible ligature, or the powerful memory of one. She coughed and coughed and coughed, then sneezed and sneezed, and the medical machines began a chorus of eurhythmic blaring and squawking.

Rapid tick-tock footsteps sounded outside the room and I hid by the side of a large metal cupboard.

The nurse, Siobhan I assumed, gasped.

'Oh my goodness, my lovely, you're awake.'

I heard Siobhan press some buttons on the wall.

'Doctor Grundy, can you come?'

I heard her put down the phone, then dial again.

'Mrs May? Yes. It's the hospital. She's awake. Yes. Come now.'

I waited until Siobhan had left, then came out to see Petal again. Her eyes had closed.

'Petal,' I said, 'You have to help me. That's my mother and father's house.'

'What?' she said, eyes flicking open.

'In the future. But we can stop him. Me and you.'

'Where am I?'

'Cumberland Infirmary. Carlisle.'

'How did–?' She thought for a moment. 'Oh yes. That…'

She began to cry and I held her hand, staring at the unpunctuated whiteness of the hospital walls.

'He said he was taking me to a party, but there was only him. I don't remember anything else just – I don't remember. Are you a doctor?'

'Don't you remember me?' I said. 'We've been... I've been helping you.'

'Oh.'

'Yes. And you've been helping me. Don't you see? While you were in the coma.'

'Have I been helping you? Have I? I like to help people. Have you seen the man? He was at the pub, he said there was a party. Have they got him? He's not here, is he?'

'They'll get him, don't worry. Look,' I said. 'This is why you chose me.'

I lifted my shirt to show her the metal lesions.

'They're disappearing,' I said. 'The metal things. Every time he shoots, another one disappears.'

'You're a weirdo,' Petal said. 'I like you. You're funny. My mind is all melty. I can't really see. It's a nice feeling. But melty and drifty. Like Angel Delight, blancmange, custard, tapioca.'

'He's outside my parent's house. Now. Mam and Dad's – don't you see, Petal? You have to help me.'

'I feel like at the dentists. You know, the gas?'

I grabbed her shoulders and stared right into her eyes. I shook her lightly and she looked shocked but didn't cry out.

'Are you from my school?' she said. 'Are you Ralph Dunne?'

'No, I'm not Ralph.'

'I used to like him. Years ago. Not years, two years maybe. He took me for a go on his tractor. It was great. You can drive a tractor when you're fourteen. On a farm, you can. He took me on it.'

She lay back against the pillow.

I looked at the machines, the wires trailing off to sockets in the wall. I looked at the monitoring equipment with its white lines on a green screen, at the blood pressure device that tightened around her arm every few minutes, and at all the beeping and booping equipment. I looked at the spare pillow on the plastic chair next to her bed, at the drips sending syrups and potions into her tiny frame, at the knobs that regulated the amounts and the mixtures and the richness of the doses. I looked at her mouth and at her nose, at the tubes running up into her nostrils which must have been helping her breathe when she was in the coma. I saw a face-mask – oxygen, I assumed – ready for if she needed additional support.

I thought about my mam and dad, and felt happy, happy that my parents were still together, thirty years in the future, happy that the Marion Crow incident was resolved, and more and more certain that Petal and I must save them. A precious, fragile thing was in my hands. That's why I had been chosen. That's why I had the metal lumps. That's why Petal had tethered me. Everything had been working towards this.

The sibilant rush of the ventilator's pump was like the pounding of surf and it disguised the metallic click of the switches.

After I was done, I watched the tortured pink of her skin slowly heal to grey, and visualised her falling into a lazy, swirling pool. I closed my eyes, and went there too, diving with her, a vortex tugging us down together, deeper and deeper into a darkness darker than anything I had experienced before. I was alongside her and we were slipping through the pitch as fast as fish and then her fingers touched mine and, as if the wing-tips of two jet planes had kissed in the air, we flew apart and away, spinning and turning violently, out of control, until everything flared brightly and we were somewhere else.

A windowless space the size of a church, yet as antiseptic as an operating theatre. A pale grey turbine blade the size of a whale's tail was suspended above a polished concrete floor, clinically spot-lit as if in an art gallery. Weights and cables made it flex slowly up and down, gracefully.

'I feel a lot better,' Petal said, 'sort of more settled in what I am.' She glanced down at the red wetsuit, which today looked damp and glistening. 'More real. And cleverer, like I just passed a big exam.'

'You were two halves,' I said, 'and now you're one.'

The only sound was the hum of the air conditioning and a low burble of conversation from two distant figures in dust-coats on the other side of the room. There was a door at the front and we went out of it and found ourselves next to a row of tall shiny blue-grey sheds on an industrial estate, and the Defiant was waiting for us.

We tore up the road to my parents' house where the diver was still outside, sounding his horn.

I could tell that the diver thought it was the house of another person, another diver, in fact. Recalled voices went bit-bat, bit-bat, to and fro inside the diver's head.

It was fine, he was safe. He just wanted to see the gnomes

You let him go too deep, man. He's a novice

Don't tell me what's right

Since the police moved the grotto, we can't go down that far

Next time I'm down there I'm gonna move those little fellers deeper so that even the Cumbria Constabulary can't reach them. Police divers have a legal limit of 50 metres. That's where I'll put them. And then those gnomes will be laughing at them knobheads in their ex-Army flippers

The laughing gnomes

Funny

You're the laughing gnome, mate

I jumped off the scooter and ran past the diver's car and into the hall.

My mother seemed tired and confused. She looked much older than I had thought she would. She was wearing a thick, quilted dressing gown and big slippers, and she was frail, and smaller than her younger self. Her face was wrinkled and bony and her hair, which had been brown, was dyed a champagne blonde colour with bits of grey poking out. My dad was sitting on the sofa in the back room looking through a magnifying glass at the racing pages.

'Who is it?' Dad called out. My father seemed shrunken too, his face furrowed with wrinkles, his neck skinny in a shirt that was too big. Patches of tufty white hair on his head, gnarled, liver-spotted hands, protruding veins on his arms and a sack of empty flesh under his chin that sagged. But his eyes glittered with cheeky humour as they always had.

'I don't know,' my mother said. 'He keeps sounding his horn. It's a taxi. We didn't order a taxi.'

My mother pulled back three bolts, turned two keys and opened a latch. She went down the steps and approached the diver's car.

You're the laughing gnome, mate

I knew that the diver was looking for someone else. But I also knew he would shoot anyone if he wanted to. To the diver, everyone in the town was against him.

A man and a dog were coming along the pavement and I ran towards the animal. I shouted at it and the dog reared up, terrified. It was a huge thing, a Newfoundland, the size of a bear, and it pulled its owner onto the ground and dragged him a few yards until the owner had to let go of the lead. It lolloped off towards me where I was standing between my mother and the diver's car, and began to bark at me.

You're the laughing gnome, mate

It kept on barking, its fur rising high in spikes, its lips stretched back a long way, showing spittly gums and yellowy teeth.

My mother was frightened and ran back into the house.

You're the laughing gnome, mate

The diver lifted his gun and pointed it at the dog, but he didn't pull the trigger.

He sped off again, and Petal and I followed. This time through Egremont and back along the dual carriageway to Seascale. He shot more people. *Whump, whump, whump*, smiling slightly as he did so.

He had begun to like the whump of a bullet and the way it could turn a head to dust.

He shot an estate agent.

He shot a mole catcher.

He shot a rugby player.

He shot a pub landlord under a narrow bridge where a convex mirror showed what was coming the other way. By this time, he had nearly done enough.

Near Holmrook he looked at a poster on a tree advertising a chamber music concert at Gosforth Public Hall with violinist Victoria Sayles. He noticed there was a strawberry fair at Haile Hall and he saw adverts in a window for guitar workshops, Babies and Bumps, Slimming World, and a botanical walk at Eskmeals Dunes led by the Cumbria Wildlife Trust.

He would not attend any of these events. They would happen anyway, happen without him.

In some recess of his mind, his life now made sense.

He drove round the corner where the road ran between the sea and a row of tall pebbledashed houses with neat walled gardens where nothing seemed to grow but ornaments and shells and antique fishing paraphernalia. The tide was in. The wind – swollen with the mewling of seagulls, the howl of sirens and the *wop-wop-wop* of helicopter blades – was whipping the top of the sea into cream. The diver stopped for a moment to look at the furrows of the waves as they materialised and dematerialised before him. A woman was walking along the pavement with a bag of Betterware catalogues she was delivering door to door, singing a song softly to herself as she made her way down the street. The diver switched off his engine so he could better hear the tune. Her soprano warbling, with the sigh of the sea behind it, made the diver think of heaven.

A luxurious floating hotel

He believed the woman to be carrying a message to him. She stopped nearby for a spell, setting her bundle of catalogues down on a wall so she could watch a small bird, a finch, pecking at a sunflower head. As she crumpled to the floor, the diver looked at her sadly, the way a vandal gawps at the unfixable smithereens of a bus shelter he's just booted in.

He drove on. He drove through hills and valleys and past rivers and miniature railways lines. On the way he shot more people, but no one else died.

He went to Eskdale, to Boot, and there he crashed his car into a bridge and got out.

They saw his eyes.

A family walked past him and saw his eyes and asked if he needed help.

His eyes looked at them.

'You're all right,' he said.

His eyes had already forgotten that the world existed apart from his connections to it, and soon, far from its brittle edges and uncaring silence, tiredness felled him, and in a shallow scoop of grass that had been carved out by prehistoric ice, he laid himself down and didn't move again.

I looked for clues in the air, on the ground, in the mountains, in the fields, in the trees, in the sky, in the universe, and found none. That a life could be forfeited in an unnoticed instant. I thought of the randomness of it all. The wrong turnings, the poor decisions, the unfortunate coincidences, the lucky breaks, the last-minute changes of plan. A few degrees' deviation in any direction could have saved all of them, and killed as many others. I lay down on the grass next to the diver. I was bone tired. Petal lay down with me. We looked up at the clouds scudding by and listened as the policemen and ambulance men tidied up the scene around us.

I thought of sad things. A woman peeling potatoes on her own in Meldrum's chip shop. Stacks of broken boxes outside the fish factory. An old man squinting at graffiti on the walls of Whitehaven baths. Rain on a river seen through the window of a train to Millom.

When everyone had gone, Petal and I were still lying there, there in the little scooped-out hollow. Blades of grass were bending upwards again as the blood soaked into the soil.

The sun went down and the wind came up and the rain started in and the sky went dim and all was quiet but for the *chit-chit-chit* of a caterpillar munching on a leaf.

17

On the day of Philomena May's funeral, the town felt as though it had given up; even the pines, even the rocks, even the lakes had an air of submission.

Finny wouldn't speak to me at first. He'd been cleared of all suspicion when Moggsy returned from Spain, but the whole thing had taken its toll on Finny's fragile teenage psyche. He'd been staying in bed a lot – sleep was an escape – and in the short periods of wakefulness, the bad thoughts were concreted over with cider and his brother's strong dope.

To try and bring him round, his mum and dad bought him a trials bike, a big, rangy, superspeedy thing, 250cc, which he shouldn't have been allowed to drive until he was seventeen, and today, a day where, for obvious reasons, his family were lying low, Finny agreed to see me. We took the trials bike and the Defiant to Ennerdale Water, a long way from St Mary's Church in Cleator where the ceremony was taking place.

Finny had a six-pack of Woodpecker, me, four red cans of McEwan's, and we sat on a hill looking down on the lake. It was sunny, which didn't seem right for this sad day, and a light wind made dark olive ruffles in the grey surface of the water, which did.

We didn't say anything for a long time, just worked our way through the drink and listened to the sounds of nature and outdoor industry; the small flat stones clicking together at the hem of the lake, the buzzard shrieking above us and, from a long way off in the woods, the anxious gnashing of a chainsaw. Yet, despite these sounds, everything was permeated by a brooding silence, a nothingness, like a vault door between us. Something was very different. A lot had happened, of course, and I knew that it had been – and still was – a tough time for Finny and his family. But Finny and I were friends. And friendship doesn't die. A friendship like ours would last a lifetime. Our atoms were arranged the same way. True, Finny and I had nothing in common. But sometimes that's what makes it. You do different things. You have different interests. You don't compete – you share.

I wondered why I didn't feel more upset about the funeral. But in reality, I had never truly known Philomena May. I knew only Petal, and Petal? Petal was still around. She didn't appear to me any more, she didn't speak to me in that wispy low voice, I didn't feel her hands on mine, or her breath on my neck, and she didn't take me into the future. But I always knew when she was around.

'They say there's a giant pike in there,' I said after a long time and three cans of beer. 'A bit like a Cumbrian version of Jaws.'

'They say there's pine martens in the woods too,' said Finny. 'People like to think things exist that aren't there.'

'You're gonna have to get over it,' I said.

'You've changed,' said Finny. 'What happened to the folk music?'

'All music is folk music, really. Apart from classical,' I said.

'So all people are the same too, are they? The same feelings, the same wishes, the same faults? I don't agree. Some people are better than others.'

'The police always knew it wasn't you. They were throwing a bone to the papers to keep them off the scent. Make the real guy relax and think he's safe. Normal police tactic, I heard.'

'It nearly killed my mother. Her brain is still fogged with those tablets. And now, with the cousin Siobhan thing, that's a new dimension.'

The chainsaw in the woods screamed louder.

'When's the trial?'

'She got bail. Because, obviously, she's not a danger to anyone else. But who knows? She says that if she did it – and she knows that she definitely didn't consciously do anything wrong – but if she did do it, it would have been a mistake, an innocent mistake.'

I picked a small stone off the grass and tossed it down to the lake where it bounced off a rock before slipping into the water. 'Your mum still doing the kung fu?'

'You can cause rock slides like that. It's dangerous.'

'That Mrs Finn talking?'

'Fuck off.'

'Sorry.'

Cloud shadows slid across the hills opposite.

'You've got a fucking nerve. Showing up on this day. What did you think I'd say?'

'You're my best – and only – mate. Come on, Finny.'

'I just don't know who to believe any more.'

Finny stood up and went over to the edge where there was a long drop down to the lake. He stared into the water as if he could see something there that no one else could see. The water was deep at this place; I knew because I'd been in swimming before. Deep and also dark and cold because of the overhanging trees.

I picked up a can of cider and a can of McEwan's, went over to Finny and batted him on the shoulder.

'You want this?' I said. 'Last one,' holding up the cider.

Finny went to take the can and I jerked it away from his outstretched fingers. We locked eyes for a few moments, saying nothing. Then I lifted it over my head and threw it into the lake.

Pshunk it went, and disappeared into the grey folds of water, re-emerging to bob about on the surface.

Finny looked at it. Then he grabbed the can of McEwan's off me and threw that in after it.

The cans bobbed about and we watched as the breeze on the lake pushed them further and further out towards the middle.

'Why are they floating?' I said.

'Alcohol is lighter than water.'

'So it's a good way to keep them cool?'

'Not good for the environment, if we don't get them back. Not good at all.'

'Will a little stickleback get his head stuck in the ring-pull? Go and get them, then.'

Finny looked at me, then at the cans, then at the drop below us.

He took off his shoes.

'Fine,' he said, and jumped off. He hit the water with an enormous *sploosh* and went under.

Finny was a good swimmer. He would often leap off high bridges into deep rivers and he was an expert at staying under a long time to frighten everyone else. I looked at the surface, at the scarf of bubbles which showed where Finny had gone in. I squinted at my watch. The limit was a minute or two. I counted one minute. The patch of water which had indicated Finny's entry was now undetectable.

There was no sign of him anywhere.

The chainsaw moaned, the buzzard squealed, the stones went plink-plink.

I counted two minutes. Then two and a half. I looked down the shore, to see if Finny had swum underwater and climbed out further along.

Nothing.

I took off my shoes and made the leap.

The water was freezing, sending my body into shock, and I worried for a few moments that I might disappear in the same way. Then I felt Finny's hands grab at my legs and I kicked them away and surfaced.

Finny emerged next to me, laughing, sucking in massive breaths like a vacuum cleaner.

'Come on,' he said. 'Let's see if we can get to the weir.'

'There's no way I can go that far,' I said, 'I'm out of practice.'

We trod water, looking at each other in our sopping T-shirts, with our dripping hair, and laughed again.

'We are fucking idiots,' said Finny. 'Come on.'

The barman in the Fox and Hounds turned on the radiator and we leaned against it to get dry. A wood fire spat sparks. We didn't speak much. A shadow lay over us and I didn't know what it was. We drank a lot, way too much to ride motorbikes legally, or safely, but at the end of the night, after we'd been chucked out of the Fox, we decided to drive anyway. The rural habit.

Midnight had draped the fells in black and mauve, and there wasn't a sound apart from the distant hiss of a thin stream dawdling down the mountain to the lake.

I was so drunk I could hardy get the Defiant fired up, but I did, and once we got going Finny raced up every straight and curled around every bend like it was a speedway, and I feared for my life. I was no longer in the magic bubble with Petal so I gripped the handlebar of the Defiant hard and tried my best to focus on the dark tarmac as it unrolled in front of me.

Finny was heading towards St Bees. It was dark now, but there was a full moon which meant you saw everything in outline – dark shapes saturated in violet and indigo hues – with Finny a darting grey fish in front of me, leaning dangerously into every curve, at one point pulling a wheelie in the centre of the road.

At a blind bend, Finny decided to overtake an old man in a Hillman Imp, tearing past with no care as to whether anything was approaching, and I had to follow, I just had to, and, as I swerved past the Hillman, it felt like jumping over a wall with no idea how far the drop was going to be on the other side.

A few moments later a coach packed with Sellafield late-shift workers steamed past, which would have flattened the two of us and our steeds had it been sooner. Then, as we approached the turn to Woodend, Finny swung deep into a curve and lost control. His back wheel swayed under him and he and his motorbike slid into the bushes and disappeared.

I was relieved. No longer forced to tear along in this lunatic's slipstream. I stopped the Defiant and ran over to the hedge and pushed through it – only to find myself staggering on the edge of a precipice with a dizzying drop below into a blacksmith's yard; a junk-heap of jagged metal, rusted tools and half-finished wrought-iron artefacts.

I peered into the darkness. I could see the shape of Finny with his bike on top of him, and could hear him groaning and making loud breathy noises like an overheated dog.

I half-slid, half-fell down the bank.

Finny had landed on a mangled panel of wrought-iron fencing. A lot of blood was coming out from around his thighs and lower body, and I could see the tip of a steel fence post poking out of his side. I tried to move the bike, but as I tugged, Finny shrieked in pain.

I looked at the dark blood pooling on the cobbles, at Finny's face, white and silvered with sweat.

'I'll go and get help.'

'No. Don't leave me. Stay here. I'm fucking scared, Barry.'

'There's a phone box on the corner. I'll use that. Just stay calm.'

'Someone else will ring. Wait with me. Please.'

'No one saw you go off the road. No one else knows you're here.'

'Just, just a few minutes, then.'

I knelt down next to him. Should I take Finny's hand in mine? I had never done that before. I gripped his upper arm instead.

'I'm sorry I've been weird with you, mate,' Finny said. 'But I think I know what you did. I think I know about you.'

'What do you know?'

'I know about you and that girl.'

'Finny, I didn't do anything.'

'I have to tell them, Barry. The police. Tell them that you did something. You switched something off, twisted a knob, or flipped a switch. Something. She came round but someone sent her back. And she didn't come up again. You have to tell them. Or I will.'

'That's not how things are, Finny, not how they are at all.'

'My cousin, Siobhan. She said something funny. She said that a boy turned up at reception with a message for her, but this boy never materialised on the ward.'

My stomach tightened, my heartbeat quickened.

'How could I have been there? I was on the other side of the building. Different floor, different ward.'

'A few odd things happened that evening. They found the clipboard off your hospital bed in the flowers. Someone tried to break into the hospital and pulled the drainpipe off the wall. Your mother says you got away and hitch-hiked home and they had to drive you back.'

Finny began coughing. He could hardly talk, his voice had become high-pitched and rasping. Blood was running out of his mouth and his nose.

'Nothing makes sense. It couldn't have been cousin Siobhan. She's a trained nurse. She would have known which valves did what. The person who did it randomly twisted every valve.'

His head jerked up and he coughed again, retching, like his stomach was turning itself inside out.

'The paper said she had a fit, a bad fit, and that they had to give her a drug to stop her fitting, and then she never came round again,' I said.

'That's the papers,' said Finny.

'Maybe she's happier?'

'What?'

'As a ghost.'

'A ghost? Don't start that again.'

'As a ghost, she would have no memory of all the bad stuff that happened to her.'

'Don't talk that shite about fucking ghosts. Those metal things you think you've got all over. They've infected you, man. They've made you go mad. There are no fucking ghosts.'

'Look, I'll go to the phone box. Stay awake, that's the main thing. Stay awake.'

I clambered up the bank and at the top turned to look down on the tangle of flesh and wrought iron and motorbike below. Even from there, I could see the puddle of gore creeping out.

I grabbed hold of the Defiant, dragged it into the hedge, and pushed it down the slope the same way Finny had gone. It narrowly missed my friend, bouncing twice before sliding across the yard and smashing into a pile of wrought-iron owls.

I set off walking. At first quickly, then more slowly as I became accustomed to the silence and the moonlight. A car swept past, its headlights bleaching the hedge of colour, but I didn't flag it down. It would be quicker to get to the phone box on my own. It would take me too long to explain to the driver what had happened, and anyway, no one would stop at this time of night.

The phone box smelled of cigarettes and piss. I found a ten-pence piece in my pocket and picked up the receiver but the dialling tone, although you could hear it, was feeble, much fainter than it should have been. This phone wasn't working well enough to make a serious call which would involve describing exactly where Finny was lying.

I would walk to the next kiosk, in Egremont town centre. It would take me half an hour.

I strolled past a row of dark houses with no lights on. The people inside would be in bed. They would not welcome a knock on their door at midnight from a panicking drunk boy with a story about motorbikes flying off the road and splatting down in backyards. They would probably ignore the knocking anyway. I passed a farm where, at a far distance, I could see the silhouettes of men moving bales around in a floodlit barn. I could have gone over and called out to them. But they were absorbed in their work. Again, it would have taken me a long time to explain myself. And they wouldn't have access to a phone in a barn. It would have wasted more time. The phone box was the best option, yes. Once I'd called the emergency services, the ambulance would arrive quickly. At this time of night there was no traffic to hold it up; it wouldn't even need its siren. Then, a simple matter of patching up Finny with a few stitches. Stitches? They didn't even use stitches now, they used glue, I'd heard. Glue or surgical sticking tape. He'd be fine. Finny wouldn't talk to anyone about Philomena May. He'd be so pleased that I had saved his life, that he wouldn't continue to gabble on and on about that paranoid theory he'd developed. I reached the next phone box more quickly than I thought, and went inside. Someone had smashed it. The receiver was dangling on its cord, the earpiece and mouthpiece screwed off, the wires snipped and drooping. I looked at the shattered remnants and thought about Finny's dark blood moving on the cobbles, and how the liquid had heaved rhythmically as if it was being pumped out hard, and its consistency, the way, in the dark, it had looked thick, like treacle.

I thought about Philomena May's family and what they would think about Finny's outlandish story.

I thought about the police.

If they wait till you are sixteen, they can send you to an adult prison

I stood outside the phone box and tried to work out where the next nearest one was. I wondered why people vandalise phone boxes, then remembered that Finny and I had once smashed one up with a length of pipe. We had enjoyed it. It had felt creative. Was this some kind of retribution?

What to do.

I waited for clues from the universe, but got none.

Whitehaven was three and a half miles away. If I put a spurt on I'd be at the hospital in an hour and from there I could lead the ambulance to exactly where Finny lay.

A much better plan.

I crept down the slope into the deeper part of the lake, letting out a gasp as the freezing water rose up to my waist.

'It'll start to feel warmer, honestly, Dad,' said Ruby. 'That's the point of a wetsuit. It creates a thin layer between your skin and the water and then your body warms it up. We are still in the epilimnion, the upper strata, the warmest part of the lake.'

'I'm not so sure this suit is working properly,' I said.

'This is as warm as Wastwater ever gets, I promise you. I checked all the charts. It's a deep lake and that means it takes until September for the temperature to rise to this level.'

After a few days of lessons in swimming pools and a couple of professionally led sessions in a flooded quarry, this was my first time in wild water and first time without my instructor. Ruby had been diving for years, all over the world. She taught maths at Liverpool University and her diving obsession was for her an escape from that – a way of being in a world that was less controlled and less well defined.

'Now Dad, listen,' she said. 'We have the hand signals, remember. And you know about de-pressurising in stages. But you aren't going to go all the way down with me. Just take me to where you think it is – this thing – then I'll go and get it. Any problem, do this,' she sliced her finger across her throat and pointed upwards, 'and I'll know what you mean.'

It was a warm day, the sun was shining and the sky was a sort of bruised blue with a few small puffs of cloud. Perfect diving weather. My other daughter, Lydia, was in the car catching up on a piece she was writing about the flora and fauna of South Asia for *The Rough Guide to Vietnam*.

They had spent the morning with my mum and dad, who, though now in their eighties, were fit and wanted to keep up to date with everything the girls were doing. My parents were lively, modern and even used the internet – to research the weather, to buy things online and to ascertain whether celebrities were dead or not. Dad had been retired now for fifteen years. Since the Co-op removed him thirty years earlier owing to the mass closure of hundreds of small village branches, he tried out a few different business ideas to breach the gap between fifty and sixty-five, but none had taken off, or indeed satisfied him. There was the mushroom farming he'd tried to do from the shed. There was the part-share in a carwash franchise he'd bought into. There was the two-week spell as a supervisor in Brannan's thermometer factory where he had hated the way the women on the shop-floor spoke to him and the other managers, and, in fact, the way they treated each other. He had talked about cruelty and thuggery and bullying. Then, in the last few years, he'd been working at a wholesale warehouse for electrical goods. It was here that, when he'd refused to take part in, or even turn a blind eye to, a secret shrinkage scheme which involved hiding 'spare' pallets of white goods in the bushes so that someone could 'find' them by accident and sell them on, the other staff had forced him out.

My mother had stayed on at the school until she was fifty-five, when she retired, with a big concert where the children sang for her while she played the piano. Emotional stuff. After her teaching post ended, she didn't take up anything else to fill the days, so spent a lot of time visiting Manchester, helping out with Ruby and Lydia, and generally being a useful and loving grandparent. She had a few health scares on the way, and some longer, more lingering ailments, which I thought stemmed from not having anything else to do all day but examine your body and think about how your mind and organs are functioning from one minute to the next. I couldn't stand not to work. I was terrified of a day without actions and deadlines, and would invent them if I needed to.

The event. When the actual event happened, I stayed away from West Cumbria and made sure my parents did too. I tried not to watch the news, but when I finally did – I simply had to, it was inconceivable to ignore it – it chilled my blood to hear what had happened set out as I had been shown it thirty-four years ago by Petal. There were differences, yes, it didn't all happen the same way, but some of it did, and I wondered if parts of it had been preventable.

I had told no one – not Ruby and Lydia, not my friends or colleagues, and especially not my parents. Everyone would have thought I was mad. My wife? No, I didn't tell her either. When she'd met me – Fiona, Fiona Maudsley, she was called back then, and in fact is called that again now – I'd had to explain the scars from the skin condition and she was perfectly satisfied with my theory about a freak allergy. She would always love me anyway, she maintained, despite some daft superficial skin condition. Fiona was a good trusting woman, and I felt terrible to have left her the way I did. Maybe it was an age thing – the grand cliché, the operatic crisis they talk about with men of a certain vintage. The girls at the time understood. They didn't like it, they hated it, they abhorred what it did to their mother, but they also didn't like the constant arguing. They had realised that I wasn't happy, but they thought at some point, in some way, it could be salvaged. They remembered good times, as did I. The four of us walking up a mountain, making up stories about the trees and the rivers talking to each other. Singing songs which featured girls called Ruby and Lydia going into space and fighting giant insects. Putting aliens into Postman Pat stories. Making sculptures out of litter on the beach. Playing games in supermarkets. Ruby and Lydia. Clever, lovely girls. They stuck by me, thank God. Some kids toss their fathers in the ditch when that happens, especially girls. But they didn't and I respected and loved them for that.

Most of the metal lumps had disappeared, but thirteen remained, although the skin had grown over them. I could hardly feel them himself any more if the truth were known, but I knew their exact location, their size, their shape.

Thirteen dead

'Come on, Dad,' Ruby said, and we went under. I remembered the clouds of silt from last time and the fact that once you were near the bottom, it would be hard to see. But I was soon able to point out the long wire that led down to the gnome grotto and Ruby gripped on to it and edged her way to the bottom.

It took a few attempts to find the right one but when she did, I recognised it straight away. The big black plug in its base was still intact. Ruby held it close to her stomach as she ascended to the surface.

This confirmed that everything was real. This confirmed that I hadn't been temporarily insane. This confirmed.

I opened the boot and placed the garden gnome on a bin liner. Its face was now bleached of colour, its carved beard almost smooth, its round apple cheeks reminding me of Petal. The gnome's pin-prick eyes looked at me imploringly before I slammed down the lid.

'I hope all that was worth it for a gnome,' Lydia said putting away her laptop and starting the car.

'Diving is always better when there's a goal,' said Ruby. 'There's often something like that to look for on seabeds and lake bottoms. Things lost, sunken. More often than not, things put there on purpose. For some reason, people like to hide random things in inaccessible places that hardly anyone goes to.'

The first few years were the worst. The waiting, the thinking, the knowing. The fact that I couldn't do anything about it even though I knew every beat, every pulse, and every inch of what would happen. I even sought out the diver himself, went as far as getting into his cab and chatting to him. The man seemed fine, he seemed like a normal bloke, a man who cared about things, a man with friends, who enjoyed company and holidays, and fun. He wasn't like the man Petal had shown me in the future.

I got used to owning this dark memory and sealed it away in a cupboard in a back room of my mind. I decided that it had been a fantasy, a hallucination. You can't travel to the future. You can't see things in the future, and you can't affect them.

Maybe I should have found a gun and shot the diver myself. Maybe that would have been the best result for all. How would that have sounded in the court? I killed him because I knew he was going to murder twelve others in the future.

At my mam and dad's, we took the gnome out of the car and into the garden where Mam and Dad were sitting in the sun having tea. We told them all about the dive and my dad laughed at the sad, withered face of the half-drowned gnome and agreed it was a good memento of the dive, a nice thing to have in your home.

Later, I took the gnome up to my old bedroom and prised the plug out of the bottom. Inside was a plastic bag and when I opened it I recognised the fabric bundle within. It was from the undertaker's. I unrolled the yellow cloth and a set of carpenter's tools sparkled in the electric light. The tool's blades had lost nothing of their lustre, and looked sharp enough to use. I placed the cloth on the floor and laid the tools out on it in a neat row.

'Ruby, Lydia, come in here and see this,' I called down the stairs. They came up and looked.

'Wow, Dad,' said Ruby. 'What weird things to put inside a gnome at the bottom of a lake. Who put them there?'

'It was,' I said, 'a man I once met. A man who is no longer around. I wish I had known him properly and spent more time with him.'

I rolled up the cloth with the tools inside it and placed the package in my suitcase.

'Let's go and see if Granddad and Grandma need any help with dinner,' I said.

About the author

David Gaffney comes from Cleator Moor in West Cumbria. He is the author of *Sawn-off Tales* (2006), *Aromabingo* (2007), *Never Never* (2008), *The Half-life of Songs* (2010), *More Sawn-Off Tales* (2013) and graphic novel *The Three Rooms in Valerie's Head*. David has written articles for *The Guardian*, *The Sunday Times*, *Financial Times* and *Prospect magazine*.

·

Urbane Publications is dedicated to developing new author voices, and publishing fiction and non-fiction that challenges, thrills and fascinates. From page-turning novels to innovative reference books, our goal is to publish what YOU want to read.

Find out more at

urbanepublications.com

David Gaffney